When Dragons Disappear

Kimberly Ann Sechser

Fired Up Seminars and Training

ISBN: 979-8-9885208-6-3 (Ebook)

ISBN: 979-8-9885208-7-0 (Paperback)

Library of Congress Control Number: 2025912296

Book Cover and Book Design by Gable Holyoak

Printed by Fired Up Seminars and Training

First printing edition 2025.

Fired Up Seminars and Training

Ogden, Ut 84401

www.firedupseminar.com

Other Books by the Author

The Greatest Investor in the World (Book 1)
The Greatest Treasure in the World (Book 2)
The Greatest Gift in the World (Book 3)

For all those who still believe that magic is real and hope for a pet dragon

Contents

VII

1. Chapter 1   1

2. Chapter 2   7

3. Chapter 3   11

4. Chapter 4   17

5. Chapter 5   20

6. Chapter 6   29

7. Chapter 7   37

8. Chapter 8   43

9. Chapter 9   52

10. Chapter 10   55

11. Chapter 11   61

12. Chapter 12   65

13. Chapter 13   72

14. Chapter 14   81

15. Chapter 15   88

16. Chapter 16   93

17. Chapter 17   102

18. Chapter 18   111

19.	Chapter 19	119
20.	Chapter 20	124
21.	Chapter 21	129
22.	Chapter 22	139
23.	Chapter 23	145
24.	Chapter 24	151
25.	Chapter 25	156
26.	Chapter 26	161
27.	Chapter 27	168
28.	Chapter 28	171
29.	Chapter 29	176
30.	Chapter 30	179
31.	Chapter 31	186
32.	Chapter 32	193
33.	Chapter 33	196
34.	Chapter 34	201
35.	Chapter 35	209
36.	Chapter 36	216
37.	Chapter 37	223
38.	Chapter 38	230
39.	Chapter 39	233
	Acknowledgements	239
	About the author	240
	Chapter	241

Chapter 1

"Pst."

Alara heard a voice and groggily groaned, trying to turn her head, but then she remembered that wherever she was, she couldn't move. She thought back to how she got there. If there was one thing that Alara prided herself on, it was that she was independent and could take care of herself. Yet, somehow, here she was in need of being rescued. She wondered if the day could get any worse.

"It's me," the voice whispered.

The day got worse. She recognized that voice. Suddenly, the past day's events came tumbling through her pain-filled head like a stampede of wild animals. She recalled that her predicament began much the same way that most females' problems begin—with a man.

***

Alara lay back on a blue couch, resting her head on the white pillows. She stared into the lights of the chandelier that hung above her head. The ability to have light was just one of the powers that made their life a little easier. She was grateful that some people had lightning power, so they could produce energy by harnessing it from lightning and use it to light buildings, power their stoves, and have other comforts.

She thought about her own magic power and fingered the locket that she wore. The locket had been a gift from the faram—the keeper of the dragons. Like everyone else, when Alara turned sixteen, she went to a faram, who had a power that allowed them to get into the dragon realm. Because of their magic power, the faram could sense which dragons should be chosen to give powers to the person. Then the dragons that were chosen would decide which of their powers to share with the person receiving them that day. Even if a dragon was chosen, it could choose not to share any.

Even though the faram had chosen four dragons for Alara, she still only had one power—invisibility. She secretly hoped she would find out she had more powers, which is why she wore the locket, but she knew that most people received all their powers within one year.

Alara looked toward the window where a yellow bird with red splashes of color on its wings had just perched. She got up to look at it, admiring not just its beauty, but also envying its freedom. She thought about her own life. Not that it wasn't a good life, but as a princess, there were many things she didn't get a say in. She chewed on her nails, a habit her mother hated, but she couldn't help it. She was so nervous. Her parents, Queen Corah and King Teron, had asked her to meet them in the room, and she worried what it could be about.

When her parents entered the room, Alara quickly moved her hand down and sat it in her lap, hoping her mother wouldn't notice her nails. She watched her parents sit on the couch. Her mother had on a stiff black skirt and a dark red shirt. She looked serious which made Alara worry even more. "Have a seat," her mother said, motioning to a blue chair with a small white pillow on it.

Alara sat down hard and looked at her parents. They were looking at each other as if debating which one was going to tell her the news. Alara wanted to run. She could already tell that she wasn't going to like this conversation. "Alara," her father said, "now that you are eighteen, we thought it would be nice to have a party for you . . . and invite rulers from other lands and kingdoms."

Oh no. She averted her eyes. A party would be nice, but not the kind of party they were talking about. "Yes," her mother said, "and as part of this, we will hold a ball."

All Alara wanted to do was go on adventures and be the heroine, but no, she had to be the heir to the throne with all the responsibility and restrictions that came with it, including having to get married at some point. Alara shook her head. "Let me guess, there will be lots of young men that you expect me to dance with."

Her mother sighed. "That is typically the point of holding a ball."

Alara's eyes flashed with fury. "Except when my brothers turned eighteen, they didn't have to go to balls and dance with all the eligible ladies. No, they got to go on their first military adventure with Father and gather information, which is something I'd like to do. All I've ever wanted is to go on an adventure, maybe a spying adventure, but do I get to? No."

"You are not going on a spying adventure," her mother said, staring at her.

"Why not?" Alara shouted.

Her mother rubbed her temples with her fingers. "We've been over this before, and it isn't proper for a princess to be out running around in the forest getting dirty and being put in potentially dangerous situations." Her mother raised her voice slightly. "This isn't up for debate."

"Well, maybe the dance isn't up for debate either. I'd like to see either of you force me to dance with anyone." Alara stood up and ran from the room.

Once inside her room, Alara paced, breathing heavily. She walked over to her bed and pulled out her evidence papers and a pencil from under it. So far, her evidence papers mostly had problems and not many suspects or answers. Vashka had a major problem, and she wanted to help solve it. This is why she needed to go on a spying adventure.

The problem started more than two months earlier when flyn trees began disappearing from the Tykee Forest. For this reason, the forest was heavily guarded, but some people, who various councils called Magic Robbers, were using magic to get past the guards. They suspected that the Magic Robbers were involved in dark magic.

Alara bit down on her pencil and studied another section. Even worse was that the Magic Robbers were stealing omps, or objects with magic powers. The Magic Robbers had to keep stealing them because the powers they stole would become inactive after one month unless it was used by the original owner of the power. In some kingdoms, omps were being stolen so frequently that people were afraid to let them out of their sight.

Alara threw the papers on the ground. "Agh," she yelled at the top of her lungs. She was confident she could solve the problem. Besides, she should get some excitement to go with all the responsibility of being heir to the crown.

She slumped onto the brass bed and wrapped a blanket around her. Alara heard a knock on her door and a gentle voice. "It's me. Can I come in?"

Alara quickly rolled off the bed and stuffed the evidence papers under her bed and mumbled, "Come in." Her father entered and sat on the edge of her bed and looked around. "Can you please make yourself visible, so we can talk?"

Alara didn't plan on making this easy. "We can talk even if I'm invisible."

Her father sighed. "I know, but it's easier for me to feel like I am talking to someone and not to myself if I can see you."

A moment later, Alara appeared, standing a distance away with her back turned, looking out one of the windows. "It isn't fair," she blurted out. "The boys get to go on adventures, and no one tells them they can't. Why should it be any different because I'm a girl?"

"Alara, it isn't the adventure that is the real problem, and you know it."

Alara glared at him. While he was more relaxed than her mother, he still could be a stickler for rules. She saw his wrinkled forehead and how tired he seemed. He was in good shape for his fifty-two years of age, but he was mostly gray, especially in his beard. She figured her behavior had probably added a few more gray hairs. *It's his own fault. I wouldn't act like this if they weren't forcing me to do something I don't want to do.*

She walked toward him, waving her hands in the air. "Well, the boys never have to attend fancy balls to meet potential matches." As the crown princess, she knew it was expected that at some point she'd marry. There was much to do to run a kingdom, so marriage was considered a must. But she didn't want to get married. She wanted to go on adventures.

Her father stood and walked toward her. "There will be plenty of adventures in your future." She rolled her eyes, knowing he was referring to marriage as an adventure. "Look, no one said you have to marry any of the eligible men at this ball. We only said you have to attend, dance, and be *civil.*" She glared at him, but he continued. "We don't want you to be miserable. You know that you don't have to marry anyone you don't want to marry. Also, unlike many kingdoms, we are a lot more relaxed about who you can marry. If you were in some kingdoms, you could be forced to marry a particular person or have your choices limited to people of certain titles. Life could be much worse."

Alara flipped her head. "Well, there isn't anyone I want to marry." Her voice turned to pleading. "I just want to continue the way I am. Please let me; I'll be miserable if I have to marry someone."

"Marriage isn't a prison sentence."

"Why can't we be like most of the other kingdoms and have the heir be a male?" She pouted. "Then I'd be free to do what I want, and one of my brothers would have to deal with all of this. Or why can't I wait until I'm much older before I have to start dating potential suitors? You and Mother are young; it will probably be years before I have to worry about being the ruler."

"We've been over this before." Teron shrugged. "Sometimes things that are beyond our control happen, and you need to be prepared just in case. Not only do you need training for the important role of queen, but whoever you marry will need training in his role as king. Understanding the intricacies of the military is a huge endeavor, and that's only a part of what he'll have to do. This isn't something someone can just step into. It takes a lot of preparation. The sooner you get married, the more time you both will have to be ready for when you do take over."

Alara puffed out her cheeks. This conversation was getting her nowhere. Her father went to say something else, but she cut him off, went invisible, and headed for the door. "If you need me, I'll be riding. And don't you dare try to stop me." She slammed the door shut.

***

Teron left and walked slowly down the hallway. He gazed at the pictures on the wall of those who had fought to keep their kingdom free and lost their lives. He stopped at one in particular. It was his friend Havid who had died in battle years before. "Going to battle would be easier than dealing with Alara." He imagined Havid would laugh, pat him on the back, and tell him it would all work out.

He continued his walk until he found Corah. She was standing in the main foyer looking out the window. "Do you think there's any hope for her?" Corah asked as Teron sat on the couch.

He smiled and motioned for her to sit down too. He put his arm around her shoulders. "I'm sure there will be . . . eventually—that may be in thirty years—but eventually."

"Why can't Alara be sensible. Her and her adventures." Corah chuckled. "I had way more adventures after I married and had kids than before." She tilted her head sideways. "Alara has seen to that all by herself."

Teron smiled. That was true and even truer after Alara got her powers. She made life more than a little interesting and kept them on their toes. "Remember when Alara first found out she could go invisible."

"Yes, she had broken a vase and was holding onto it, wishing she could disappear, when suddenly she and the vase disappeared. After an hour of not being able to go visible, she finally approached us to help her and confessed what had happened."

"After that, the real fun began. She disappeared whenever she wanted to, which was anytime she was mad at one of us or wanted to play a trick on her brothers."

"Or any other person she was mad at. Remember how she used to run away from the castle when she didn't want to do something?" Teron nodded, thinking about his interaction moments ago and how some things never changed. "You don't think she'll try to skip the ball, do you?" Corah asked.

Teron wiggled his fingers. "If I need to, I will use my immobilization power so she can't. Having this power has worked wonders with Alara." Teron hoped it wouldn't come down to that though. She could make the evening pretty miserable for everyone if she wanted to.

Chapter 2

Zarium patted the thick black gloves he was carrying which allowed him to go invisible. The king loaned them to him to help with the latest assignment he had done. He had been doing assignments for the king and queen since his dad had died a few years earlier.

He glanced in the direction of the Tykee Forest, though he couldn't see it through the buildings of the city of Vashka. The Tykee Forest had flyn trees that had a special bark that increased one's magic when it was attached to an omp. The royal family owned the trees, and they didn't let just anyone have an omp, but he really wanted one.

He wondered if he could get into the forest if he used the invisibility power. He debated. Even if he got past the guards and got into the forest, he'd still have to find the pieces, and that wouldn't be easy to do in such a short time because there wasn't any known pattern as to where the pieces would be on the tree. He pulled out his pocket timekeeper. The king wouldn't be expecting him for more than an hour. That was enough time to at least try. He slipped the gloves on and used his place-transport power to get him quickly to the forest.

An hour later, Zarium picked himself off the ground, wondering how anyone else was getting into the forest without serious injuries. So far, he had been thrown up in the air, attacked by snakes, and nicked with a guard's sword. He looked at the forest again. Today, it had won, but he was determined that in the future, he'd figure out how to get a piece of bark.

A servant showed Zarium to the Red Room, where he sat down and waited for the king and queen. As he waited, he looked at a brass dragon statue on top of a red table runner. Like other smaller meeting rooms, there were no windows or pictures. Under the table was a rug, in this case, red, since it was the Red Room. The other smaller meeting rooms were similar, except the color of the table runner and rug matched the room name.

The door opened, and Zarium stood and bowed as King Teron and Queen Corah entered the room and shut the door. "Zarium, welcome back. I trust everything went as planned?"

Zarium handed the gloves to the king. "It did."

"Good." King Teron and Queen Corah sat down. King Teron motioned for Zarium to sit. Teron shifted in his chair. "Zarium, I've known you for a long time, and I knew your father even longer. You have done every assignment asked of you, and in many cases gone above and beyond what I asked."

"I try, Your Highness."

King Teron put the gloves on the table. "I feel like we can trust you. At least I hope that is true." King Teron stepped closer to Zarium, his eyes probing deep. "Can we trust you?"

Zarium nodded. The king clutched his shoulders. "Can we trust you with *anything?*"

Zarium took a step back. This was an intensity he hadn't seen when being given past assignments. He turned toward Queen Corah, but she said nothing. Zarium spoke, but his voice cracked. He cleared it and spoke louder. "Yes, I'd gladly serve you any way I can." Zarium made his voice deeper. "You have my word."

King Teron drummed his fingers on the table. Zarium gulped, wondering if he should have been so confident before. At last, King Teron spoke. "We will be holding a ball for Alara in a few weeks. You will receive an invitation by the end of the week." Zarium nodded his head, and King Teron continued, "You can track people when they accept a gift from you, correct?" Zarium nodded. King Teron rubbed his chin. "Good, I want you to make sure that when you dance with Alara, you give her a gift, so you can track her."

"You want me to . . . to spy on Alara?" Zarium questioned, shocked at the suggestion.

"Yes," Queen Corah said. "After the dance, it is imperative that we know where she is and who she is with."

"You do realize that under normal circumstances, I can only track someone for a day."

King Teron reached his hand into his robe and pulled something out. He put his hand on the table and opened it. Zarium's eyes widened, and he nearly gasped. There was a two inch piece of smooth orange flyn bark. "How long could you track someone if you had this?"

Zarium fumbled for the words, excited at the prospect of having a piece of bark. "I'm not sure. I've never tried it before."

King Teron reached out his hand toward Zarium. "I want you to use this when you give Alara a gift the night of the dance. After that, I want you to give me the bark back." Zarium was disappointed but fought to keep his face the same as it had been, so King Teron wouldn't notice. Zarium reached for the bark. King Teron pulled his hand back slightly. Zarium looked up at King Teron, who said, "I don't want you using this for any other reason right now. Do you understand?"

Zarium nodded, even more disappointed than before. King Teron dropped it into Zarium's outstretched hand. Zarium fingered the bark. "I don't know how to use this. How do I attach it to an omp?"

King Teron pointed to the table. "Put one of your omps here. Zarium took off a metal bracelet that had his tracking power and put it on the table. King Teron continued, "Take the bark and put it on it."

Zarium lowered the bark, and much to his surprise, the omp pulled at the tree bark like a magnet right before it was about to touch. "It's like a magnet."

"The bark is naturally attracted to magic, and they create their own force. They will stay together pretty easily until you pull them apart. Also, I recommend you keep the bark hidden when using it, like putting the bracelet in your pocket. That way, no one will know you have the bark."

"Okay. Do I just use my power the same way I always do?"

"Yes," Teron nodded, "any questions?"

"No, I understand."

"One more thing," Queen Corah said. "We want you to ask Alara about the Tykee Forest."

"The forest? Why?"

"That isn't your concern," Teron said firmly but with a smile. "That is all; you are excused." Zarium stood up and headed for the door.

Chapter 3

Alara tapped her foot impatiently as she waited for the stable boy to finish saddling her horse, Thunder. As soon as he finished, she got on her horse and steered him toward the countryside. Alara looked out at a sea of flowers in the tall grass. The purple ones were her favorite. She knew she was lucky to live there and that she was fortunate to be her, but she wished she were born to a less prominent family.

"It isn't fair." Thunder snorted, and she reached down and stroked his black mane. "I want to go on daring missions and be the hero." Thunder nodded his head. "I want people to sing about me for generations to come about how I was the protector of the innocent." She raised her hand in the air. "But alas . . . I'm just a girl." Her hand fell limp. She lay back on Thunder and felt the warm sun on her face.

Thunder turned his head and nudged her with his nose, bringing her back to reality. She grabbed the reins and steered him toward Nori's house. Nori was the faram in Vashka and who she had received her powers from years earlier. Alara had visited Nori many times over the years to get advice or have someone listen to her, and Alara felt like Nori understood her.

At Nori's house, Alara hopped off her horse and tied it to a nearby apple tree. Then she walked up the cement path to Nori's. The paint on the house was nice, but a boring white—the same white it had been when she first met Nori two years earlier. Alara knocked on the door, and soon Nori opened it. "Alara, what a pleasant surprise. Come in and have a seat."

Nori was the one thing in Alara's life that never changed. She still didn't have any better furniture than she had years earlier. Alara sat down on a wooden stool, and Nori sat beside her in a worn chair. "Now tell me. What can I do for you today?"

Alara went through all of her issues lately—the dance and the lack of adventure in her life. She braided a couple of strands of hair. "Besides all these problems, I still only have one power. Couldn't I have at least two? I've tried not to let it bother me, and I know I should be grateful I have one, but I still wish I had more."

"And what would more powers do for you?"

"You know . . ." Alara swallowed hard. "I'd feel like I really matter. It seems like the dragons didn't find me worth their magic." She paused, but Nori didn't speak. "Maybe my parents would give me more freedom if I had more powers, and they'd see I'm capable of taking care of myself."

"I'm pretty sure everyone in the kingdom knows you can hold your own," Nori snorted.

Alara smiled and undid the braid. Last week, she had been at the market when someone stole some produce. Even with only her invisibility power, she managed to single-handedly take care of the problem.

Nori continued, "It seems you put more importance on the powers the dragons gave you than on the power you have within yourself." Nori pointed at Alara's heart and head. Alara frowned. She hadn't come here for some pep talk on how amazing she was. She wanted answers that would help her persuade her parents to let her live her life without all these regulations. Nori interrupted her thoughts. "Has it occurred to you that you have everything you need to have the life you want and to rule the kingdom?"

Alara's head shot up. Then her shoulders slumped. "Maybe, but I'd still be tied down to the kingdom and not be able to do what I wanted to do. Even if I'm capable of going on an adventure, it doesn't mean I'll be allowed. What good are powers if I can't even enjoy them?"

Nori smiled. "Do you know why the dragons share their powers with us?"

"Of course, we studied that in history class. Centuries ago, our ancestors saved the dragons from the invaders. In return, the dragons share their powers with us."

Nori nodded. "Yes, that is part of it, but more importantly, the purpose of any power is to help us best accomplish the things we will do in life. The dragons knew you'd be queen someday, and you will get what you need when you need it. Remember, the powers never come too early or too late. They always come at the perfect time."

None of this made Alara feel any better. Especially not the part about her being queen one day.

Nori got up and stirred some food in a pot over the stove. As she stirred, she hummed. Alara relaxed as she listened. She closed her eyes until she had the best idea. She couldn't go to a far-off place to investigate these issues, but she could do some investigating around town. Alara told Nori goodbye and climbed on her horse. She smacked her lips together, and Thunder moved forward.

As they entered town, Alara saw familiar shops and the road that would lead to Berica's house. She wished she could visit her friend and ask her for advice, but Berica was out of town, visiting relatives. As Alara rode through the streets, her horse snorted and tensed. "Whoa, boy, it's okay." She gently patted his dark brown neck.

But Thunder didn't calm down. He started stomping his feet. Alara pulled the reins tighter. Thunder snorted again, but this time she saw why and turned Thunder away from the scene to calm him down. She steered Thunder behind a building, tied him up, went invisible, and walked out from behind the building to face the problem.

Rulon, the twenty-year-old bully, was on a rampage again. He had a habit of picking on people because he liked making others look like fools. At this moment, he had stolen the school bags from some little kids and was tossing them to the only friend he had. Alara clenched her fist.

A few feet behind Rulon was a trough that was full of water. Alara grabbed a bucket sitting near the trough and filled it up. Being as quiet as possible, she snuck up behind Rulon and threw the water on him. Rulon yelped, "What the—" he spluttered. "Who's there? You'll be sorry for that."

Alara laughed to herself and ran to the trough again. She had just dipped the bucket in when suddenly the water sprang up and soaked her. She fell, sputtering and coughing. "Looks like I outsmarted you, whoever you are." Rulon raised his hands in victory and started walking toward the trough. "Now, you'll be sorry when I get my hands on you."

Oh yeah? Alara gritted her teeth. She was glad she was invisible, so she could run to a different spot without being seen. While he was searching for her by the trough, she gathered some rocks and threw them at him. Rulon covered his head and ran behind a building. While he was distracted, the children were able to get their things back. "Just you wait," Rulon yelled as the children ran away, "next time, no one will be here to help you."

Yes! She fixed the problem, and no one knew it was her. *Oh no. H*er dress was wet, muddy, and had a hole in it from her fall—she wished for the hundredth time that she had the power to fix holes in clothing, or at least make them instantly clean.

Alara rode back to the castle and left the horse with the stable boy. As she climbed the castle steps, she wondered what the guard must think of her outfit, but as usual, he didn't say anything. He just stood there. She thought his job seemed pretty boring. The guards were important though, and made sure that no one got into the castle unless they were on the official approval list.

Alara opened the door to the castle and shut it as quietly as possible. She tiptoed past the entrance area and turned to go down a hallway, hoping to avoid her mother seeing her. "Alara." She cringed as she heard her mother's voice. She turned around. Her mother's eyes widened. "What have you done to your dress? You get plenty of *adventure* just walking out the doors of the castle."

Alara told her what happened with Rulon. She braced herself for a scolding, but curiously enough, her mother came closer. "I'm proud to have a daughter who cares about others." Stunned, Alara stammered a thank you. Her mother smiled and continued, "It's one of the traits that will make you a great queen someday. The people are lucky to have someone who can easily relate to them because she is often among them." Alara wasn't sure if that last part was a compliment or criticism.

That night at dinner, Alara kept quiet at first, formulating a plan to go on a spying adventure. She bit her lip and tapped her toes. How could she make it advantageous for her parents? What did they most want?

She examined her parents at the far end of the table. They sat in the same two spots every time, but she enjoyed switching it up. Today, she sat on the exact opposite end of them.

A servant brought in roasted chicken, rolls, carrots, and pudding. Alara picked up one of the golden forks and stabbed a piece of chicken and stuffed it into her mouth. As she chewed, an idea popped into her head. *Surely, I can come up with a better idea.* She swallowed the huge bite. *Nope, that's what they want.* She took a big bite of her roll, hoping for some last-minute inspiration. She didn't have the power of persuasion, so she couldn't use magic to help her. And much to her dismay, she hadn't been blessed with it as a talent either, at least not where her parents were concerned.

Let's get this over with. She cleared her throat, "While I was out riding today, I was thinking..." Her parents looked up at her. She had their full attention. She proceeded, choosing her words carefully. "... about the disappearing trees in the Tykee Forest."

They continued to stare at her, though it felt like more of a glare. She went on, but the rest came out sounding like one big word. "What if I agree to go to the ball without any fights and you allow me to do some investigating?"

Her mother put her hand to her forehead. Alara quickly continued, "I promise I will gladly try on dresses and allow my hair to be done all fancy ... and I promise to not do anything that could ruin my outfit or hair." They said nothing. *Tough crowd.* It pained her, but she heard herself say, "I will also be nice to the gentlemen and dance with anyone who asks ... Oh, all right, I will engage in polite conversation ... and not go invisible," she said sheepishly. She crossed her fingers and hoped they said yes.

Her parents were silently passing a white, black, and red unsharpened pencil back and forth. Her mother had the power to thought-receive. Anyone could send thoughts to her as long as they were within a short distance of her. Like most people, her mother had transferred the power to a different object than the one she got from the faram, so she could share her powers with others. It also allowed them to have an entire conversation without Alara knowing what they were saying.

At last, her parents stopped passing the pencil. "We will agree to your proposal with two more stipulations added," her father said. Alara held her breath; she hoped it wouldn't be too bad. "Someone must accompany you on your spying adventure." *Okay, not bad.* "And you must agree to see one of the suitors at least three times after the ball."

Alara nearly choked. *Well, I could always make those dates really bad,* she consoled herself.

"On your dates," her mother continued, "you will behave the same way you have promised for the dance, and you will go on all three dates before you can go on your adventure." Alara nodded, thinking to herself that she could do all three dates on the same day, but her mother dashed those hopes. "And each date must last for at least an hour, and you will not do more than one date in a day." Alara eyed her mother, who chuckled. "And no, I'm not reading your mind. I just know you . . . too well."

Alara weighed her options. What choice did she really have? This was a battle that could only be won by compromising. She clenched her teeth. "Fine, I will accept your terms." She stood up. "But I refuse to like any of the young men." Alara hurried out of the room before anyone said anything else.

Chapter 4

Two weeks later, Alara was up before dawn to get ready for the ball. Her mother brought the royal dresser and hair stylist into her room and began the process of getting her ready. She tried on so many dresses that she was sure she wouldn't want to change clothes again for at least a month. Each time she was hopeful it would be the last dress, her mother would disapprove of it and more would be brought in.

She was as pleasant as possible, though, by the end of the day, she had to bite down to avoid saying anything she shouldn't. She didn't want to go to all the work but blow it by being impatient and still not be allowed to go on her trip.

By the time of the ball, Alara was dressed in a beautiful, dark purple gown with sparkles on the top and a stitched flower pattern around her waist. Extending from the waist to the bottom of the dress were gold swirls. She was quite pleased that the one her mother liked happened to be purple since that was her favorite color.

Her mother walked toward her. "You look radiant. I have a surprise for you." The queen clapped her hands, and one of the royal dressers brought a box over. Her mother opened it. Alara craned her neck, trying to see what was in the box. Her breath caught when she saw it.

It was something she had loved since she was little and saw her mother wear it—a diamond necklace. It had small diamonds going down each side with seven larger diamonds in the middle forming a diamond shape. "It is time you have this, and it will go well with your dress," her mother said.

Alara turned around so her mother could put it on her. Then she remembered the locket. She hesitated, not sure she wanted to take the locket off. Her mother noticed and said, "Don't worry. You can put it back on in a couple of hours." Alara nodded, took the necklace off, and gently placed it on her bureau. Her mother put the other necklace around Alara's neck and adjusted it. Alara glanced at her locket again. *Stop being silly*, she chided herself.

Alara fingered the new necklace, hardly able to believe it was hers, and turned to hug her mother. She still wasn't happy about the dancing situation, but at least something good had come from it.

***

Zarium finished putting on his black suit and stood before his mom. She brushed it and had him turn once slowly. It had been a suit of his dad's, and his mom had kept it in the closet for something as special as a royal ball. A couple of weeks before, they had taken the suit to a tailor they knew, so Zarium could have a perfect fit.

His mom looked up at him, her eyes glistening. "You look so handsome, just like your dad did when he wore this."

Zarium looked in a nearby mirror. The black color looked nice with the red vest and collar scarf. He folded his arms and turned to the side. "And you think my hair looks okay?"

"It looks perfect."

He walked into his room and took the flyn bark off of a shelf he had put it in. He took off his metal bracelet and attached the two together and put them in his pocket. This way, he would be ready to give Alara a gift whenever an opportunity presented itself.

***

An hour later, Alara paced by the window of her room as guests arrived—so many horses and carriages. The men and women who got out of the carriages looked so proper and perfect with flawless movements. Alara felt like she was suffocating. She had never been good at being perfect. She reminded herself why she was doing this and that it was going to be worth it.

She noticed the guards. Whenever there was a big meeting or event, more guards were stationed in the front to make sure everyone was safe.

A smile spread across her face. Her brothers would be arriving shortly, except for Jarius. Jarius, who was twenty-five and the second oldest, had been gone for months on a secret mission. A thrill went through Alara—soon she could be joining him. The rest of her brothers lived at the castle some of the time. They had many other responsibilities and traveled a lot, so she didn't see them much. But they each popped in from time to time.

Alara's thoughts were interrupted by a knock at the door. She smoothed the front of her dress and called out, "Come in."

Her father walked in. "You look beautiful." He kissed Alara on her forehead. "The guests are here, and it's time for me to present you. Are you ready?"

Alara sighed and grabbed her gold crown with diamonds going around it, leading to a large purple sapphire in the middle which was chosen from her collection of crowns because it matched her dress. She put it on and took her father's outstretched arm. "As ready as I'll ever be. Might as well get this over with."

Chapter 5

Two guards stood in front of the large gold ballroom doors. They opened them wide, and a hush fell over the room as Alara and her father entered.

They waited at the entrance until the guests had lined up. Alara felt a small tinge of excitement. The gold walls of the room looked even more stunning with the purple silk ribbon that lined them. On the ceiling hung stunning chandeliers made of the most exquisite crystals that danced as the lights hit them. Various statues of past leaders lined the outer edge of the room.

The people bowed as the king and princess passed. Alara focused on the front of the room and avoided making eye contact with anyone. Her mother was already standing at the front of the room. When Alara got to the front, she stood next to her mother.

Her mother thanked everyone for coming, gave a few instructions, and officially started the dance. With that, the musicians in the large orchestra started playing. As her father whisked her mother onto the dance floor, her mother whispered to Alara, "We'll be seeing you on the dance floor." Alara knew it was a command.

Alara swiftly made her way to one of the food tables. As she did, she watched the people dancing. There were rulers and other people from lands within the kingdom as well as from other kingdoms close by.

At last, she made it to the table, and no one had asked her to dance. The food table had chocolate truffles, cookies, pie, fruit, and cake with white frosting and purple flowers on them. She quickly grabbed a cookie and slowly nibbled on it.

Alara didn't see her twenty-two-year-old brother Levon until he bumped into her, nearly throwing her off balance. *Of course, he would be in the food area.*

Levon loved food and would never turn down an opportunity to eat, and it showed in the extra pounds he carried.

Levon reached out and steadied her with his hand. She nudged him. "Just getting a snack, huh?"

He shrugged. "I think we can both agree that the food is the best part of a ball."

Alara nodded. "I would think you would be dancing with Berica." Alara had spent so much time over the years with Berica that she had caught the attention of Levon, and they had been dating for the last ten months. Alara hoped that one day Berica would be her sister-in-law. Alara looked around. "Where is Berica anyway?"

Levon ran his fingers through his wavy blond hair and laughed. "You can't tell me that you thought she would be on time. We both know she is late for everything."

Before Alara could say anything else, her parents were close by. "Alara," her mother whispered, "if you stand here talking to your brother all night, none of the other young men will dare ask you to dance." Alara rolled her eyes but nodded.

She looked at Levon and wanted to wipe the smirk off his face. He pulled his lips in, trying to avoid laughing. "Sorry," he said. "I guess I'd better let you go."

After he left, she nervously stood alone, feeling more like a display than a person. She wasn't alone for long, however, before a young man with brown hair and a black suit made his way toward her. She recognized him from some of the meetings and knew that he was the son of the governor of Zarothan. She couldn't remember his name and was relieved when he bowed and introduced himself as Hans. She curtsied, smiled politely, and accepted the dance.

She found out quickly that he considered himself to be one of the best men in the land. It was no surprise to Alara that he was still an eligible suitor since he spent the entire song bragging about all his great feats.

"May I cut in?" Alara smiled at the familiar voice and turned to see Ian dressed in a white suit. Ian was only a year and a half older than her and was her favorite brother, and saving her from her situation made her like him even more. He was also single, and Alara believed it was only because he hadn't found someone good enough for him. Alara waited until her Hans was out of earshot before whispering, "Thank you for saving me from him."

"How is it going so far?" Ian asked.

"About as well as you can imagine," Alara groaned. "And it won't be long before our parents are over here to tell us that if we're dancing together, the other men here can't dance with me."

He got a mischievous grin. "And since when do you care about what our parents think?"

She huffed. "Since I want to go on an adventure trip, and to do so, I must dance with the young men tonight."

A boyish grin spread across his face. "Well, you're in luck. I'm a man, and I'm young."

"You know what I mean." She jokingly slugged him. "Besides, saying you're a boy might be more accurate."

He backed away, holding his hands up in front of him. "All right, since you insist, I'll leave you so you can dreamily dance the night away." She stuck her tongue out at him.

She quickly turned around, nearly running into someone approaching to ask her to dance. "Oh, pardon me, princess." He quickly bowed. "I am Zarium of Camden. May I have this dance?" She eyed him. She had seen him once in a while before in meetings. He mostly attended meetings where people received assignments. He was thin, though muscular, and had dark hair that looked nearly perfect. *More perfection. Probably not any better at dancing than the last one.* Still, she curtsied and accepted.

She stood before him in ready position when he reached inside his suit and pulled out a bouquet. Alara eyed it suspiciously. "Were those inside your suit all night?"

"Well, not exactly," Zarium laughed nervously, "it's one of my powers."

"You have the power to produce flowers whenever you want?" *Sheesh, the dragons have a sense of humor.*

He cleared his throat. "No, what I mean is I can picture objects and pull them out from behind something." Alara raised an eyebrow. "Like I can pull them out from under tables, behind trees, out of a river, etc."

"Can you make them disappear too?" She curtly asked.

"Uh, no . . . I don't have—"

"How do you want me to dance with these in my hands?" Alara asked as Zarium turned red. Alara's parents waltzed by, and her mother cleared her throat. Alara smiled at Zarium. "Thank you. They're lovely. Hold on a moment while I set them on a table." She walked back to the table and sniffed the pink flowers.

At the table, Ian stopped her. In a low voice, he said, "Are you going to dance with Zarium?"

"I suppose. He did ask after all." She motioned to the flowers. "And he gave me these, so I think I should probably dance with him."

Ian moved in closer. "Be careful around him. Whenever he's around, it seems like things happen. I don't know if he can be trusted."

She frowned. "What kind of things?"

"Like things getting broken or people near him slipping and falling. Just be careful." She saw her parents coming her direction and excused herself and returned to Zarium.

Zarium took her hand in his and began to dance. She noted that at least he had conversational skills, a huge improvement over her last dance partner. His dance skills were better too—a couple of times he even twirled her without missing a beat. She was surprised when he blurted out. "Princess, I wonder if I might ask you some questions about the Tykee Forest?"

"Why do you want to know?" As far as she knew, only her family and the guards specifically knew about the disappearing trees. They had been trying to keep it a secret, so as not to cause alarm in the kingdom.

"You see . . . ," he stammered, "I uh have a—" A loud crash, mere feet away from them, caused them to jump. One of the pedestals, holding a vase filled with flowers, had tipped over. Two of the guards, who were positioned close by, moved closer when they heard the crash. Seeing no problem, they moved back, and some servants immediately arrived and cleaned up the broken pieces. Alara's mother told everyone not to worry and to continue dancing. She gave Alara a look. Alara mouthed, "I promise I didn't do it."

Before Zarium could ask any more questions, Alara said, "I'm going to get a drink and rest for a minute." She left Zarium standing in the middle of the floor. *Ian said strange things happen when Zarium is around. Was this his fault?* While she drank, she watched Zarium. He awkwardly made his way to the wall and stood there. *I need to find out more—*

"Excuse me, Princess." She looked up and forced herself to smile as another young man asking her to dance. She accepted, and off they went to the dance floor. She didn't need an introduction to this one. She knew exactly who he was—Asher. His blond hair was down to his shoulders and pulled up in a neat tail. He always wore fancy clothing so everyone would know how important he was, and he walked with his head high and shoulders back, making it easy to ignore anyone he wanted to. Today, he had on a white suit, with a black vest, and a collar scarf. She looked at his shirt as he took her hand in his and noticed he had diamonds for the buttons. Alara wasn't impressed.

Her brother Claud had been friends with Asher for years. Asher was on the military council and attended meetings from time to time. His father had been a duke before he had been killed years earlier in a battle. Asher pulled her closer. "I do hope you weren't hurt or frightened by the crash earlier. We can't have anything happening to you."

"I assure you, I have faced far more dangerous things than that." She hoped he understood she didn't need suitors sweeping in to rescue her.

"Of course, and I'm sure you will face even more dangerous things in the future when you get to go on a spying adventure."

Alara stopped dancing. "How would you know about that?"

"From Claud. We discuss many topics, including his beautiful sister."

Alara blushed and shook off the compliment. "Claud doesn't know when to be quiet."

"Still, he has great ideas for the kingdom."

Alara fought not to laugh. She and Claud had very different ideas for the kingdom. She would argue with Asher, but she wasn't going to blow her promise to her parents on him. She chose a lighter tone. "As I recall, the two of you got in trouble a few times for your not-so-brilliant ideas."

"No more trouble than you did for some of your ideas," he countered, winking.

Alara was thinking of something clever to say when the song ended. *Thank goodness.* She turned to leave, but Asher grabbed her arm. Reluctantly, she turned toward him. "Princess, I am wondering if you'd like to take a walk outside for a moment."

She had no desire to be alone with him. "My parents insist that I must stay in here and dance for the duration of the dance. They're watching me like a hawk, and if I go out there, trust me, they will be close behind."

He reached for her hand and brought it to his lips before gently kissing it. "Perhaps after the dance, we can talk more, or maybe next week when I come for meetings."

Alara avoided saying what she really thought. "Perhaps." When he turned around, she wiped her hand on her dress.

Alara felt a tap on her shoulder and prepared herself for yet another dance invitation. Upon turning around, she squealed with delight. "Berica!" She threw her arms around her friend.

"You look so beautiful." Berica twirled around in her peach dress with frills going down the skirt all the way to her ankles. Her curly hair cascaded down her back with the sides pulled up. "But you are late as usual." Alara wagged her finger. "And I've been stuck here without an ally."

"I got here early enough to see the last two men you danced with. That first one was so good-looking," Berica teased. Alara shot her a look. Berica put her hands on her hips. "Oh, come on, you can't tell me you didn't notice."

"Even if I did notice, and I'm not saying I did, I'm not here to find a husband." Alara flipped her hair as if that made it final.

"I know. You want to go on an adventure." Alara and Berica talked until Levon interrupted them. "Berica, we'd better leave Alara alone, so she has plenty of time to dance. We wouldn't want to keep her from all the fun."

Alara playfully punched him in the shoulder. "I'll show you fun."

Levon led Berica onto the dance floor. Alara watched them; they seemed happy, and Berica didn't act like she was trapped, but Berica also wasn't as adventurous as Alara.

Alara was disappointed when another well-dressed young man interrupted her. Honestly, she was bored with all of them and didn't see anything too special about them, but she continued to dance with each eligible man throughout the night. Her feet were killing her. She glanced at the century-old timekeeper on the wall—only an hour more. She could make it.

Grateful for a small break, Alara dashed to the side to sit on a chair at one of the guest tables, where she slipped off her black shoes. The table had a black tablecloth with crystal glasses and plates. In the center of the table, there was a miniature fountain with flower petals sprinkled around it.

Upon further observation, she noticed a small fish, swimming above brightly colored rocks. She was so enthralled with the fish that she didn't see her brother, Claud, sit next to her until he said, "What did you think of Asher?" He moved his eyebrows up and down.

Alara's head jerked slightly. Claud was the oldest at twenty-eight. He had a trimmed beard and wore a dark blue suit. Alara wasn't in the mood for his teasing. "The mere fact that he thinks highly of you is all the information I need to know that I don't want to choose him." She lightly elbowed him.

"What?" He feigned being offended. "I'm a model citizen, and anyone I know would be an excellent choice for you."

Alara's mother came by again and reminded her about her responsibility to dance. She stood up and waited for the next man to approach her. After five more dances, she was grateful when a servant rang a bell and her mother made an announcement to end the ball. She thanked everyone for coming and for making the night truly special for Alara. Alara forced herself not to roll her eyes.

Alara and her family stood by another set of doors and said goodbye to each person. The doors went directly outside and down a small stone path that led the guests to the place where their carriages were waiting, ready for them to leave.

When the last person had left, Alara walked toward the doors they had used when entering the ballroom that night. As she walked, she slipped her hand inside a pocket of her dress. *What's this?* She pulled out a folded-up piece of paper. "Be careful." She glanced around, wondering who could have put it there without her knowledge. *Is it a warning or is it a threat?*

Her thoughts immediately turned to Zarium and the conversations she had throughout the night. She debated showing the note to her parents but decided against it. She didn't want them coming up with any reasons why she couldn't go on her adventure trip. This would be her little secret. She could add it to her evidence papers.

Alara saw her mother coming and quickly slid the paper back into her pocket. Her mother wrapped an arm around her. "I'm proud of you for handling tonight so well. Did any of the suitors catch your eye?"

Alara glared at her mother. Even if they had, which they hadn't, she wouldn't let her mother know anyway. "No, but I will pick one to fulfill my obligation." Her mother's hopeful expression quickly changed to disappointment. Seeing her father, she took the opportunity to change the conversation. "Did you figure out what made the pedestal fall?"

Her father's forehead creased slightly, but he quickly smiled and shrugged. "Probably just a breeze." He wiggled his eyebrows. "Or maybe it was from all the twirling and spinning you and that young man were doing."

Berica and Alara's brothers were quick to join in, teasing her about their favorites. Disgusted, she said, "If you all liked my dance partners so much, why don't all of you marry them?" They laughed, but Alara didn't find any of this funny.

She wanted them to hold a ball for her brothers. She'd love to go to a ball like that. Alara heard Ian behind her whispering with her father. She slowed her pace until they were walking next to each other. When there was a lull in the conversation, she nudged Ian. "So, besides the ability to make objects appear out of thin air, do you know if Zarium can also make them appear in random places?" She fingered the note in her pocket.

"I don't know. Why would I know that?"

"I thought that since you seemed to know so—"

"Alara," Claud interrupted, "Asher asked me to see if you'd meet him outside for a few minutes." *Boy, he's persistent.* She was racking her brain for a good excuse when her mother came up beside her.

"It's late, and Alara still needs to get out of her ball attire and get ready for bed. She can talk to Asher some other time."

Alara had never been more grateful for her mother's timing. Alara turned to Claud, "I guess we'll have to talk some other time."

When Alara got to her room, she said goodnight to the guard, though she knew he wouldn't say anything back. A guard always stood watch at each of the rooms of the royal family and any guests at night. She took the note out of her dress and set it on her bureau, pondering what to do about it. How had it gotten in her pocket? She remembered the crash. She bet Zarium caused the crash, as a distraction, so he could put the note in her pocket. Maybe he was behind the disappearing trees. He did mention the forest.

Chapter 6

The next morning at breakfast, Alara rambled from one subject to another, talking about anything to keep the conversation off the dance. If her mother knew she was avoiding the topic, she clearly didn't care. "Have you decided which young man you will be seeing?" Her mother asked.

Alara's shoulders slumped. "No, I only met them last night, and I've been sleeping until about thirty minutes ago. When did I have time to think about it?"

"Would you have thought about it more if you had thirty days?" Her mother asked sarcastically.

"It wouldn't matter how long I had to think about it because there wasn't a single one that interested me." She saw her parents' expression and really dug in "Not. Even. A. Little."

Her father fidgeted and changed the subject. "Does everyone remember that we have a meeting later this afternoon?"

Alara shifted uncomfortably and said as casually as possible, "Remind me who will be there." Out of the corner of her eye, she saw her mother's cheek twitch.

"This is a meeting with the rulers from Clim, Shara, Kova, and Thoren," her father answered. Alara remembered that they were meeting today because the leaders of the five largest kingdoms, which made up an alliance and council called the Great Five, were already there from the dance the night before. Alara was excited for this meeting. She hoped that because multiple kingdoms were having similar problems with magic being stolen that someone would have some information that would give her a better lead.

After breakfast, Alara took out her evidence papers and put the note from her dress with them. She wrote down each person's name who she had contact with, the events that happened, and what she suspected as a result. It was a start. Whether her parents liked it or not, she was determined to solve the mystery.

She flopped onto her bed, remembering she still had to pick someone from the dance to see. She knew that eventually, she'd want to, so she could get more information by going on her spying adventure trip, but for now, she could continue to find out information around town and make the whole situation a little more painful for her parents, who surely thought she'd choose more quickly. She smiled to herself, glad to have such leverage.

She scratched the back of her neck and remembered her locket. She looked on her bureau, but it wasn't there. She was certain she had placed the necklace there the night before. Frantically, she searched around her bureau and bed, but it wasn't there. Her pulse quickened. Tears stung her eyes. Her throat felt like it was closing off. She should have never taken it off. She ran out of the room and didn't stop until she'd found her mother. Through her tears, Alara said, "I've lost the locket. I can't find it anywhere."

"I remember you put it on your bureau last night."

"That's what I thought, but it isn't there anymore."

Her mother seemed unfazed by the issue. "I'm sure it will show up somewhere. Perhaps this will give you a good reason to clean your room." Alara scowled and walked quickly back to her room, trying to remember if she had done something else with it after the dance.

She scoured her room, but she didn't find it anywhere. With no hope, she leaned against a wall and slid down it, folded her arms across her knees, and put her head into her arms. *Probably a sign that I will never have more than one power.*

Her thoughts raced. She was positive someone had taken her necklace—maybe one of the servants who cleaned. Though her parents had always made them make their beds and pick up after themselves, the servants still dusted and took the sheets off the bed once a week to wash them. If they were in her room searching for things, maybe they found it. *My evidence papers. What if someone finds those?* She gathered up her evidence papers and headed to her secret room. It wasn't entirely secret, but no one had used that room in a very long time, so that made it secret enough.

She walked quickly through the hall until she saw the painting of the castle. Underneath it, she ran her hands over the wall, feeling for the smooth stone. She pushed it in and pulled the door open to reveal a set of stairs. She closed the door behind her and walked down the stairs.

At the bottom of the stairs, she turned left and went down a hallway that led to a room that had the belongings of past leaders. Either her parents didn't like the stuff in the room, or they didn't have room to display it anywhere else, so they stashed it down there. She went to the back of the room, pulled on one of the stone blocks. It was attached to a circular metal piece, and she twisted it. The door opened into a room, which she entered. She put the evidence papers next to a chair. When she was finished, she walked through the secret door and shut it, turned the brick, and pushed it back in.

Later that day, on her way to the meeting, she was stopped in her tracks by angry shouts coming from the White Room. She went invisible and stood by the door eavesdropping. Claud and her father had been fighting more frequently lately. She heard an angry outburst from Claud. "I don't see why I can't come to the meeting!"

"Because this is a meeting for the rulers of kingdoms."

"Alara isn't a ruler either."

"She will be someday."

"Good luck turning her into a queen." Alara wanted to barge in there and give Claud a piece of her mind, but she remained still. Claud continued, "Why don't you change the rules and make the oldest son the heir to the throne? It would make more sense. Alara doesn't even want to be queen." Alara shivered. While she often wished she wasn't the heir to the crown, it sounded different when someone else suggested it.

"That's not the point." She heard her father raise his voice a little more.

"You're right. The point is this kingdom is struggling, and it's because we're stuck on tradition and never move forward with new ideas."

"New ideas that will put the people of this kingdom in danger are what you want. Why? For your *own* selfish gain." Alara heard a hand slam on the table and flinched. She couldn't see her father, but she knew his face was bright red. He didn't often get angry, but when he did, everyone had better watch out.

"Maybe you're the one who is selfish and doesn't want to try new things," Claud fired back. "Because you're afraid of losing some of your power. What? It's okay to talk about my faults, but not about yours. You believe you do everything perfectly, but you don't, and the forest issues are proof."

Her father was eerily quiet. Alara wondered if something was wrong until she heard him say in a calm voice, "The fact is, you're not going to this meeting and that's final." Alara jumped back as the door slammed open and Claud stormed out. Alara began walking away, but her shoes squeaked. *Stupid shoes.*

"Alara," her father called out, "you can go visible. I know you're there."

Alara appeared and stepped inside the room, blushing. "I . . . uh . . ."

"How much did you hear?" Her father asked.

Alara hung her head. "Enough to know that Claud doesn't think I'm capable of being queen someday."

"I wouldn't worry too much." They both turned in surprise at her mother's voice. "He isn't in a position to make any changes to the law, so it doesn't matter anyway." Her mother turned to her. "I know we don't always see eye to eye, but I have every confidence you will make a great queen." Alara was relieved to hear that her mother believed in her. "And that you will be the next ruler." Alara caught the tone and knew her mother was reminding her that it was her responsibility, not choice.

"Thank you, and I know," Alara said.

"Now," her mother said, "let's get to the Grand Council Room to greet the rulers." Alara and her parents stood at the door and greeted each person who entered.

When the last ruler was seated, Alara, her parents, and a guard entered the room. Alara and her parents sat down, but the guard stood in front of the door.

They only used this meeting room when there was a large group, since it could hold up to fifty people, when they met with royalty from other kingdoms, or for special occasions, and it was refreshing to be in. It was larger and fancier than any of the small meeting rooms.

Alara moved her chair in toward the large brass table in the center of the room. On the table was a gold table runner laden with fruit and cheese on silver trays. She reached out and grabbed an apple slice and a piece of cheese from the silver trays that sat on a gold table runner. She glanced at the wall of the flags of every kingdom their kingdom was associated with. The Vashka flag hung in the middle and was larger than the others. It was white and red with a black dragon holding a sword.

On the wall directly in front of Alara, there was a huge mural depicting the mountains in the kingdom. The purples, greens, and blues were vibrant and beautiful. It had been painted nearly eighty years earlier, but without any natural light in the room, it stayed well preserved.

Her mother opened the meeting. "Thank you for coming to this meeting and for coming to the ball last night. It is always a pleasure to associate and work with each one of you."

Alara's mother looked at her. She had asked Alara to also thank everyone. Alara rose. "Yes, thank you for coming. You truly made the evening a special one that I will remember for years to come."

Alara looked at her mother, who nodded, and Alara sat down. "Now," her mother said, "are there any new developments the council needs to know about concerning problems with people losing magic?"

A king named Exor from Thoren said, "As you know, we've been having a problem with magic in our kingdom. We thought we were getting the problem under control, but it is getting worse."

"Why do you believe it is getting worse?" Her father asked.

King Exor eyed the room and hesitated as he licked his lips. "A faram from one of our cities is missing." Everyone in the room erupted into chatter.

Alara's mother raised her hands, and all went silent. "What makes you believe he or she is missing?"

"No one has seen her for six days. It is extremely unusual for her to leave without telling anyone. No one has come forward having the power to control the dragons. This has to mean she is still alive. I see no other answer besides someone used some sort of force, whether physical or magical."

The princess of Kova asked, "What about the dragons? Are they still there?"

King Exor nodded. "We are fairly sure that they are all still there and alive because no one has completely lost any of their powers. The powers are just unpredictable, which as you know, is common when something serious happens to a faram. They work part of the time or at half-strength. This is also why we suspect that she has been taken against her will. The dragon's magic wouldn't be acting up if she were still capable of accessing Mirum."

"Maybe we all need to increase the security of our farams," Alara's father said. "I know many of them may not like having guards at their door and having restrictions, especially not if they are young and have children at home, but maybe for the time being, this would be in their best interest."

"I don't know if that will really help," King Exor said. "You have guards around the Tykee Forest, yet people still get in. We can put guards around the houses of the farams, but until we actually stop the Magic Robbers, I don't think it will help."

"I agree," the King of Clim said. "Why waste our resources? The best thing we could do is figure out how this is happening and who is involved. We don't even know who is in this group. I'm sure we could all take guesses, but does anyone know for sure?"

"Thank you for your thoughts," Alara's mother said. "Does anyone have some ideas for what we can do to figure out who is part of the Magic Robbers and how to stop them?"

"We can send out more spies and see what we can do," King Exor said.

Alara felt a surge of excitement. Maybe she could talk her parents into letting her go on a spying adventure if it would help everyone. When the meeting ended, Alara lingered to talk to her parents. "We can't stand by. Please let me see what I can do," she begged.

"No," her father replied.

"If we wait too long, we could lose everything."

"Right now, we don't have enough information," her father countered. "If we rush in, we *will* lose everything. Sometimes being a good ruler isn't about taking action, but taking action at the right time."

Alara tried again, using a different tactic: "What if there is a traitor among us who is stealing our trees?" She saw her father's expression change and knew there was something they weren't telling her. "You already know, don't you? Why don't we do something?"

"Whether I suspect a traitor or not, it doesn't matter. More lives could be lost if we don't do this cautiously." Alara watched both her parents carefully. She could tell they were debating whether to tell her something.

"Alara, we haven't heard from Jarius for over three weeks," her father said. "And now we suspect the letters we received before weren't really from him." Alara took a step back as she registered the news. He continued, "I want to find my son and protect him, but at the same time, I know that it isn't time yet."

"How will you know when it is the right time?"

"We just will. You are dismissed; I need to talk to your mother."

Alara wanted to argue but knew it wouldn't help. She went back to her secret room to update her evidence papers.

***

Teron closed the door tightly behind Alara. He turned to Corah. "I didn't want to say something during the meeting, but right before the meeting, one of my guards reported to me that Asher has been seen shapeshifting into another person."

Corah hung her head. "So, we do have a good idea who is part of the magic robbers."

"At least a couple of them." Teron saw Corah's head jerk. "Corah, you do realize there is a high chance that Claud is too. He and Asher are best friends. Besides, we already suspected he could be because of how he has been acting lately."

Corah put her hand in front of her mouth. "I know, but as long as we didn't have evidence, I had hope that he wasn't. When are we going to tell Alara?"

"I don't know." Teron rubbed his hands together. "For our plans to work, it may be necessary to not ever tell her."

Corah moved closer, her eyes narrowed. "You mean we're going to let her be surprised when she is in the middle of it, with no warning?"

"If that is what's best, we must do it." He rubbed his face, wishing there was a better solution.

"No!" Corah's jaw tightened. "I will not have my daughter used as a pawn . . . as some sort of bait."

Teron walked toward her and held her shoulders with his hands. "I don't like this any more than you do, but I guarantee you that the other side is going to use her as a pawn no matter what we do. Our only chance is to figure out how to use what they see as their greatest advantage against them."

"And what's your plan to protect her?" Corah moved so that Teron's hands fell from her shoulders.

"I'm working on that."

"What if she's killed?" Corah asked. Teron took a deep breath and wrapped his arms around her, pulling her in for a hug. Corah pulled back. "I hope we don't have to lose our whole family to save the kingdom."

Chapter 7

Alara spent the next couple of days attending meetings about education and taxes and did research about powers and farams disappearing. One afternoon, Alara was sitting in her room reading when she heard a knock on her bedroom door and found Berica standing there.

Alara pulled Berica into the room. "What are you doing here?"

Berica nudged her. "What do you think I came for? I want to find out who you will be seeing from the ball."

Alara's shoulders fell. "I haven't chosen anyone. I'm trying to make it as painful as possible for my parents."

Berica looked upward and put a finger on her chin. "Doesn't doing that prolong your pain of not getting to go on an adventure?"

Alara puffed out her cheeks and blew out the air. "Yes, but I can do a little bit of spying in the area."

Berica's eyebrows shot up. "Do you have suspects?"

"Mostly one suspect. Zarium has a lot of suspicious activity, and I want to see if I can find out more about him."

"You are in pursuit of a man!" Berica put her hands in the air and jumped up and down.

Alara put a hand on her shoulder to stop her from jumping and put her finger from her other hand to her lips to tell her to quiet down. "No . . . I mean yes . . . I mean . . . why did you have to say it like that?" Alara folded her arms.

"So, I could see you get flustered," Berica laughed with delight.

"All right. Enough of all this talk. Let's play a card game." Alara grabbed some cards from her shelf.

"Oooh. You're avoiding the topic."

"And if you don't stop, I might avoid you." Alara poked Berica in the rib, tickling her.

***

The days following the dance, Zarium used his tracking ability and focused his thoughts on Alara. He closed his eyes and pictured her in as much detail as possible. Each time, in his mind, a small view of Alara's general surroundings would flash through his mind. Most of the time, she was inside the castle.

Like normal, the scene would be a little hazy, but he never saw anything that gave him reason for concern. One day, he tried using the bark and nothing happened. Now he knew. He could track someone for three days with the bark. That same day, he received a message saying the king and queen wanted to talk to him.

Zarium waited for King Teron and Queen Corah in the Black Room. He put his hands in his pockets and rubbed the piece of bark. It had been tempting to test it out on his other powers, but he had resisted. He had pulled it out a couple of times, thinking that what the king and queen didn't know wouldn't hurt, but each time, he had chosen not to use it.

The door to the room opened, and King Teron and Queen Corah quickly entered. They sat on the opposite side of him. Zarium handed Teron the piece of bark. "Good work, Zarium," he said.

Zarium raised an eyebrow. "What do you mean?"

"I can track people when I give them a gift," King Teron said. "When I gave you the note at the dance, I put a tracker on it, so I know you only used the bark for the purposes I asked you."

You've got to be kidding me. Zarium nervously laughed. "So, you already knew how long I could track someone with a piece of flyn bark. Why did you need me to give Alara the flowers and put a tracker on them if you could've done it?"

"A test."

Zarium thought back to how many times he nearly failed that test. He felt heat in his face and neck. He had almost blown it.

Queen Corah picked up the bark and held it in front of him. "Now, we know we can trust you with more important responsibilities." He wondered if this was his reward for being loyal. Maybe he'd finally get a piece of bark for his own. Then Queen Corah dashed those hopes. "We have another assignment for you that is different from anything we have ever asked of you." Queen Corah bit her upper lip. "If you accept, you will be given this bark to help you."

Zarium listened attentively as they explained their idea and what they wanted him to do. He couldn't believe what they were asking. When they finished, they asked him if he would do it. He avoided eye contact. After a long silence, he told them that he'd think about it.

***

The next couple of days didn't improve Alara's investigation efforts. Her evidence papers didn't look any different than they had a week ago.

Early one morning, Alara went invisible and walked around the city. Normally, she loved the smell of the bakeries in the morning and the bustle of people doing what they loved.

But this morning, she couldn't stop thinking about her abysmal options. Her parents were hounding her at every meal to choose someone—she got indigestion just thinking about eating. Besides, if she didn't choose someone soon, her parents would select someone for her. Also, she hadn't been successful in her attempt to spy on Zarium. Every time she tried to follow him, he would disappear. She needed a different plan.

She stared at the ground as she walked and saw a beautiful purple rock with yellow bands. She stooped to pick it up, hoping this was a sign of good things to come. After all, it was her favorite color. She would add it to the other rocks she had been collecting ever since she could walk. She loved all the different colors and shapes of rocks. She walked on as she admired her rock.

Suddenly, she bumped into someone and turned in time to see the person fall to the ground. Alara made herself visible. "Sorry, I didn't see you."

The man stood up and brushed himself off. "That's all right, I was just thinking before heading off to a meeting, and I wasn't paying attention."

Alara gasped. *Flower boy.* "Oh," she said as flatly as possible, "it's you again."

He looked around nervously. "I'll uh see you around sometime."

Alara only glared at him and walked away. She was about to go invisible and follow him when she heard her name. She turned around and saw Levon.

"What are you doing here?" She asked in dismay, realizing she was losing her suspect.

"I'm on my way to see Berica. I was a little surprised to see you out here."

"I love walking, especially in the mornings." She put her hands up and did a quick twirl. "It's my favorite time of day. What about you? I know mornings aren't your favorite time of day."

"I have a breakfast date with Berica."

"Breakfast." Alara took out her timekeeper. "Drat. I've got to go or I'll be late."

***

Zarium followed a servant toward the Black Room. He was nervous and could hardly think. He had changed his mind ten times that day alone. It had consumed his thoughts over the last week until he couldn't stand to think about it anymore.

Zarium was escorted into the room. He bowed and approached the king and queen with his head held high and his shoulders back. Queen Corah invited him to sit, but he remained standing. He had been nervous and preoccupied all morning, and he just wanted to get this over with. "I've thought about what you asked." He saw them both lean in slightly. "I've pondered over the potential consequences . . ." He took a breath. "And I will agree to do it."

King Teron sat back in his chair, but Queen Corah reached her hand toward Zarium. Zarium reached his hand forward, and Queen Corah pressed a piece of flyn bark into his palm. Zarium didn't look at it or rub his fingers over it. He shoved it into his pocket, bowed, walked out the door of the meeting room past the guard, and didn't stop until he was outside, where he transported to his house.

***

Alara changed into an outfit more appropriate for breakfast, knowing her mother wouldn't approve of the casual dress she had on earlier while walking around. The dresses her mother approved of were stiff, restricting, and uncomfortable. Her mother told her that it was to ensure she kept good posture and didn't fall asleep during meetings. Alara preferred dresses that were loose, so she could easily ride horses or climb trees.

After she changed her dress, she decided that she had enough time to go to her secret room and look at her evidence papers. She walked quickly down the hall, pushed the smooth stone, and went downstairs.

Once in the room, she analyzed it, noting that Zarium had more suspicious activity than anyone else. First, there was Ian's warning, and of course, there was the crash. She thought back to the note—she suspected he had put it there when the crash happened. Also, he had acted awfully strange that morning—nervous and in such a hurry to get away.

Alara pondered an idea that entered her mind. It would allow her to fulfill her obligation and enable her to do a little spying on Zarium at the same time. She stood drumming her fingers on her cheek, racking her brain for a better idea. After deliberating for several minutes, she reluctantly consigned herself to this fate. She headed to the dining room.

As they ate, she grew more and more nervous until finally she just had to bring it up. "I've been contemplating this whole suitor thing."

Her mother eyed her suspiciously. "Really?"

"Yes, and I have decided on one." Alara twisted her fingers nervously.

Her father wiggled his eyebrows. "Who is this young man?" The smile on his face nearly made her sick. Her mother still looked skeptical, as if she suspected she had an ulterior motive.

"It's Zarium. The one I was dancing with when the pedestal fell over. I'm not saying I want to marry him; I'm just saying if I must choose someone, he is the one I choose to fulfill my obligation."

Her mother leaned back in her chair, staring at her. After several uncomfortable seconds, her mother called for the messenger and dictated a letter.

Chapter 8

Zarium was deep in thought when he heard his mom say, "Zarium, sit down. What is with all this pacing? You are making me nervous."

Pulled back into reality, he stopped pacing. "It's nothing."

She smiled at him. "Zarium, I'm your mother; I have known you long enough to know it isn't 'nothing.'"

He puffed out his cheeks. The king and queen had asked him to become friends with Claud and Asher. How was he supposed to become friends with Asher? He fingered the bark in his pocket. What had he gotten himself into?

Zarium had been snubbed by Asher since his father died. The rumors surrounding the death of Zarium's father resulted in many people treating him and his mother poorly. Ever since Zarium was allowed to sit in on some of the council meetings, Asher had harassed him and tried to make him look like a fool.

Zarium told the king and queen that he'd rather rid the kingdom of venomous snakes or something not as difficult. On a serious note, he told them this could be the most impossible task ever. If that had been all they asked, it would have been okay, but no, there was more.

They gave him a piece of flyn bark that once again he couldn't use for himself, but when it came time, and Claud and Asher trusted him, he was to give the bark to them as a sign of his loyalty to them. He was also to act more and more like he agreed with them in meetings.

He sat down next to his mom and bounced one of his legs as he pondered. He heard his mother again. "Does this have to do with the ball the other night? You haven't been the same since you returned." He ran his fingers through his hair. His mother placed her hand on his shoulder. "I bet it has something to do with Princess Alara."

His face brightened. He could certainly use that as his excuse, and it was something his mother would actually believe. "I wanted to impress her, but I think I blew it. I even gave her flowers, but she didn't seem too impressed."

"Really? You gave her flowers?" Tannah raised an eyebrow.

Zarium avoided eye contact by turning the bracelet on his wrist. "Yes, can't I give a gift without having ulterior motives?"

"You could, but over the years, I've learned that you don't."

He waved his hand in the air and busied himself fixing a chair that had broken the week before. A few seconds later, out of the corner of his eye, he noticed she was still looking at him.

Zarium reflected on the day his father died. His body had been brought in a wagon, where it was left while attention was given to those who were injured. Zarium had run to his father and sat in the wagon next to him.

He had barely received his powers a couple of months earlier. Though he knew his dad was dead, he'd tried healing him anyway. He was his son, after all. Nothing he did worked, and he had been devastated.

Due to the chaos of the injured and the death of many, he was uninterrupted for nearly an hour. Because he was in the presence of the dark magic for so long and was quite young, it was possible that it could change him and make him desire more dark magic, even if it didn't happen until years later.

Coming in contact with a dead body that had dark magic on it was one way to gain dark magic. Another way was to do something truly evil: killing, betraying a trust that led to dire consequences, or making an oath with others who were evil.

A knock at the door pulled Zarium back to the present. He answered the door, surprised to see a messenger with a letter for him. It had the official stamp of the queen on it. He quickly opened it. His mother was immediately at his side. "It says my presence is requested at the castle."

"Do you think it has to do with the princess?" His mom asked, smiling. "Perhaps she was impressed with you at the dance."

"Maybe, but I was sure she didn't have an interest in me. To be honest, she didn't seem like she was interested in anyone, or even that she was enjoying the ball. I guess I should hurry and see what this is about."

He heard his mother cough and turned around. "Don't you think you should change your clothes and look a little more presentable in case it is about Princess Alara?"

"I guess I can," he shrugged, "but I'm pretty sure that isn't why they want to see me. They will probably want me to take care of some problem, and I will ruin my good clothes."

His mother smiled and nodded. "I know but humor me."

Ten minutes later, he presented himself for her approval, wearing a nice pair of pants and a button-down shirt. He had even brushed back some unruly strands. His mother smiled. "Much better."

Zarium waited for five minutes inside the Blue Room before he heard a loud booming voice. "It's nice of you to join us and in such a timely manner." King Teron walked to him and shook his hand.

Zarium bowed. "The pleasure is all mine. How can I be of service?"

"Today, we have an opportunity for you that perhaps you will find enjoyable." Teron motioned toward Corah. "It seems our daughter would like to get to know you a little better after meeting you at the ball. We are giving you official permission to spend time with her."

Zarium's head shot up. "Really?" King Teron laughed at Zarium's surprise. Zarium wasn't convinced, especially after his encounter with her that morning. Was it a trick? He recovered from the shock and politely said, "I would be honored to spend more time with Princess Alara."

"Good," Corah said, "we hoped you might say that." She turned to the servant at the door. "Tell Alara she can come in."

Alara walked in with her head held high and curtsied. Zarium bowed. "I am pleased you'd give me the honor of getting to know you better."

She flashed him a big smile. "You did stand out at the dance. You were, after all, the only person to give me flowers."

"I wasn't sure if you liked them. I'm glad they suited you."

Teron and Corah excused themselves and left Alara and Zarium alone. Well, almost. With all the guards around, Zarium still felt like it would be hard to get to know her. He looked out the window of the room and saw that the sun was shining brightly. "How about we go for a walk through town?"

Alara looked in the direction of the guard. "That sounds like a good idea."

Once outside, he turned to Alara. "I was a little surprised to receive the invitation."

Alara turned toward him. "I feel like I should mention why I really wanted to see you." He avoided eye contact as Alara said, "You see, I made an agreement with my parents that I'd go to the ball, and choose one of the young men to spend time with at least three times."

"And what do you get out of this agreement?" Zarium asked, trying to sound like it didn't bother him at all.

"I get to go on a trip I have wanted to do for a little while now. My mother doesn't approve of me going, so I made her a deal." She shrugged and sped up slightly.

"I suppose you're telling me this so that we both know what to expect up front?"

She bit her lower lip. "I figured you'd rather I be honest and not lead you on. Furthermore, since this is not a romantic endeavor, we will call these meetings and not dates."

He laughed. "It seemed kind of strange when I got the invitation. You didn't show any interest in me when we bumped into each other earlier." She felt the color rising in her cheeks as he said, "What are we going to do on these meetings of ours? It seems getting to know each other isn't really on the agenda."

Alara was quick to reply, "Oh, but if I must be here anyway, we might as well find out more about each other. It certainly can't hurt, and I don't want it to be . . . awkward." She winced.

"It's a little late to not be awkward?" He chuckled. "Tell me, Princess, wouldn't it be easier if we did three short meetings in one day?"

She raised an eyebrow. "You clearly don't know my mother. Trust me, that would never work for her. Besides, each meeting must be at least an hour."

As they walked, she asked him several questions. He mentioned that his father had served as an advisor representing the city of Camden. "Our fathers sat in many meetings together."

"Did your father retire? I don't remember ever seeing him in meetings."

Zarium didn't want to have this conversation with Alara, but he figured she could get access to the information if she wanted.

He grabbed a dried corn snack at the vendor nearest them and offered part of it to Alara, though Alara politely refused. "My father was killed seven years ago in an . . . accident. Ever since, it has just been my mom and me."

"I'm sorry. That must have been hard." Trying to lighten the mood, she nudged him. "You were too much on your parents, so they only had you, huh?"

He had barely taken a bite and was grateful for the chance to gather his thoughts. He took his time chewing before saying, "I did have another sibling, but he uh well umm . . . that is he . . . sort of . . . disappeared. And we have never seen him since."

Alara covered her eyes with her hands. "I didn't mean to bring up a painful topic."

"It's fine." He shoved the empty package into his pocket. "My brother disappeared two years before my father was killed. He was seventeen. It's been hard on my mother, but she's strong."

When Zarium believed it couldn't get worse, he saw Asher walking toward them. When Asher got to them, his foot skidded to a halt and kicked some dirt onto Zarium's shoe. Zarium knew it was on purpose, but he didn't want to make a scene. "Hello, Asher," he said as politely as he could. Asher nodded but said nothing, making Zarium regret that he acknowledged him at all.

Asher turned to Alara. "Princess, it's good to see you." Alara nodded and asked him where he was going. Asher told her he had some meetings and excused himself. With Asher out of earshot, Zarium said, "Not exactly the friendliest person."

"He has always been friendly to me, both in meetings and at the dance."

Zarium pressed his lips together to keep himself from saying something he shouldn't. All at once, he heard shouting. A wagon and horses were headed their way without a driver. Zarium grabbed Alara and shoved her several feet away. The horses turned around and headed for them again. They both jumped. No matter where they went, the horses followed them.

Alara went invisible and jumped onto a fence. Zarium pulled an object out of his pocket and thrust it out in front of him. Frightened, the horses turned sharply, causing the wagon to tip over and break. People ran toward the horses and calmed them down.

A man ran toward them, apologizing and saying he had hit a strange bump in the path that knocked him off the wagon. He bent over to get a closer look at his horse which had a bleeding leg. Zarium pushed past the horse owner and gently put his hand over the horse's wound. At first, the horse fought against his hand, but then it relaxed. A few seconds later, Zarium removed his hand, and the wound was gone.

Zarium stood up and turned to Alara. "Are you okay? You disappeared. I didn't know you could go invisible."

"And thank goodness. Those horses seemed to be after me. How did you turn them away?" Zarium produced a fake snake. Alara pulled a face. "Interesting. That was smart thinking. Speaking of having powers, I didn't know you were a healer."

"Yeah." Zarium motioned toward the castle. "I think we should head back to the castle. I don't want to cause alarm, but I think we should play it safe."

Zarium saw Alara look at her timekeeper. "What if we walked around the courtyard instead? No runaway wagons should be able to get to us from there."

He thought about telling her no, so she couldn't use him just to get her time in for the day, but instead he muttered, "I guess."

Soon, they stepped through a metal gate attached to a gray stone wall. They walked along a cement path that curved around the castle and throughout the orchards and gardens. As they walked by a stone fountain, Alara brought up the dance and asked him why he was interested in the Tykee Forest. "Who wouldn't be interested?" He shrugged. "They're the most unusual trees, both in color and function. What other type of trees do you know of that enhance powers?"

She leaned in closer. "So, you want some of the bark?"

"I think anyone would love to have a piece. When I asked about it at the dance, I was just curious about a few things that were going on. I like a good mystery."

"How do you know that there is a mystery about the trees?"

"Your parents have me do a lot of things in the kingdom that would probably surprise you. I know that trees are disappearing." He smiled to himself, noticing how her furrowed eyebrows added a certain charm. He picked a leaf off one of the trees and spun it between his thumb and finger as he changed the subject and asked her about what it was like having four brothers.

Alara spoke with such enthusiasm as she told him stories of the things she did with her brothers—the injuries they got, some of the interesting pets they tried to keep over the years, the picnics they went on, and the tricks they played on people.

Alara turned to Zarium, "Do you want to know what one of my favorite tricks we played on someone was?" Zarium nodded, and Alara said, "Once there was a cranky, stuck-up ruler who always made sure we realized he was third in command in Vashka." Alara smiled. "One day, his driver went for a short walk, and while he was gone, I got in his carriage and had both me and the carriage go invisible. The driver didn't have a clue what happened. It took a while for anyone to realize I wasn't there. I couldn't leave the castle for a week, but it was so worth it." Alara laughed so hard her face went red. "You should have seen everyone's faces as they searched for this big carriage."

Zarium loved how her whole face lit up as she talked and her brown eyes sparkled. "You know, you're not bad to be around once you loosen up a bit and aren't interrogating me."

Alara locked eyes with Zarium but quickly looked away. "Perhaps we should head back inside."

***

Alara hurried up the steps of the castle. Zarium rushed past her and opened the door. She thanked him and walked inside. Zarium followed behind her. "Thank you for a great meeting."

"Yes, two more to go."

"Right." Zarium turned to leave when Alara's parents came around the corner and asked them how their walk was. Alara quickly replied that it was good, but Zarium said, "Umm, there was a small incident where we were, but no one was hurt."

She watched the expressions on her parents' faces and wanted to punch Zarium. *Why did he bring that up?* He definitely was not going to be the type to go on an adventure. She wondered if he brought it up because he knew why she wanted to go on her trip, and he was trying to stop her. *That little sneak.*

"What kind of incident?" Alara's mother asked.

Alara quickly jumped in. "It was just a runaway wagon. The owner fell off when his horse got spooked. It wasn't anything too dangerous and certainly not anything worth mentioning."

She wanted to kick Zarium when he wouldn't let it go. "Well, what about—"

"Don't worry. Even though today was a shorter meeting, we can make up for it next time with a longer one." Her parents glanced at each other, and she nudged Zarium and mouthed, "Be quiet." She was relieved he didn't say anything else.

Zarium cleared his throat and asked, "When would you like to meet again?"

"Tomorrow," Alara responded a little too quickly. She tried to recover. "I mean, tomorrow would work for me. Would it work for you?"

Zarium's eyes shifted back and forth for a couple of seconds. "How about if we do it the day after tomorrow?"

"Okay, how about two o'clock?"

"I will be here. Well, have a good rest of the day." Zarium bowed to the three of them and left.

Her mother closed her eyes partway. "I see you refuse to call the time you spend with Zarium a date."

Alara ducked her head for a moment before standing back up straight and tall. "A date would imply I'm interested." She pulled her shoulders back and flipped her hair. "And if you recall, I'm not doing this because I'm interested, so we're just having meetings. Meetings, I hope to get through very quickly."

As she walked away, she thought about Zarium and felt her cheeks grow warm. The way he smiled at her while she told him about the prank she did made it seem like he really understood her and what made her tick. The only other person she felt like she could truly be herself with was Ian.

Chapter 9

When Zarium got home, his mom was in the kitchen cutting up meat. She slid a cutting board, knife, and potatoes toward him and told him to have a seat. He told her about his day, or at least most of it. "You didn't spend very much time with her today though. Did it go okay?"

How does a mother always know when something is up? What should he tell her? He examined a spot on a potato. "Well, it was only our first meeting, and I wouldn't want her to get bored of me already."

Tannah raised an eyebrow. "Meeting?"

"Yes," he sighed, avoiding eye contact, "that is what Alara calls them because she doesn't like referring to them as dates."

Tannah put her hands on her hips. "Why wouldn't she refer to them as dates?"

He explained what Alara told him. Tannah raised one eyebrow. "Still, couldn't you spend a little more time at each of these *meetings*? I'm sure you could win her over."

"We probably could spend more time together." He put some potatoes he had cut into a pan. "Today just didn't work out."

"When will you see her next?"

"In two days."

"That's so soon," Tannah said with wide eyes. "Are you sure she doesn't like you?"

"I told you. Alara wants to get all these done as quickly as possible."

Tannah pursed her lips and furrowed her eyebrows. Then she smiled. "Why don't you bring her to the house, and I will cook a wonderful meal for the two of you." She waved the knife in the air as she spoke. "It will help you both to relax."

"Is this your way of saying you want to make sure I don't blow it?"

"Well, someone has to help you." She winked, adding the meat to the pan.

The next morning, Zarium used his ability that allowed him to person-transport and work on his assignment from the king and queen. Besides being able to transport to a place, he could think about a person and transport close to them. Similar to the place-transport power, the person had to be within a certain distance of him for it to work.

He focused his mind on Asher first. Much to his surprise, he found himself on a path that led to the forest. He didn't see anyone else within a hundred yards. Was it possible Asher was inside the forest? Zarium walked through some tall grass and bushes and sat down, looking intently at the forest. Did he dare?

He crawled on his stomach toward the forest, only sitting up when he got to another set of bushes to hide behind. He stayed low to the ground and went around the perimeter of the forest looking for a spot that he could sneak past the guards. He was surprised when he saw his opportunity—a guard had fallen asleep. Under normal circumstances, he'd report this to the queen, but today he was grateful for this chance and snuck up slowly, hoping the other two guards who were each about one hundred yards from the sleeping guard wouldn't notice him.

He was almost inside when he checked above him to make sure there were no snakes about to chase him or loose branches that could fall on him like the last time. He pulled out his sword and stepped into the forest. He didn't feel any different, and nothing had happened. He wasn't sure where to go. He wondered if his power would take him to Asher now that he had found a way into the forest. Zarium thought about Asher again and found himself standing behind a tree. He threw himself to the ground, hoping no one saw him. He lifted his head slightly, looking around him, trying to locate Asher.

He didn't see anyone, but he did hear voices. He immediately recognized one of them as Asher. "Great job stealing this. Now let's see if Alara has any untapped powers that perhaps she doesn't know about. Everyone, be quiet."

Zarium didn't hear anything for nearly a minute and wondered if they had left and what untapped power they were talking about. *Even if there were powers she didn't know about, how would Asher get them? Could it be dark magic? Or was it somehow one of Asher's gifts?* He was going to have to do some research later. He heard Asher curse. "There isn't any power in this stupid locket. Can it be true that Alara only has one power?"

Another voice asked, "What if she has more powers but has put them on other objects and hasn't told anyone?"

"Come on," Asher sneered, "Alara isn't smart enough to keep a secret like that."

The whole group laughed, and someone grunted as something fell to the ground several feet to the left of Zarium. He still didn't know where the voices came from and didn't dare move. He waited for over an hour until he was sure the people were gone before getting up. He walked to the spot where the object fell and saw a locket. *This must be Alara's.* He picked it up. He would figure out a way to return it to Alara later.

Chapter 10

The next morning, Alara sat in the Grand Council Room eating a cookie, waiting for the meeting to start. About twenty local leaders of cities within the kingdom were in attendance. Her mother opened the meeting by asking if anyone had any items of business. Alara listened until a movement caught her attention—Zarium had nodded. He wasn't talking to anyone, and there wasn't anything being said that would warrant him nodding. She struggled to concentrate and found herself entirely focused on Zarium.

She watched every hand and facial movement. Then she saw it as Zarium's hand moved over close to her father's hand—her mother's pencil. She focused on the meeting again as the governor of Zarothan said, "More people are having problems using magic, with certain powers not working at all. Also, there is a lot of activity in Zarothan lately."

All eyes were on Alara's mother. When she spoke, it was deliberate, with each word being spoken carefully. "We are aware that more things are happening and feel the need to tell you that we recently found out that two farams from neighboring kingdoms are missing at least one dragon. As a result, a lot of people have lost powers and won't get them back until the dragons are returned to Mirum."

"If they can steal one dragon, they can and will steal more," the Governora of Durco said. "This is more serious than missing farams. The dragons are mortal if they aren't in their land. If they die, it will take away a lot of people's powers permanently."

"How about if we each agree to put a guard at the house of the farams in our cities," the Governor of Camden said.

Her father wrote in his notebook. "I agree that this would be a good idea. We tried bringing it up in a meeting of The Great Five, but it was shot down because no one believed it would be effective, but we could try it within our own kingdom and see. All in favor, say 'aye.'"

A resounding "aye" was heard from the people in the room.

When the meeting finished, Alara started to leave but was stopped short by her father. "Alara, Claud, Ian, and Zarium, I would like each of you to stay, so we can discuss the meeting."

Once they were all seated, Claud didn't waste any time speaking his mind. He stood up and pounded his fist on the table. "I still say we need to start looking at the leaders of other lands and kingdoms. Surely, one of them is waiting until we are in confusion, so they can attack. Every minute we spend sitting here waiting, we are in danger of losing everything. Even one of the leaders who were here could be a traitor. How would you know?"

Ian slammed his hand on the table. "Why is it that every time we have these discussions, your plan is to go raid someone? We don't have any evidence that any of them are doing it."

Claud leaned in and countered, "Well, it is either people from other kingdoms or people within our own. If it is someone in our own kingdom, we should figure that out. Where is Levon anyway? He has missed several meetings over the last month. Don't you think it is suspicious that he is gone more often while the rest of us are sitting here? He could be out meeting with others and preparing to attack."

"He has his reasons why he isn't here," Teron said. "We aren't going to start blaming other people on the council today."

Zarium interrupted the conversation. "You know, maybe we should consider what Claud is saying." Alara's mouth dropped open. Zarium shrugged. "I'm not saying we should necessarily raid other kingdoms, but what if we did a little spying on them? I know Alara would like to do some spying. This doesn't have to be dangerous. It could be as simple as being invisible and following some of the leaders back after meetings and listening to their conversations. What are they really thinking after the meetings? That type of thing."

Corah looked at Zarium. "That's certainly an interesting idea. However, that could get out of control really fast. What if someone heard something out of context and it caused more problems? We don't want someone taking it upon themselves to orchestrate an attack because of a misunderstanding."

Alara's father leaned back. "Do you have a plan for how this could work, accounting for human error?"

"I don't. But if you give me a few days, I can come up with some ideas," Zarium replied.

"All right," Alara's mother said. "We will look forward to your plan. Perhaps, Claud would also like to give you input on how some of this could work."

Claud seemed confused but pleased. "Yes, of course. I'd be happy to see if we can come to a workable solution."

Alara's mother ended the meeting. Alara saw Claud nudge Zarium and tried to listen while looking like she was busy doing something else. "Thank you," Claud said, "for speaking up for me in there. It's nice to have someone see reason." Claud lowered his voice. "It seems like it's always me against them. We should meet up in the next couple of days and discuss some possibilities for my parents."

Zarium checked his timekeeper. "I have time right now."

"All right. Follow me." Claud and Zarium stood up and walked toward the door.

Alara stood up to follow them when her mother reached out and touched her arm. "Don't go anywhere. We have something we need to discuss with you."

The tone was serious even for her mother. Alara reluctantly trudged over to a chair and sat back down. When everyone left the room, Alara's parents shut the door and sat next to Alara. "Claud invited Asher over earlier today," her father said, "and he asked to—shall we use your words—have a meeting with you."

This was not at all what Alara was expecting. "I hope you told him no."

"I gave him permission." She looked up, but her father wasn't smiling. He was serious. Alara felt like she had lost control of her life over the last week and a half. *Ughhh! Leave it to men to make my life complicated and stress me out.*

Alara opened her mouth, but her mother spoke first. "Asher will be here in a little while to ask you, and I would like you to accept."

"Why can't I tell him no?"

"Because we would like you to use your spying skills to get more information on him."

Alara held back a grin. Her mother was finally speaking her language. Her mother continued, "We need you to put the date—"

"Meeting," Alara interrupted.

"Meeting." Her mother rolled her eyes. "Put it for the day after tomorrow."

"That's really soon."

"We would do it tomorrow, but we didn't want to ruin your plans with Zarium. Also, I don't feel comfortable with you going with Asher alone, so we will put some precautions in place, like having guards go with you."

"You trust me with Zarium but not with Asher? You think Asher is behind the problems?"

"At least involved in some way." Her mother handed her a piece of paper. "We want you to ask him some questions while you are with him. Memorize them. When you ask him, pay attention to his body language and tone of voice."

Alara left and sat in the main foyer, and let a servant to bring Asher in there when he arrived. She picked up a book and pretended to read it. In a short time, Asher entered.

"Princess, I am delighted to see you." He walked closer to her.

"Hello, Asher," she said, without looking up from the book.

"I was wondering if I could talk to you."

Seeing how she didn't have much of a choice, she closed the book. "Yes."

"Do you mind if we go for a walk?" Asher asked.

Alara blinked; he was already trying to turn this into more. "All right." Asher smiled. Alara put the book on the couch. She walked toward Asher and hoped this got over with fast.

They walked out the front doors and onto the main path around the inside edge of the castle wall. Asher wasted no time. "Princess, I wanted to talk to you for two reasons." She turned toward him and nodded. He continued, "The other day when I saw you and Zarium together, I was a little surprised."

She turned her head sharply. "Surprised? Why?"

"Well, for one, given the possible scandal associated with his father's death."

"What scandal are you referring to?" Alara asked, perking up. "I know the family believes it wasn't an accident."

"Did you know that when they found his body, it had traces of dark magic everywhere? It seems that it is likely Zarium's father used dark magic or got involved with the wrong people, and it backfired."

She made a mental note to add that to her evidence papers later.

"Not to mention that when he found his dad, Zarium sat there for some time. They say with the amount of time he spent with the dark magic at such a young age, that it could impact him." *Could it be possible? Was this why Ian was warning me?* Asher furrowed his eyebrows. "I don't want you to get hurt, Alara. Be careful if you are going to be around him. You never know what he could do."

Asher moved closer, and Alara had to force herself not to take a large step back. "Now, I've been wondering something else." She braced herself. "I am wondering, or rather hoping, that you would allow me to spend time with you getting to know you. I enjoyed the dance with you, and I would be honored if you would go on a date with me."

She wanted to say no, but she forced a smile. "I have time the day after tomorrow."

"Oh, I was thinking it would be a few days out, but I can make that work."

"By the way, I don't go on dates." She twirled a piece of hair on her fingers.

"What do you mean?"

"I do meetings. I meet with men, and if they spark my interest, I go on a date with them."

Asher blinked a couple of times before saying, "I look forward to seeing you for our meeting." With that, he walked her back to the castle doors and bid her farewell.

Alara walked inside the door where her mother was waiting. "How did it go?"

Alara sighed. "I agreed to meet with Asher the day after tomorrow." She shivered. "I want to make it clear that I'm not happy about it."

Chapter 11

Zarium and Claud went inside the White Room and closed the door. "Thanks again," Claud said.

"Well, you're right, something needs to happen."

"I've been trying to explain that to my parents for a while now." Claud put his bag on the table. "But they refuse to see that we are stuck in tradition and need to do something else. We have been doing things the same way for five hundred years or more. Meanwhile, times keep changing, and they're going to keep changing."

"If you've been thinking about this for a long time, you must have some ideas."

Claud opened up his bag and took out a notebook. "I do. I have a whole notebook full of ideas."

"What's first?"

"How we choose a ruler." Zarium worked not to smile—he wasn't the least bit surprised this was Claud's biggest concern. Claud kept going. "Why is the next ruler the oldest female? Why not the oldest male? Or the youngest? Do you know what I really think we should do?" Zarium shook his head. Claud slammed his fist on the table. "My father is always speaking about representing the people, so maybe we should let them choose the next ruler."

"That is an interesting idea, and it does seem like it would make things fairer for everyone. No one would get stuck ruling if they didn't want to. I know Alara hasn't been the most excited about being queen—"

"And another thing," Claud said as if Zarium hadn't even been speaking. "There are so many other things we could use our magic for."

Zarium leaned forward and rubbed his chin. "What do you mean?"

"There's the magic that we all have, and there's the dark magic, but there is something else too."

Another kind of magic? Zarium raised an eyebrow. "I didn't know there was anything else."

"Yeah, I learned about it during some of my travels to other *very* distant lands. It's possible to use our powers for things that can only be done with dark magic, as long as it is only for good purposes. It's called gray magic."

Zarium tried to wrap his mind around that idea, but had no idea what Claud was talking about. And what distant lands? Claud continued, "Take shapeshifting. We can't shapeshift into another human with regular magic, but with gray magic, it is possible to shapeshift into a human if you are using it to help another person."

"Okay, but how does one get access to that power?"

Claud stretched his arms out in front of him and laughed. "That Zarium is a discussion for another day, but think about what I said."

Zarium shifted nervously. "Okay. Well, I have an idea of my own that I got when you brought up what you did in the meeting earlier. We could go to the cities where farams or dragons are disappearing and use the tracker power to give gifts to people who we suspect could give us information. We could even put trackers on invitations for meetings that would track the rulers for a few days. I think your parents would let us do that."

Claud smiled. "Zarium, I underestimated you. This is the kind of thing my father would go for." Claud stood up and walked toward the door. "I have somewhere else I need to be, but we'll be in touch."

Zarium's head overflowed with thoughts about the gray magic when he left the room. He walked slowly down the hall. He was overwhelmed and needed time to process what he heard. Could using dark magic for good work? What would be the consequences?

Zarium walked toward the front door. As he walked past the room they had met in earlier, he saw that Corah and Teron were still inside. He asked if he could meet with them for a few minutes. He sat down. "Earlier today, I had some time, so I used my person-transport power to find Asher. It led me right to the forest. I walked around for a few minutes, looking for Asher, before I discovered there was a guard asleep. I guess it's possible he fell asleep, but I'd be willing to bet that some people used magic to put the guard to sleep, so they could enter the forest. While I never saw Asher, I have reason to believe that he was inside."

Zarium hoped they wouldn't ask him any more questions about the forest. He didn't want them to know that he had entered the forest himself. He nervously watched the queen take notes.

Corah spoke to Teron. "We need to find out what happened with the guards." She turned back to Zarium. "What about Claud? You were just meeting with him. Did he come up with any plans?"

Zarium was relieved that they didn't ask any more questions about Asher. He told them about Claud's ideas for electing a leader and his ideas about giving gifts to lots of people and tracking them.

"So basically, he wants to take away the privacy of everyone?"

Zarium chuckled uncomfortably. "It was me who came up with that, but Claud was definitely supportive of it. I also responded positively to his suggestions and encouraged him to explain more. I'm sure there is more he will tell me when he trusts me more. I will try to spend more time with him." Zarium debated telling them about the gray magic Claud told him about, but he decided that for the time being, he'd keep that to himself.

Corah thanked him and told him that they had some information for him as well. "We have a situation that has come up. Asher has asked to be able to go on a date with Alara."

Zarium gripped the table. "What did you tell him?"

"We gave him permission and told him to talk to Alara."

"You think Asher could be involved in dark magic, yet you are okay with him going on a date with Alara?" Zarium's head spun. They had to be joking.

"We aren't doing this lightly," Teron said. "You and Ian will go using an invisibility power that we will borrow from some soldiers. Also, we will have a couple of soldiers go, who will ride just a few feet from the wagon. We suspect that at this time, Asher just wants some information."

Zarium's heart beat faster. "You suspect? You are doing this on nothing more than a suspicion? A lot could happen even if Levon, I, and some soldiers are there."

"Calm down," Teron said. "We have concrete evidence to believe she will be fine."

Zarium took a deep breath. "What if he wants to see her while I'm gone?"

"We already told her to put it for the day after tomorrow, so arrange to make yourself available. You can leave to go to Zarothan after that," Corah said. "Now, we have other matters to attend to, so unless you have more questions, you may go." Zarium had at least a dozen questions, but he knew he would get direction as things progressed. It was the way the king and queen worked.

Chapter 12

The next morning, when Alara got to breakfast, Ian was already seated, scarfing down his porridge. It was the first time in over a month that he had been around to eat breakfast with them. Alara was determined to talk to him. As he got up to leave, she ran after him. "Would you have five minutes that I could talk to you?"

"Yeah, but it may cost you," he joked. "Just kidding. What can I do for you?"

She pulled him out into the hallway. There was a guard there, so she led Ian a few feet more. "Do you remember the dance when we were at the refreshment table and we talked briefly about Zarium?" Alara bit her nails. "Do you think there is a chance Zarium could be behind some of the problems we are seeing?"

"I suppose it's possible, but I don't have any reason to think that."

"But the night of the dance, you told me—"

He rubbed his neck. "Maybe we can talk later. I have to go right now." He darted away.

He's acting strange. Alara went to her secret room and wrote down that dragons were disappearing, Zarium had defended Claud, her mother trusted Zarium but not Asher, and how Ian responded to her questions.

Later that day, Alara sat in the main foyer, waiting for Zarium. She felt nervous, but she told herself it was only Zarium and no reason to feel nervous since she wasn't even really interested in him. But he was handsome, and at times she did find it hard to focus on anything else when he was near. *Enough of these thoughts*, she chided herself. *I can't fall for him.*

Finally, Zarium arrived. He bowed and walked toward her, "I wondered if today, you'd be willing to go on a small trip?" Zarium asked.

Alara raised an eyebrow. "Where will we be going?"

"I thought it would be fun for you to see where I grew up and uh . . . And meet my mom. She wants to have you over for dinner."

There was an awkward silence, then Alara said, "I will have to ask my par—"

"Ask us what?" Her mother interrupted.

Alara turned around, surprised to see them standing there. "Zarium would like to take me to his home to meet his mother," Alara said flatly.

Her mother raised her eyebrows, and her father grinned like he'd won something. Alara shook her head. "The trip would do you good," her mother said. "How will you be going?"

Zarium cleared his throat. "Actually, I was hoping Alara could borrow your place-transport feather."

Alara's mother took the feather out of her dress pocket and handed it to Alara. "Make sure you're careful with this and that you put it where it can't get lost." Alara nodded and took the feather.

With that, Zarium led her outside. "I'm guessing you've never been to my house?" Alara shook her head, and Zarium said, "I just need to be touching your arm or something, so I can think of where we are going and have you go to the same place."

"I know how it works." Alara held out her hand, and Zarium placed his hand on it and thought about his house.

When they appeared on the doorstep, Zarium's mom was waiting. "Welcome, Princess Alara, I'm Tannah, and I am so happy to meet you. We've actually met before at palace parties, but you were young, so I bet you don't remember me."

Alara smiled. "The pleasure is all mine."

Tannah motioned toward the inside. "Please come in and have a seat."

Alara walked inside. It was a simple yet nice home. After the entrance area, there was a cozy room with a couple of chairs with black cushions on them. Next to each chair was a small table with a lamp on it. Alara noticed a nearby table with a game she didn't recognize. She glanced at a wall and saw some paintings. She walked over to them. The first couple were just of Tannah and Zarium.

Further down was one that she assumed was of Zarium's brother and father. Tannah walked to the side of her. "That one," she pointed at the person standing next to Zarium, "is Kursek. And the other one is my late husband, Havid. Aren't they handsome?"

"Oh no," Zarium slapped his head and teased his mom, "we'll never stop hearing stories now."

Tannah pointed to another picture. "This is of the two boys when they were younger. Zarium followed Kursek everywhere. It drove Kursek crazy, but Zarium wanted to do everything he did."

Alara smiled. "I guess that's like me and my brothers."

Tannah chuckled. "I bet your parents loved you following your brothers all around."

Alara stepped away from the pictures. "About as much as you can imagine."

Tannah pointed to the kitchen. "Let's go in there, and we can talk while I make dinner."

Tannah was warm and chatty, and Alara immediately felt comfortable. Alara couldn't help but notice the huge table in the middle of the room with an assortment of vegetables, chicken, and a bowl with liquid in it. The large table seemed out of place compared to the size of the room. Tannah pulled out a chair for Alara and invited her to sit down.

Tannah got bowls and mixing spoons out of the cupboards and drawers. Alara ventured to ask a question. "Have you always lived here?"

Tannah winced slightly and smiled sadly. "No, we used to live in a much bigger place. I would entertain people all the time, but after the accident and the rumors, we moved here." She ran her hand gently over the table. "I kept this table as a reminder of when our family and friends had all been together around it. We had such a happy life—we ate, laughed, sang, and played games around this table."

Those last words hung in the air. Zarium got up and put a hand on her shoulder. "What can I help with?"

She shooed him away. "You don't need to help. You can visit with Alara."

"I insist. I can visit and help at the same time."

"Okay. Go wash your hands, and you can help."

Alara was impressed that he'd help his mom with the cooking. She felt a flutter in her stomach—he was good-looking, with his toned sun-tanned arms, he treated his mother well, and he could cook. Then she reminded herself that she was only meeting with him, so she could go on her adventure. She figured there was no point in her sitting there, so she got up and asked what she could do.

Tannah shook her head vigorously. "Oh, no, you must sit and enjoy yourself. You are a guest in our home and a princess on top of it. You shouldn't have to help."

"This is kind of new for me. It isn't every day I get to help prepare or cook food, so it will be a nice break from my normal life."

Tannah looked at the stuff on the counter and back at Alara. "Oh, all right, you can help with mixing and rolling out the dough."

Alara washed her hands. Then she stared at the bowl and the ingredients, unsure what to do. As a kid, she'd sneak into the kitchen and watch as the cooks prepared meals, and sometimes they'd let her be the taste tester, but she never made anything. She was always fascinated by all the different meals the same ingredients could make.

Tannah walked toward her when Zarium stepped in front of her. "I'd be happy to help Alara." Tannah smiled.

Zarium stepped to the side of Alara and showed her how to mix the ingredients. He handed her a measuring cup to add the flour to a bowl with some water in it. When she was finished, he said, "Now, take the wooden spoon right there and stir it." When it came time to knead it, he carefully showed her what to do and watched as she made a good attempt.

He laughed and moved behind her. "You've almost got it. Just do this." He put his hands over hers and moved them. Alara's breath caught, and she went beet red. Zarium took his hands out of the dough and went back to his own job. His mother nudged him and winked. Alara pretended she hadn't seen that.

About an hour later, they had warm rolls, pork, and lots of vegetables to eat. Tannah got out some glasses and put a little water in the bottom of each, which she turned to ice.

Alara turned to Tannah, surprised. "You have a water-freeze power." Alara clasped her hands together. "Do you have other powers?"

"Yes," Tannah said, pouring some peach juice into each glass. "I also have a fire-lighter power, so I can focus on an object and have a flame appear on it."

"Hmm . . ." Alara mused, "Two nature powers."

Alara couldn't wait to see if her bread really turned out. She took a bite and sighed. It tasted wonderful, especially with the raspberry jam that Tannah had made.

Tannah turned to Alara. "What about you? What powers do you have?"

Alara twisted the bracelet that she had transferred her invisibility power to. It had been a gift from Berica. "The dragons only gave me the ability to go invisible. I used to hope more would be revealed eventually, but the older I get, the less I believe that will happen."

She fingered the spot where her locket used to hang. "Besides, my locket, which the dragons originally put my power on, has been lost, so any chance of having another power is gone."

"You know, Alara, it doesn't matter how many powers you have. What matters is how you use those powers." Alara figured Tannah was trying to make her feel better, and she didn't want to complain, so she smiled and told her she supposed that was true, but deep down, she still wished she had more.

When the meal was done, they cleared the dishes and moved into the living room. Zarium motioned to the game Alara had seen earlier. "Would you like to play a game of Chork?"

Alara nodded, and Zarium moved the table in front of his mom and grabbed a foldable wooden chair for Alara and him. The game had a large wooden board with small holes drilled around it. He got out some marbles and gave each of them a different color. Alara had never played before, so he explained the rules. On a person's turn, the person could place their color of marble on the board and move one of their opponent's pieces to another spot. The person who could get three of their pieces in a row was a winner. Alara learned the game fast and enjoyed playing.

Zarium won the first round with Tannah taking second place. "It is so nice having you visit and play Chork with us," Tannah said. "We haven't played it in a while, but it was one of Havid's favorites."

"I'm glad you taught me how to play." Alara studied the board. "Maybe next time, I will give you both a little competition." Alara picked up one of her pieces. "Today, I didn't fare very well, but we'll have to do it again sometime." Alara was surprised that she meant it. She had enjoyed her time there, not that she'd let anyone else know that.

Alara noticed it was getting dark outside. She checked her timekeeper and told them it was time for her to return to the castle. Zarium and Alara said goodbye to Tannah, who made sure Alara knew that she should come back soon. Alara and Zarium transported to the castle gates, where he opened the gate for her.

They stood there awkwardly for a moment before Zarium said, "Thanks for a great day. My mom will undoubtedly want you over again." He walked her up the stairs to the door and turned to leave.

"Aren't you coming in? Mother will find it strange if you don't come say goodbye before leaving." She saw Zarium smile. She shook her head. "Don't read too much into the invitation."

They walked in, and Alara asked the servant if her mother was available, and soon she came. "How was your . . . *meeting*?" Her mother asked as awkwardly as possible. Alara glared at her.

Alara told her about making bread and learning the game of Chork. She handed her mother the feather. Alara turned to Zarium, "By the way, how did you know my mother had a feather she uses for place-transporting?"

"Because I have been at meetings before when your father has needed it. On one such occasion, I happened to be walking past as she handed it to him. Your father later told me that he often uses it to check on affairs within the lands of the kingdom."

A reasonable enough answer, she supposed. "Will you be available tomorrow for another day out?" She saw her mother glance upward and sigh.

"I will be leaving tomorrow for a few days," Zarium said. "But we can do something when I come back?"

Alara agreed because she had no other choice. She told him goodbye and curtsied to let him know she was done. Zarium bowed and walked out the door. Alara stood for a moment, staring at the spot where he was standing., *I wonder what I will do for the next few days.* Alara noticed her mother watching her carefully and rolled her eyes.

Chapter 13

Alara awoke before dawn and went to her secret room to look at the evidence papers. She shuffled papers around and rewrote some of it in different orders and even directions, trying to make sense of what was going on with Claud, Asher, Ian, and Zarium, but she still wasn't sure what to make of it. She decided that she needed another perspective. She checked her timekeeper—seven o'clock. It was a little early to go to Nori's, so she went downstairs to breakfast.

"Alara, what is the rush?" Her mother looked disgusted.

"I'm going to Nori's in a few minutes."

"That's fine, but couldn't you still at least chew your food?" Her mother's forehead creased.

"Sorry, no time." Alara got up and shoved one more bite into her mouth and left the dining room.

Once outside, Alara went invisible and walked to Nori's house. When she got there, she saw the guard and thought that it seemed so strange to see one there. She went visible and knocked on Nori's door. She waited and waited and waited. She called out to Nori through the closed door, but there was nothing. She was getting worried when she turned and saw Nori coming from the direction of the forest. *What would she be doing?*

Alara walked toward Nori. Nori went off the path and picked up some flowers. Alara caught up to her. "Good morning."

"Oh, good morning, Alara."

"What are you doing?" Alara asked.

"Just collecting flowers and herbs. What are you doing?"

Alara hesitated, but she really only had one reason to be there. "I was actually coming to talk to you. Would it be okay if I asked you some questions while you gather flowers?"

"Of course. What's on your mind?"

Alara wrung her hands and told her about the accident at the dance several weeks before. She wasn't going to mention the note, but before she knew it, everything tumbled out. She mentioned what her brother had said about Zarium and the horse accident which also happened when Zarium was around.

When she finished, Nori didn't say anything. "Well, what do you think it all could mean? Do you know anything about Zarium? Do you suppose he could be behind the missing trees since he's so interested in the forest? It was suspicious that the accident happened right after he was struggling to come up with a reason for asking me questions." Alara paused, out of breath.

Nori stood up and signaled to Alara to move in closer. Alara took a step toward her and leaned down. Nori whispered so quietly that Alara could barely hear her. "Perhaps, you should be careful around Zarium."

Alara waited for Nori to say more, but she didn't. "Are your dragons still safe?"

"I haven't checked on them today, so perhaps I will after I go to the market today."

Alara watched Nori head down another path. *What a strange conversation.* It was then that Alara saw Zarium walking away from the direction of the forest. *What is going on? Is this why he couldn't see me today?*

She walked behind a tree. When Zarium got closer, she called out, "Zarium." His body jerked in surprise. Alara asked. "What have you been doing today?"

"I was . . . going for a walk. What are you doing?"

"You took a walk to the forest and back?"

Zarium folded his arms. "I didn't know there was a law against someone walking along this path."

She wanted to ask more questions, but he told her he had to be going and transported away. Alara was frustrated with him and wished she could somehow follow him.

On the way to the castle, she went invisible and walked through the market-place. She saw a most unexpected sight at one of the shops. She went visible and called out to Nori, "Nori, is that you?"

Nori turned and waved. "Alara, how good to see you today." She walked closer.

"You sure got here quickly."

"What do you mean?" Nori asked, adjusting her bags.

"We were just talking a few minutes ago at your house, and now, here you are."

Nori surveyed the area and leaned in. "I don't recall seeing you today." Alara didn't know what to say. Nori grabbed Alara's arm and put the bags into her hand. "Follow me."

Alara followed Nori to her house. Once inside, Nori checked each of her rooms and opened every closet and cupboard. This was the most frantic Alara had ever seen Nori.

Alara went to the counter and put the bags of food down. Then she sat down and waited for Nori. When Nori was finished, she sat down next to Alara. "Now, tell me about this conversation you say you had with me earlier."

Alara recounted everything that had happened. When she finished, Nori asked her if in their conversation, she had given her any advice. Alara told her about the warning concerning Zarium.

Nori sat silent for quite some time, thinking. "I'm not sure what is going on, but I assure you, I didn't talk to you this morning. I was at the marketplace for a couple of hours today."

"But if you weren't here, who was?" Alara shivered and rubbed her arms.

"I don't know, but it wasn't me. Perhaps someone shapeshifted into me."

"But one can only shapeshift into an inanimate object."

"Normally, that's true." Nori's voice dropped to a barely audible whisper. "But if someone were using dark magic . . ."

"I've been wondering about that, actually. Is there any way for someone to know if someone is using dark magic?"

Nori bobbed her head. "Perhaps there could be someone who has that magical power, but otherwise the only way to know if there is dark magic is if someone dies who was using dark magic or was killed by it or you catch a person using magic in a way that could only be done through dark magic like shapeshifting into humans. In the first one, whether they were using dark magic or if it was used to kill them, it lingers around the dead person like a cloud of dust. It's almost as if the magic is lost and doesn't know what to do or is looking for someone else to settle on."

Alara remembered her discussion with Asher. "Hmm . . . interesting. Does that happen often?"

"I don't know if I'd say often, but it has been known to happen." Nori stood up and pulled her food out of the bags. Next, she got a knife and a cutting board and started chopping up the vegetables from her bag.

Alara watched Nori chop for a minute before asking, "Is there something I could help you with?"

Nori handed her a pot. "Could you fill this with water and start it boiling?"

When the pot was filled, Alara turned on the stove and put the pot on it. She stood next to Nori, watching her chop the last of the carrots. "There's something else I wanted to talk to you about as well. Have you heard about farams having their dragons stolen?"

Nori turned away from Alara and stirred some carrots into the pot of water. "I heard about one such instance a few days ago from one of my friends."

"Do you have any idea how the dragons are being stolen?"

Nori said nothing, but took out some meat and started cutting it as well. Alara stirred the pot, hoping Nori would say something. Finally, Nori spoke. "I'm gathering information and trying to figure it out."

"What about another faram?"

Nori stopped cutting and turned to her. "Are you asking if I suspect that a faram is a traitor?"

Alara ducked her head. "It would make sense if it were an inside job."

Nori dumped the meat into the pot while Alara continued stirring. "Though I have wondered about it, it would only be speculation, and nothing good comes from spreading rumors." Nori motioned for Alara to step aside. She stirred the pot and added some powder to the soup. "The one thing that doesn't make sense is that each faram has their own special way of opening up Mirum. I'm sure they wouldn't share that with each other, so I'm not sure how one of them would find that out to steal dragons."

"Is it possible that multiple farams are involved or stealing their own dragons?" Alara asked, peering into the pot.

Nori dumped some peas into the pot. "Not necessarily, but maybe someone is using magic to gain access. Maybe even dark magic is being used to help a person with a thought-receive power to get into the thoughts of people when the person doesn't want someone to receive their thoughts. But, I don't know." Nori poured some celery into the pot. "Just guesses."

"What would happen if a person the dragons chose to be a faram later became evil?"

Nori turned the heat down and let it simmer. She walked to the main room and sat down. Alara joined her. Nori leaned back and closed her eyes. "There are often multiple people who could be a faram, though more than one will never be able to fill the position at a time over a specific colony of dragons. Ultimately, the dragons determine who will be the next faram. When it is time for a new faram, the dragons give the current faram a dream, and the faram contacts the new person. The faram will teach them how to enter the Mirum, and the new person becomes an apprentice until the time comes for the faram to turn over the care of the dragons to the new faram. In a case where the faram dies unexpectedly, the dragons will reveal, through a dream, the secret of how to get into their land to the next person who will be the faram, and the person gets thrown into it, though they could ask for help from farams in other cities. The dragons wouldn't choose someone who wasn't good."

"Ever?"

"Such deep topics for this time of day," Nori said, with a penetrating gaze. Alara continued to look at her expectantly. Nori ignored the looks of Alara for a time before saying, "If the dragons were evil, they could choose a faram who shouldn't be in power."

"How does a dragon become evil?"

"Same way a human does."

Alara stood and took out a piece of paper and wrote some notes. She tapped the pencil on her cheek before saying, "Would you know if any of your dragons were missing?"

"I take care of many, but yes, I'd notice if one was missing."

"And so far, yours are all here?"

Nori got up and stirred her food again. She tasted it, scrunched her nose, and added some more powder to it. "My dragons are safe."

"But isn't it possible that while you are opening up the land of the dragons, someone could read your mind without your permission and get access to the dragons?"

"I suppose that would be one possible way to do it," Nori seemed unfazed by the concern.

"How can you protect your dragons, so they don't get stolen?" Alara asked. "Doesn't it alarm you that someone could be listening to our conversation right now?"

Nori just continued to stir. Alara moved closer and whispered, "Well?"

"If a faram could hide their thoughts or scramble them, that faram wouldn't have to worry about it." Nori winked.

Alara pondered over that information as Nori tasted her soup again. Alara had more questions, but it was clear she wasn't going to figure it out from talking with Nori. *How can she always be so in control of her emotions?* "Thanks, Nori. I'll let myself out."

Alara left Nori's and went to Berica's. Alara covered her ears as Berica screamed with delight. She invited Alara in and took her to her bedroom. "I'm glad you came to visit. What brings you here today?"

"Can't I just come to visit my friend and have fun?"

"Yes, but knowing you," Berica raised her eyebrows, "you have multiple reasons for coming today."

"Okay, my life is getting complicated. You know that I had a meeting with Zarium the other day." Berica nodded and lightly nudged her, though Alara assured her that she was only seeing him out of obligation.

"This may be the only time I ever get to tease you about a man."

Alara shook her head. "No, I need to marry before I can officially take over the kingdom. It's the rule of the land. It wouldn't matter whether I was a male or a female; the ruler must be married."

"Does this mean you're finally accepting that someday you'll be the queen?" Berica asked, bouncing on the bed.

Alara avoided looking at Berica by playing with a spot on the bed. "I believe I can do a lot of good as queen, and I'm seeing the situation differently than I used to." Berica put her hand on Alara's forehead. Alara swiped her hand away. "Don't make a big deal out of this," Alara told Berica about some of her discussions with Nori and how it was changing her perspective.

"Still, I can't believe *you* would actually agree to marry."

"That will probably still be the challenging part."

"Only you would see a proposal of marriage as the end of the world. Do you think Zarium could be the one?"

"Actually," Alara paused for suspense, "that's partly why I came to talk to you." She saw Berica perk up. "But not in the way you're thinking." Alara laughed as Berica playfully slapped her arm.

Alara picked up her bag and rummaged through it, pulling out the evidence papers. She unrolled them and explained what she had. Berica interrupted her. "Wait, you went on two dates with Zarium in three days? Why didn't you tell me you went on another date?"

No matter how many times Alara corrected her, Berica insisted on calling them dates. It annoyed Alara a little, but Berica was the only person she'd let get away with it. "Maybe because I knew you'd tease me about it. And before you say anything else, I'd do a third meeting soon, if he didn't have appointments. I want to get them over with and go on my trip. It is purely an obligation."

"Now, it's even more interesting because there is Asher," Berica giggled.

"I'm only going with him, so I can get more information." Alara intentionally left out the information about her parents wanting her to spy on Asher. She trusted Berica but knew that the fewer people who knew about things, the less chance there was that the plan could get into the wrong hands.

"Isn't that what you said about Zarium?"

"Yes, and it's still the only reason I'm seeing Zarium."

"Are you sure?"

"Yes," Alara said in exasperation. "Now, what do you make of all this? If you were me, what would you do next?"

Berica grinned. "I'd definitely go on another date with Zarium."

"I'm serious." Alara put one hand on her hip and rolled her eyes.

"So am I."

Alara let out her breath. "Okay, but what about the other stuff?" Alara asked in a tone that let Berica know she was done with the joking.

"I'd let it play out and see what happens. The way I see it, there are only a few ways you can get the information you want: someone confesses, you overhear the information, or you gather more clues as things play out naturally."

Alara bit her lip. "I wish someone wanted to confess more information. Or if I could just talk my parents into letting me go on a spying adventure . . ."

"Where would you go for this adventure?" Berica arched her eyebrows.

"I would go to Zarothan since interesting things have been happening there."

Berica leaned in. "What kinds of things?"

Alara hesitated for a moment, wondering how much she should leak out. She figured this was something she probably heard from Levon anyway. "Zarothan is one of the lands where a faram has gone missing."

Berica seemed lost in thought before saying, "Interesting, I wonder if all of this has something to do with why Levon left yesterday?"

"He went to Zarothan?" Alara said in surprise. "When is he coming back?"

"He borrowed a place-transport power, so he could get there quicker, but he said he would be there for a couple of days."

Interesting. Alara wondered if the reasons Zarium was going to be busy were related to Levon's trip. Alara stood up. "If you hear any more information, will you let me know?"

"Of course." Berica got a huge grin on her face. "As long as you tell me if anything happens between you and Zarium."

Alara threw a pillow at her. "You're impossible."

Chapter 14

Alara returned home and went to her room to get ready for her meeting with Asher later. She had only been there a few minutes when a servant knocked on her door and told her that her parents wanted to see her immediately. She quickly headed downstairs. The servant led her to the Blue Room. Once inside, she closed the door and sat down.

"We have important news to discuss with you," her mother said. Alara took a deep breath and waited for the worst. Her mother continued, "Earlier today, we were notified that the King and Queen of Faskin are missing their son, Shem, the heir to the throne." Alara's head shot up, a million questions going through her mind. "We want to keep it a secret for as long as possible. Only a few rulers know about it. In the meantime, we want you to be more cautious."

"Okay, I understand."

"Additionally," her mother said, "a group of guards will go on your outing with Asher. A couple will ride in front, with two more about ten feet to the side of you and two more directly behind you. The rest will follow thirty or so feet behind you. Hopefully, they're close enough to protect you, but far enough away that the two of you can still talk. I don't know what powers Asher could have on him. In case he has the ability to person-transport and is using dark magic to allow him to transport another person with him, I am giving you this string." Corah tied the string around Alara's upper arm under the sleeve. "I've placed a tracker on it, so we can find you if anything happens."

Alara raised her eyebrows. "That's reassuring. You tell me I'll be safe, but you tell me that I may not be."

"It is just an extra precaution. If I believed it was likely to happen, you wouldn't be going today. The guards will be enough to keep Asher from trying anything. Did you memorize some of those questions I gave you?"

"Yes."

"Now," her mother said, "shouldn't you get dressed for your *meeting?*"

"Yeah," Alara mumbled.

Alara tried on several dresses before finding the perfect one. She wanted to look presentable but not look like she put too much work into it. She chose a simple blue dress that hung loosely on her and went down to her midcalf. She brushed through her brown hair but didn't put it up.

When she was satisfied with how she looked, she pulled out the card of questions and tips her mother gave her. She saw that it said to bring up doubts about Zarium and that she suspected he was into dark magic. She wasn't sure why they wanted her to bring that up, but she would do her best.

Soon, a servant knocked on the door to tell her that Asher was there. *Great. Let's get this over with.* She looked in the mirror one last time and went out to face her fate.

***

Zarium and Ian met with Corah and Teron to go over the last-minute changes with extra guards being there. Zarium felt a little bit better about the situation. Before they left the room, Corah handed each of them an omp with invisibility power that they had borrowed from a couple of soldiers. Zarium and Ian walked outside the gates where the stable boy had left their horses tied to a couple of trees. They got on their horses and went invisible.

They saw Asher come out the door and hold it open for Alara. Zarium clamped his jaw. Alara and Asher climbed in the carriage and headed out. He and Ian stayed about thirty feet behind Asher and Alara at first, riding several feet to the right of the soldiers.

He couldn't wait until they got on the soft dirt, so they could move closer without being heard. It was clear that Alara and Asher were engaged in conversation, but Zarium couldn't hear any of it. Zarium pulled at his shirt, feeling hot from the full sun.

Zarium shook his head as Alara laughed and Asher moved closer. He felt a nudge and Ian whispered, "Asher is going to hear your frustrated sighs if you don't stop doing them."

Great, I get caught being jealous. He whispered back, "Sorry. I will be more professional."

After several minutes, Asher turned the carriage onto a dirt road. Zarium and Ian moved up until they were close enough that from time to time, they could hear parts of the conversation. Zarium heard Alara say, "Yes, I'm glad I came."

"Would you rather it were Zarium?" Asher asked.

Alara scooted closer, "No, I'm enjoying being here. Besides, I sometimes wonder if Zarium isn't involved in dark magic."

"Why do you think that?"

Zarium leaned forward on his horse. "I mean, you warned me about him, and Ian warned me about him, and strange things do happen when he's around. Plus, I've seen him coming from the forest many times."

Zarium wanted to ask Ian why he warned her, but he didn't dare say anything. Asher didn't miss a beat when it came to putting Zarium down. Zarium frowned. This was the worst date he had ever sat through.

Alara changed topics. "What do you think is going on with dragons and people's powers disappearing?"

"I don't know, but obviously there are some pretty smart people out there. If we aren't careful, it could be us losing our powers. Speaking of powers, what are the most interesting powers that you have heard of that your friends have?"

"Well, one friend can heal people."

"Oh, are you referring to Zarium. I know all about his powers. What powers do others of your friends have? You know, your real friends." Zarium clamped his jaw down. *Real friends? What makes him think I'm not a real friend?*

"I know someone who can turn water into ice."

"Who can do that?"

"Just someone I met one day. But what about you, do you have a favorite power or maybe something you wish you could do with your powers if you had a piece of flyn bark?"

Zarium listened to them both go back and forth for some time before realizing this was going nowhere. Asher didn't ask her out because he wanted to go on a date or even kidnap her. He was only looking for information.

Zarium had never been so glad for a date to end. At the castle, he waited for Asher to take Alara in and for him to come back out. Asher disappeared as soon as he was on the castle steps.

Zarium and Ian got off their horses and headed into the castle. Zarium told Ian to follow him to the Blue Room.

"Okay, what was that? You warned Alara about me?"

"I can't explain right now, but trust me, it isn't what it seems."

"Fine, whatever," Zarium said.

Ian asked a servant to get his parents. When the king and queen got there, Zarium and Ian gave them back the invisibility powers and updated them on what happened. Ian started telling them about how Asher had asked questions about Nori's dragons.

"What are you talking about?" Zarium asked. "I don't remember this being mentioned."

"I have the object-communication power which gives me the ability to split an object in half, like a rock, and then I can give one half to a person and keep the other half for myself. It allows me to hear sounds near the half of the object that is with the other person."

"Really?" Zarium said, surprised. "But weren't we a little far back for that?"

"Normally, it would only work within about twenty feet, but with a piece of flyn bark, I could hear it even when we were thirty back."

Corah thanked them for the information and excused them. Zarium had many more questions, but he was frustrated about the whole situation and left the castle and transported home.

***

Shortly after her meeting with Asher, Alara and her parents went over what she had found out. She explained her frustration and how he didn't give her any information but tried hard to get information from her. "He even had the nerve to ask me about what powers my friends have and about Nori's dragons and if any were missing. I guess the questions he asked give us some information, but he wouldn't directly answer any of the questions I asked. By the way, he seemed kind of nervous throughout our meeting. I don't think he'll ask me out again."

Her father rubbed his hands together. "That is relieving."

"I suppose. By the way, I was wondering . . ." Alara swiped her hand in the air. "Do either of you know where Zarium is today?"

"We know where he is, but that doesn't mean we are going to tell you."

Alara could feel her temper flaring again. She told herself to calm down, but the anger got stronger until Alara couldn't hold it in. "I am the crown princess, and yet I feel like you are keeping stuff from me. If I must be the queen someday, shouldn't I know these things? I recently discovered that Levon is in Zarothan. This is the exact place I want to go on my spying adventure, and it is where a lot of stuff is happening, and I want to know why he's there. Is this where Zarium is too? Why am I not included in this?"

Alara's mother stepped in with her voice slightly raised, "You can't only be the crown princess when it is convenient and suits you, and not be it when it doesn't fit in with your plans. If you want to know more about what is going on, start acting like you are the crown princess and take your responsibilities seriously."

Alara opened her mouth to refute it, but what could she say? There was a lot of truth in that statement. Angrily, she turned and stormed out.

As she was walking past the library, she saw a glimmer of light out of the corner of her eye. Curiosity got the best of her, and she headed to investigate. Alara saw Ian sitting in a green chair, close to one of the many windows, reading a book under a lamp. She walked up to him and read the title out loud. "'How to Disengage the Magic of an Enemy.' I see you are doing some light reading," she joked.

"I was curious what it would say about dark magic." He thumbed through the book to another spot. "People who use dark magic can do some things that we are limited in doing, yet the world isn't being taken over by the dark magic that has existed for thousands of years, so obviously, it isn't more powerful than good magic even if people use it to do more than we can with good magic. I want to understand why." Ian closed the book. "What did you come in here to talk to me about?"

"So, I know Levon went to Zarothan this week."

"You know about that?"

"Why wouldn't I know about that?" Alara folded her arms.

"Hey, don't get upset." He tapped the book. "I just wasn't aware that very many people knew. Did you have a question about it?"

Alara knew this was a big risk, but it was her best chance. "Do you know when he and Zarium will be returning from Zarothan?" She tried to appear as confident as possible.

"I'm not entirely sure." A smile spread across Ian's face, and his left eyebrow went up. "It's only been a day since you saw Zarium, and you're already missing him?"

"No, I just want to finish my three meetings and go on my spying adventure."

"It sounded like from the council meeting the other day that you could have plenty of spying adventures without even going to Zarothan."

"Yeah, maybe. Thanks for the information." Alara turned around and left.

In five minutes, Alara had gone from frustrated to on top of the world. She still had one meeting left, but something was going on, and she wanted to know what it was. With or without the three meetings or permission from her parents, she was going to go to Zarothan and spy on general conditions as well as see if she could locate Zarium.

She knew it would probably prove her parents' point that she was too spontaneous and didn't think things through, but at that moment, she didn't care. She came up with a plan. She needed to get out of the castle without drawing attention to herself. She considered sneaking out with her invisibility power and stealing a horse, but she worried that would alert them faster. The best way would be to do it right in front of them.

She realized this would make it impossible for her to take extra clothes or food with her, but the city of Durik was fairly close, where she could stop and get provisions. If she told them she was going to go riding, she could take water with her, and it could buy her a couple of hours before anyone would start to worry.

As she went to bed that night, she was filled with excitement and nervousness. She hoped everything would go as planned.

Chapter 15

Zarium ran as hard as he could through the crowd of people. He looked back to see if the mysterious person was still following him. *Curses.* He ran between several shops. Then he saw his chance. There was a table outside one of the food tents that no one was sitting at that had a black cloth hanging over it all the way to the ground. He hoped nothing was under the table to impede his plan. He slid and grabbed the grass to stop himself from sliding all the way through. He took deep breaths, trying to slow his breath and not make a sound. He wished he could see what was going on.

Earlier that day, he had been exploring Zarothan, doing an errand for the king, and looking for clues. From the city, he could see the largest mountain, Mt. Fraton. Something about it lured him to it. Once he got to the mountain, he felt something he hadn't felt in a long time. He searched his memory. *Evil.* A part of him wanted to leave the area, but another part of him had to know what was there. He put on a cloth mask he had brought.

He climbed up a ledge and peered over it. There was a group of people standing around a fire, with more people walking out of a nearby cave. He started to inch closer when he heard something. He looked up toward the sound and saw a hooded man staring at him. He immediately transported into the city. He was sure he was safe, but the hooded man appeared a mere fifteen feet away.

He had run through groups of people, weaving in and out, but the man always seemed to find him again. That was when he saw the table. He was sure no one would find him.

Zarium's heartbeat faster and faster when he heard someone asking questions about a man who was running. He heard a "thank you." Zarium prepared to bolt.

He saw someone's shoes, barely visible under the sheet. He went to run out the other side of the table, but he couldn't move. He tried harder to move, but nothing worked. His heart pounded. He grabbed his knife, ready to attack.

The sheet lifted, and there stood a man with a sword. The man jumped back a few feet. Zarium tried to run away but couldn't. He lunged toward the man. Zarium tackled him to the ground. The surprised man dropped his weapon as he fell to the ground. Zarium kicked it several feet away with his foot.

Zarium had the man pinned down. The man was clawing at him, but Zarium held his arms tight. One of the arms got loose, and the man grabbed the mask off his face. Zarium heard a gasp. "Zarium, is that you?"

The man lifted his hood. "Levon?" Zarium quit fighting. He'd never been so glad to see anyone. "What are you doing here?"

Zarium released Levon and helped him up. Levon spoke, "My parents sent me here to check on things. What are you doing here?"

"I came to deliver some provisions to some men your father has stationed here." Zarium brushed the sweat off his forehead. "I'm pretty sure I lost five years off my life today. I thought you were with the group of men on the mountain."

"I thought the same about you," Levon said. "I don't suppose you got a good look at them, did you?"

"No, they all had some form of covering over their faces."

"Or," Levon mused, "they were using powers to make it appear like they had masks over their faces."

Zarium felt a throbbing in his arm and saw blood dripping from his elbow. "Looks like you got cut," Levon said.

"What gave you your first clue?" Zarium joked. "Probably happened when I flew under the table or tried to escape. Speaking of which, I tried to run from you when you got close to the table, but I couldn't. Why?"

"My father has an immobilization power. He let me borrow it for this trip. I couldn't use it on the mountain or while we were running because you weren't close enough."

"Okay, that makes sense." Zarium put a hand on his hip. "How did you find me after I left the mountain?"

Levon smiled. "That was luck. I was using a place-transport power from someone I knew, and I took a chance that you went to Zarothan and hoped for the best. If you were one of the Magic Robbers, I didn't think you'd go too far from the area."

"But the city is so big. How did you find me?" Zarium asked.

"I have the location-vision power, which means I can close my eyes and think about a person who is within a certain range of me, and I can see them and their surroundings. I told some people I was meeting someone here and described the scene. After several tries, someone led me here. From there, it was a matter of keeping an eye on you and asking around. When you hid under the table, all I could see was the ground and darkness. That's when I began asking if anyone had seen someone running, and that led me to you."

"I didn't stand a chance." Zarium ran his fingers through his hair. "I hope the evil people don't have that power."

"They probably do. Well, after all this running, I'm famished." Levon patted his stomach. "We could grab some food."

"I'm starving, but it would probably be better if we traveled to Durik and ate there. I don't want to be around if someone else catches us. I've had all the excitement I want today."

Levon tousled Zarium's hair. "You've got to grow a bigger backbone."

Zarium swatted Levon's hand away. "All right. Let's get going."

***

Alara woke up early, prepared what she could, and headed to breakfast. She wanted to get started early, but she knew her parents would be suspicious if she didn't show up to breakfast. She was grateful when the cooks brought the meal before anyone could start to question her or give her another lecture.

She was careful not to eat too quickly or act differently, but she was so nervous. She was sure she was doing a good job until her mother spoke up. "Alara, is something bothering you?"

Startled, Alara fumbled for a response. "No, of course not, why do you ask?"

"You seem extremely preoccupied this morning," her mother replied

"I've been pondering the issues with the trees and the farams and dragons. You know that my three meetings are almost over, and I was thinking that maybe I could find something out."

Maybe too early considering how yesterday went. She tried again. "I have also been thinking a little about Zarium . . . ," she hesitated, "on a personal level." Both her parents looked at her. "I mentioned yesterday that I'm a little confused about him. He's always nice when we do things, and he seems genuine, but there are things that make me wonder if that is real or not. I worry a little about the whole situation."

"Are you thinking of seeing Zarium beyond the three meetings?" Her mother questioned.

"I don't know." Alara resumed eating and tried to ignore the looks her parents were giving her.

After Alara waited for what she considered to be an appropriate amount of time, she asked to be excused and told them that she was going for a ride to think about things. They agreed that it would do her good to get some fresh air.

She grabbed some water and a small snack from the kitchen and walked to the stables, where she asked the stable boy to saddle her horse.

She tried to wait patiently, but he seemed to be taking forever. She was positive it never took this long. When he arrived, he handed her the reins.

She thanked him and jumped on the horse. Once outside the courtyard, she went to an area that didn't have as many people and made herself invisible. She didn't want anyone to see where she was going as she rode toward Zarothan.

Without place-transport abilities, it would take her about two days to get there. She was grateful that Durik was close and that she could get food.

As Alara approached Durik, she made herself visible and pulled the hood of her riding cloak over her head. Durik was smaller than Vashka but still full of people bustling around. She figured she'd go unnoticed. She walked around the shops buying food, clothes, and other supplies.

Chapter 16

When Zarium and Levon got to Durik, they grabbed some food from one of the food huts. They sat down at a table and talked about what they discovered in Zarothan. "So," Levon said, "did you happen to find any clues about Jarius or anyone else that has gone missing lately?"

Zarium shook his head. "I entered several tunnels and caves in the mountain and explored, but I didn't find a single other person until I saw the small group."

"That makes me wonder more if they're using power to make it so what we see is distorted."

"Yeah, it would make sense. From what I understand, it is how they steal the—" Zarium squinted his eyes. Levon turned his head to look where Zarium was looking. Zarium was sure his eyes were deceiving him.

He stood up to get a closer look. Levon turned, trying to figure out what Zarium was looking at. Zarium muttered, "Is that . . . no it can't be . . ." Zarium squinted again. "It has to be."

Zarium stepped over the bench he was sitting on. Levon stood up. "What's wrong?"

Zarium pointed. "Please tell me that isn't Alara."

Levon threw his hands in the air. "That's her. What is she thinking?"

They both headed toward Alara. She was absorbed in what she was doing and didn't notice them sneak up behind her. They waited until they were inches from her, and Zarium shouted, "Alara!" She jumped and nearly fell over. If he weren't so angry, he would have laughed.

She turned, clearly shocked to see the two of them. "What are you doing here?"

"No, the real question is, what are you doing here?" Levon said. "I have a feeling our parents don't know you are here."

"I am a grown woman, and I don't need everyone's permission to go somewhere when I want to."

Levon shook his head and pointed his finger. "Alara, it's not safe to be going places without telling someone where you are going, especially at this time."

"What do you mean *especially* at this time?"

"You know what I mean." Levon kept his voice low. "Someone obviously is plotting something, and since you are the crown princess, you are at risk."

"So, what are you going to do now?" Alara asked.

Levon cleared his throat, "Hopefully, Zarium will lend us his place-transport power, so I can take you home."

"What if I refuse to go home?"

"Alara, we can do this the easy way or the hard way." Levon pulled a rope out of his backpack.

Exasperated, she spat out the words, "All right, I'll go back the easy way."

Shortly after, Levon arrived and handed Zarium back his knife. Zarium transported to the castle. He asked a servant if he could get an audience with the king and queen. He waited for nearly an hour, but finally, he was led to a room where they were waiting.

Zarium updated Corah on what he saw in Zarothan. He told her that he believed that something was happening at Mt. Fraton. Corah nodded. "What evidence do you have that the location is correct?"

"I have nothing but a feeling. It feels different there, like there is so much dark magic you can feel its presence in the air. I suspect the Magic Robbers are using dark magic to somehow hide everything from us, and if we could see it, we would find dragons in cages, and somewhere we would see Jarius. I know a feeling doesn't help you, but I remember how I felt when I found my father. The dark magic was palpable, though I didn't know that's what it was at the time. Anyway, those mountains give me that same feeling."

"You didn't see any sign of Jarius?"

Zarium shook his head. "No, I'm sorry. I could go back and scope the area out if you'd like."

Corah thought about it. "No, let's hold off for now."

Zarium bowed and left. At the front door, as he opened it, he heard his name and turned to see Alara. "Are you still coming back tomorrow?"

"I'm surprised you'd even want to see me after what happened today."

"I still have to finish the third meeting if I want to go on my trip."

Zarium wasn't sure he wanted to go. Maybe he could tell her that she had to do her three dates with Asher. That would certainly serve her right. It really would be funny. But he swallowed his pride. "I'll be back tomorrow." With that, he shut the door before Alara could say anything else.

Zarium left and transported to Nori's to get her thoughts on some things. As he knocked on the door, he heard her say, "Just a minute." A minute ended up being five minutes. He noticed a purple flower in her yard. *Alara's favorite color.* He considered picking it, but wasn't sure if that was an activity the guard would approve of or not.

When Nori opened the door and saw Zarium, she excitedly invited him in. "Sorry," she panted, "I was finishing up with the dragons. I'm glad you stopped by. How's my favorite nephew?"

"I'm your only nephew." Zarium grinned.

"True, but I have a feeling you'd be one of my favorites even if I had several. Now what can I do for you?"

"How are your dragons doing? Have you had any problems with any disappearing?"

"No, so far my dragons are safe, and no one has figured out how to get in."

"Does it worry you that someone might?"

"I try not to worry about what I can't control," she replied. "I do my best to keep my dragons safe and hope it is enough."

"I'm not sure that hope is a very good plan."

"Perhaps not, but sometimes, it's all we have. I have a feeling you didn't come here to discuss dragons today. How about if you tell me what is really on your mind."

Zarium laughed. "You're right. I didn't come here to talk about missing dragons. I came here because I'm confused. I don't know who to trust and who not to. I'm not even sure if I trust myself anymore. I feel like so much depends on me, and I worry I won't be able to live up to the expectations put on me."

"Ahh, finally we get down to the stem of the problem."

He tilted his head to the side, "Don't you mean the root of the problem?"

Nori sat down in a chair. "No, I don't believe you have given me the root, just the stem."

Her gaze seemed to go right through him. He sighed. She was right. "Okay, I give in. My problem has to do with . . ."

"Alara?"

"How would you know that she has anything to do with all this?"

Nori smiled. "I pay attention. Alara comes to see me from time to time, and we have discussed you, though probably not in the way you would want. She's been trying to figure out if you are behind the forest and dragon problems. It didn't help that she saw you coming from the direction of the forest a couple of days ago."

Zarium didn't say anything. He wondered how much he should tell his aunt. "After the questions I asked her at the ball, and the fact she saw me near the forest, I can see how that would make her curious." He rubbed his neck and paced.

"Well, does she have any reason to be worried?"

He pondered what he could say. He had to be careful, even if she was family, that didn't mean he could tell her everything. "There are a lot of things I can't explain to her at this point. I want to make sure that no matter what happens, Alara will be okay."

Nori smiled. "I have a feeling this goes deeper than that."

"Okay, fine. You're right. I really like her, and I don't want to be the reason she gets hurt."

"Let me assure you, Alara can probably take care of herself better than most people."

"She only has one power though."

"What does that have to do with anything?" Nori asked, throwing her hands in the air.

"She's limited in what she can do."

"Now you listen." Nori stood up, shaking her finger at him, and moving closer. "I have spent years trying to convince Alara that she is as capable as anyone else and that she doesn't need more powers. She just needs to believe in herself more. Don't you go getting her all worried that her power isn't good enough. If I had to place my bet on a match between you and her, I'd bet on her!"

Zarium was surprised by her reaction. "I didn't mean to say Alara isn't capable. I'm fully aware she's strong and independent and doesn't need anyone."

"That's where you're wrong," Nori countered. "She does need someone. She needs someone to believe in her. Someone who will let her be strong, but also be strong for her. If you don't mess it up, that someone could be you. She has fears too. Don't forget that."

"Okay, so what do you think I should do?"

"That is for you to decide. If I give you all the answers, it will be my life, not yours."

Zarium stood awkwardly, wondering if she'd say anything else. Finally, he said, "Thanks for listening and for the advice."

Zarium left and thought about what Nori said. He had to get things finalized for his meeting with Alara. He needed to show her that he supported her without using his desire to protect her to stop her from living her life.

He didn't want to go into town, so he walked along the road to the Tykee Forest.

Zarium hadn't walked for long when he heard his name. He turned around and saw Claud. He stopped and waited for them to catch up. "Where are you headed?" Claud asked.

"I often walk this road when I want to think."

"Why this particular road?"

Zarium knew this was his chance. "Because I like getting as close to the forest as possible. I dream about the possibilities of having the flyn bark to give me enhanced powers."

Claud dug his toe into the ground. "What would it be worth to you to get a piece or two?"

"Are you saying you could get me one?"

"I didn't say that at all. I'm just wondering what you'd be willing to do to get a piece."

"If the opportunity arose," Zarium whispered, "I'd be willing to make a deal."

"Good, I may have some connections. I'll see what I can do." Claud paused before speaking to Zarium again. "By the way, I heard you were in Zarothan this week."

"How did you hear that?"

A smile spread across Claud's face. "*Connections.* What were you doing there?"

"The king asked me to take some supplies to some soldiers he has stationed there."

Zarium had hoped that would appease Claud's curiosity and was disappointed when Claud said, "Is that all you were doing there?"

Zarium debated. How much could Claud know? Did he already know that he had been on the mountain? "No, while in Zarothan, I was drawn to the mountains."

"Really? Why the mountains?"

"You really want to know?" Claud nodded. Zarium said, "I could feel the same power emanating off of them as what I felt on my dad the day he died. I was curious and went exploring."

Claud was clearly surprised and took a step back. "Did you find anything while you were there?"

"No, I wasn't there very long."

"I was about to meet Asher for lunch," Claud said. "Why don't you join us?" Zarium nodded and went with him.

***

Alara bit her nails as she waited for her parents to call her in. She was mad that things had turned out this way, but as she thought about the situation, she realized how badly things could have gone. She was mad at herself. *What was I thinking? Now my parents will never trust me. I could have ruined things. Why can't I do what I'm supposed to? Claud is right; I'm not fit to be queen.*

Her mother emerged from the Yellow Room and escorted her into the room. She sat in a chair, with her head down, waiting for the lecture she was sure was coming. She was surprised when her mother sat beside her and gently placed a hand on her shoulder. "Alara, we know you want to have a bigger part in what is happening." Alara held her breath waiting for the 'but' and reasons why she couldn't, but instead her mother said, "We've been discussing it, and we want you to take a bigger part in the meetings and in the decisions that are made."

Alara nearly gasped, whipping her head around to meet her mother's gaze. After what happened earlier, she didn't think they'd ever trust her again. "This means we have more we need to tell you about," her mother said. Alara tried not to look too excited, but she was about to burst. "Firstly, be careful of the thoughts you have. We believe Magic Robbers can read other people's minds and are using that information to thwart plans, steal magic, and create chaos. We aren't sure how far that ability goes. It's possible they have to be within so many feet of you, but who knows? Maybe they can even read multiple minds at once."

Alara's mind raced. It was hard enough to control the words that flew from her mouth, but how was she supposed to control her thoughts all the time? "I understand, and I will be careful. What about in the castle? None of our meetings will be safe if someone can read our minds."

"Levon has the thought-scrambler power," her mother said. "He has given us his power for a while. We are using a piece of flyn bark which makes it so that anyone within about twenty feet of us will also have their thoughts scrambled."

***

Zarium ordered himself some chicken and potatoes and stood next to Claud while they waited for Asher to finish ordering his meal. Afterward, they walked to a table that was at the far end of the eating area with no one around it. Claud turned to Asher. "Zarium is interested in getting a piece of flyn bark."

Asher raised his eyebrows. "Oh, isn't that the dream of everyone? I want the bark too, but that is a difficult feat."

"He says he's willing to make a deal."

"From my conversation with Alara the other day, it seems she suspects that you are already involved with dark magic," Asher said. "If this were the case, I bet you can find a way to get a piece."

"What if I don't have access to dark magic?" Zarium asked.

Claud grinned. "There are ways of getting that too. Surely, you know all about them."

Zarium had hoped they would give him more information, but it seemed they didn't trust him enough. "Did you get a chance to bring up our ideas to your parents?"

Claud shook his head. "No, I've been busy traveling and checking things out for my father. I'll see if I can meet with them next week when I have more time."

Zarium knew it wasn't true. Teron hadn't given Claud any trips in a couple of weeks. Zarium changed the topic and asked them questions about their interests, trying to find some common ground with them. He was grateful when it was over, and he could leave.

Later the next day, Zarium asked one of the servants if he could speak with Queen Corah. When she arrived, Zarium told her about his plans for the day and asked her if he could borrow her feather for Alara. Corah told him yes and that she had another gift for him.

He watched her pull out a fox tooth from her pocket. "This tooth has the thought-scramble power. We want you to have this on you at all times. If you are with Alara, make sure you stay close by. We don't want anyone knowing what she is doing or thinking."

Zarium took the tooth. "This takes me up to five powers. If I get any more, I will have to choose what to have on me."

"Yes, you will have to make a decision about the other ones."

"Okay, I'll do my best." He groaned as he walked away. One more thing he had to worry about. He walked until he was at the main entrance room where Alara had asked him to meet her for their third and final meeting. He felt a heaviness in his chest at that thought. He had hoped he could change her mind about him, but no matter what he did, he could never seem to win her over.

He saw Alara sitting in a chair, reading a book. She was facing away from him. He smiled and slowly, silently crept up behind her. He crouched down and slid along the floor until he was beside her and jumped up, shouting her name.

Chapter 17

Alara jumped, throwing the book in the air, and screamed. Immediately, a guard was in the room. Zarium was laughing. "You should've seen your face. I'm two and you're zero."

Alara punched him, "You scared me half to death. I have a mind not to go with you today."

"Your loss."

The king and queen burst through the door. "What's going on in here?" Corah asked. "Alara, we heard you screaming."

"*Someone*," she shot a look toward Zarium, "thought it would be funny to play a trick on me."

"Sorry," Zarium shrugged his shoulders, "I didn't know *someone* was going to wake the dead with her screaming."

The guard, seeing there was no danger, left to stand outside the doors again. Alara saw her parents smile at each other. She was slightly less annoyed than she would have been a few days ago. "What are we going to do today?"

Zarium smiled. "I have a surprise, but you will need your mom's feather again." Alara was about to ask her mother when he produced the feather.

"How did you get that?"

He laughed, "I finally bested you! I came early and talked to your parents about this."

Alara allowed her mother to read her thoughts, and soon her mother spoke, "It's okay, Zarium has the thought-scrambler power too."

"He does?" She looked at Zarium. "Since when can you scramble thoughts?"

"Since about fifteen minutes ago, when your mom gave me an omp with that power."

"They gave you the power they've been using?" Alara asked.

"No," Alara's mother said, "We were able to acquire the power from someone else temporarily, and thought Zarium would be a good choice to give it to. Since there are no problems here, we should be going." Her mother took her father's hand and left.

"You surprised me today, but it doesn't matter what you do today, I still won't be interested." She turned up her nose at Zarium and walked past him.

"I know, but I still wanted you to have a wonderful day. I need one more thing." He reached behind his back and pulled out a piece of cloth. Alara gave him a funny look. "It's a blindfold, so this can be a true surprise."

For a moment, Alara panicked. Should she let him blindfold her? *Be reasonable,* she told herself. She hesitated a moment longer before agreeing. He quickly fastened it behind her head before she changed her mind.

He took her hand and thought of the place, and the two transported to the location. Alara stumbled slightly when they arrived, but Zarium helped to steady her. She reached up to take the blindfold off. "Not yet," Zarium said.

Even though Alara wouldn't admit it, she was excited about this. Zarium told her to stand right there and not move. She could hear him talking to another man. She couldn't hear everything they said, but she could tell that Zarium had agreed to something.

When he came back, he sounded excited. "Can I lift you up? It will be easier than trying to guide you to where I need you." She nodded and felt his strong hands grab around her waist and hoist her up onto what felt like a saddle. Her hands were clutching Zarium's arm. He moved her hands forward, and she could feel soft feathers. Next, he climbed onto the seat behind her. He grabbed a rope that was attached to the halter of the bird. He pulled the rope over them, so it wrapped around his back, and moved Alara's hands to each side of the rope and wrapped his arms around her. Her heart fluttered—she told herself it was from the thrill of the surprise.

"Are you ready?" Zarium asked. She nodded.

The driver, who was seated behind them, loudly clicked his tongue twice, and they started moving.

"We are moving up?" She half exclaimed and half asked. With his one hand, Zarium loosened the cloth and put it in his pocket. She was delighted to find they were in the air. "But how . . . where did you . . ." She searched for words to explain how she was feeling, but she was speechless.

"My dad used to travel all over; as a result, he met people from different kingdoms. During one of his visits, he met Huxley, who had these giant birds called—"

"Tarocks," she cut in.

"How do you know about them? Have you been on one?"

"It appears you aren't the only one with a surprise. I've never been on one, but I have heard of them. My brother, Jarius, has seen them in his travels and told me stories about them. I never imagined I'd get to ride on one. How did you get this one?"

"Last week, Huxley was visiting some relatives of his, and I ran into him. We talked, and I asked him if he'd consider bringing his Tarock here."

She admired the beautiful bird with its purple feathers. On its head, the feathers stood up in such a way that it appeared like it was wearing a crown. It was about ten feet long with large, powerful wings that glided through the air effortlessly. It was majestic and beautiful. "Does it have a name?"

"Her name is Shyra."

Alara patted Shyra. "You're such a good bird, Shyra." Alara laughed and stuck both of her hands straight out to her side. She felt Zarium's arms tighten around her. She put her head back on Zarium's shoulder and looked straight up. "Can it go faster?" Alara asked.

Huxley laughed. "Yes, are you sure you want to go faster?"

Alara clutched the rope again and gripped harder with her legs and shouted, "Yes!"

All at once, they were moving so fast she could barely keep her eyes open, and it was hard to catch a breath. She yelled to Huxley to slow down a little. He did and said, "These birds can go twice as fast as that, but I don't think we could stay on."

"Huxley, can you tell me more about the birds?" Alara asked.

"Sure, this one is an average size for a female. The males will add about two feet to their length. She's five years old, and she loves people. Not all of them love people, and some are very hard to tame, but I got this one as a baby, right out of the egg, and she has always loved human attention. If you pet her at the base of her head, she will love you."

Alara reached down and scratched the bird. Sure enough, the bird moved her neck toward her. Zarium petted it too. At one point, his hand came in contact with hers. She went to pull away, but before she could, his hand wrapped around hers. She was enjoying his hand being there a little too much for her own comfort. She let her hand stay there for about three seconds before yanking it from underneath. *What does he think he's doing?*

She looked out at the scene before her. In the distance, she could see a lush green forest, and little beyond that was a river snaking its way through the land. She smiled wider. *How beautiful! What a perfect day!*

The people below her were so small. From up high, all her problems seemed far away. There wasn't any pressure to be a certain way—no rules—just freedom. The wind tugged lightly at her hair. She took out a pin that was in it and let all of it fall down her back. She felt like she was a child again without a care in the world, and wished the moment could last forever.

In time, Huxley carefully landed the Tarock just on the edge of town. Zarium held out his hand to help Alara down, but she ignored it and hopped off. Alara smiled as Zarium shook his head. She wasn't giving in that easily. She thanked Huxley for bringing the bird and petted it again while Zarium talked with Huxley for a moment.

"Well, would you like to walk around town?" Zarium asked.

Alara smiled at him. "Yes, that would be nice. I enjoyed today so much. Thank you."

As they walked, she thought about the fun she had and how much she was enjoying being around Zarium. She wasn't sure she should like Zarium. After all, she still didn't know which side he was really on. She decided to ask a question that gave her a chance to get to know Zarium better while still finding out some information. "Tell me about your brother, Kursek. What was he like?"

Zarium paused before saying, "I guess he was a lot like other big brothers. He teased me a lot and sometimes got on my nerves, but in the end, I always knew he had my back. If I needed something, I knew I could count on him."

"Hmm, kind of like my brothers." She bent down to pick a flower on the edge of the road they were on. "Do you mind if I ask how he disappeared? I mean, did he just not come back? Did he literally disappear while you were looking at him?"

"I was fourteen. We had been at school that day. On the way home, we laughed and joked. At one point, Kursek said he was going to stop by and get a couple of items for our mom from one of the shops. He told me to go home. An hour later, my parents asked me if I knew where Kursek was. Two hours later, neighbors and friends were panicked, looking for him everywhere. My parents kept asking me if anything seemed out of the ordinary. I told them over and over again that I didn't know where Kursek went. The shop owners claimed they never saw him. It seemed that within about ten minutes of my leaving him, he disappeared without a trace."

"Two years later, your dad had his accident, right?" Zarium nodded, and Alara asked, "Have you ever wondered if somehow your brother's disappearance and your father's death were connected?"

He ran his fingers through his hair and stopped walking. "All the time. What are the chances that two people from the same family would have something happen to them? I wonder why I haven't disappeared or been killed. And what about my mom? Wouldn't someone worry that she knew too much and want to kill her? I worry about all of these things all the time, and I don't have any answers for anyone."

Alara blurted out, "I heard some rumors about the death of your father." He didn't interrupt her, so she continued, "I've heard there was dark magic that encompassed his body."

Zarium let out the air he'd been holding in. "That's true."

"Do you have anything to say about that?"

He stopped walking and faced her. "What do you want me to say? That my father was evil and trained me, so I'm evil too. What are you expecting from this conversation?"

Alara wrung her hands. "I don't know."

Zarium's tone changed to resignation. "There's a reason there isn't much information about it, and it's because not much is known. I'm tired of always feeling like I have to prove myself to you."

Zarium wiped his forehead and started walking. Alara followed him and changed the topic. "I want to apologize for how I treated you when you found me in Durik. It was wrong of me to run away and wrong of me to be mad at you or to treat you the way I did when we got back."

He shrugged his shoulders. "I forgive you. Look, Alara, this has been hard and awkward from the very beginning, and honestly, I think it is for the best that this is our third and *final* meeting. I know doing these meetings weren't your idea and that you didn't want to do them."

It hit Alara that she never gave Zarium any hope at all, nor had she invested anything in him. He planned and paid for every outing, and she showed up and made life harder for him each time. He kept trying to find little ways to show he cared, and she brushed them all off and didn't even give him any hint that what he was doing was working. Realizing that she did care for him and was in danger of losing him, she gently placed her hand on his arm, searching for the words to say to him.

He was quick to move it away. "I don't need you feeling sorry for me. I'm fine. We should return to the castle."

Alara bowed her head. "I'm sorry Zar—"

"Zarium, Alara, over here." Tannah was standing a few feet away from them in front of one of the shops with her hands full of food.

They walked over to her and helped hold some of her things.

"Did you know about the Tarock?" Alara asked.

"Yes." Tannah grinned. "Zarium was excited and was sure you'd enjoy it."

Alara smiled. "He was right; I loved it." Alara glanced at Zarium, but that didn't even cause the corners of his mouth to turn up at all.

As they stood there awkwardly, Tannah broke the silence, "Have you two eaten yet? I have been preparing lunch, and you could come back to the house and eat if you want."

Zarium started to speak, "I really don't—"

"That would be great." Alara saw this as her opportunity to try to fix some of the mess she had gotten herself into.

Tannah was clearly pleased, though Alara noted that Zarium didn't seem pleased. On the short walk back to the house, Zarium chatted with his mother as if nothing were wrong. Alara was grateful his mother showed up.

At the house, Alara insisted on helping again, and this time, Tannah didn't argue with her. She was put in charge of cutting up the carrots for the salad. As she was cutting, the knife slipped and cut her finger. Blood oozed from the wound.

Zarium rushed over and put his hand around her finger. All of a sudden, her pain subsided, and when he removed his hand, there wasn't any sign at all of where the cut had been. "Thank you." Alara put her hand on his arm. "It doesn't even hurt a little." He shrugged and resumed cutting up some fruit.

While Tannah put some meat and cheese on bread, she told stories about Zarium and his power to heal. "He loved to heal everything. Even bugs. He has practiced a lot and gotten really good for one so young."

Curious again about this part of his abilities, Alara asked Zarium, "Do you think in time you could get good enough to heal major sicknesses or accidents?"

Alara was pleased when he made eye contact with her, "Probably not. The flyn bark is the only way I know to enhance a power, but even it has limitations. There isn't any proof that even the bark could truly give me that great of power, though sometimes I hear rumors that maybe it could." He looked away. "Most rumors are just rumors." Zarium glanced at her briefly. Alara knew what he was getting at.

Alara grabbed three plates from the cupboard and set them on the table. Tannah set three glasses, with ice that she had made, on the table and poured some apple juice into each one. As they ate, Alara asked Tannah about her life growing up. Tannah talked of coming from a poor home where her father was a leather tanner.

In between bites, Alara asked her follow-up questions. Eventually, it got around to how Tannah met Havid. Alara saw Tannah's whole face light up when she talked about meeting Havid.

"We met at a dance at the spring festival right here in Camden." Tannah took a small bite of fruit. "He was such a horrible dancer, and he stepped on my toes several times. He was so embarrassed he didn't dare ask me to dance again, so he sat along the side through several dances. But I knew he was a keeper, and finally I went up to him and asked him to dance again. He was worried about my feet, and I told him not to worry about the steps." Tannah smiled through glistening eyes. "We rocked back and forth to the beat for the next five songs, just talking." She took a few more bites of her food.

"That sounds so romantic," Alara said.

Tannah looked toward the ceiling. "It was. And marrying him was the best decision I ever made." She laughed. "He never got any better at dancing, though, but he was great in all the ways that mattered. And Zarium is just like him." She slid her empty plate to the side.

Zarium turned red. "Nah, he was definitely better than I am." He cleared his throat and picked up the dishes from the table and put them in the sink. He spoke to Alara. "I've got some things I need to do this afternoon, so I should probably get you home."

Alara thanked Tannah for another wonderful meal, and she and Zarium transported to the gate of the castle. As they walked up the stairs, Alara said, "I really enjoyed today. Thank you for putting it all together."

"No problem."

Alara nervously clasped her hands. "So, will I get to see you again?"

"I thought you weren't interested in seeing me again."

Alara stopped at the top of the stairs and turned toward Zarium. "I've enjoyed our three . . . dates, and I hope I will see you again." She saw Zarium brighten.

"Really? I thought after all those questions earlier that you were doubting me and wouldn't want anything to do with me."

"You are a good person." Alara fidgeted with her hands. "And I want to see where this can go."

Before either of them could say anything else, the door burst open.

Chapter 18

"Alara," Ian shouted, "what a pleasant surprise seeing you here. Father told me you were meeting with Zarium today." Ian picked her up and swung her around. "It's so good to see you again." He put her back down and turned to Zarium. "How are you doing? Am I interrupting your time together?"

Zarium shook his head. "We just finished, and I'm on my way out. I'll see you both later."

Alara stepped toward Zarium and gave him a hug. "Thank you for a great day."

"You're welcome," Zarium said, with a smile that spread to his eyes. Alara's heart skipped a beat as she closed the door.

When the door closed behind Zarium, Ian asked, "How are things going with Zarium?"

Alara walked toward the main foyer. "That was the third date. Now I can focus on getting ready to go on my trip." She sat down on the couch, and Ian sat beside her. "Surely, Mother and Father have to agree to let me go now."

"You and your adventures. Is that all you think about?"

She nudged him. "Well, there isn't much else for a princess to think about."

"Except for maybe a handsome man."

"I actually wanted to ask you about that."

Before she could get her next words out, their parents walked into the room. Their father looked at his timekeeper. "I see you were gone a lot longer today. How was today's meeting?"

"Our *date* went well." She saw the look of shock register on her mother's face and a small smile. Alara smiled wide. "Oh, he took me for a ride on a Tarock."

Alara put her hands in the air and spun around. "It was so much fun. I have heard stories about them, but I never saw one in real life until today."

"So, will we be seeing more of Zarium in the future?" Her mother asked.

Alara blushed. "Maybe. We don't have any definite plans, so I can't say for sure."

Ian took the opportunity to tease her more. "My little sister found someone who made her think twice about love and romance."

She gave him a shove. "What would you know about love and romance? No girl would even want to get close enough to you for you to find out what it's like."

Ian pretended to be hurt and put his hands to his chest like a dagger had been thrust in it. "Oh, you got me." He straightened up. "But at least I've kissed someone."

Well, he had her there. She playfully bantered, "Was she your horse?"

"Okay, you two," their mother interrupted, "enough of that. Before anyone touches on a nerve, let's change the subject." Alara stuck out her tongue at Ian, and he stuck his out at her.

"That's all right," Ian said. "I have some other things I need to do anyway. I will see all of you later."

Alara's mother waited until Ian was gone and said, "In all seriousness, will we be seeing more of Zarium?" Alara scrunched her eyebrows together. Her mother tilted her head. "What is it?"

"Well, I kind of blew it today, and I'm sure he's still upset about what happened in Durik. I don't imagine I'm his favorite person right now." She told her parents what happened earlier. She collapsed into the chair behind her.

Her father moved closer. "What makes you so suspicious of Zarium? Is it only the rumors?"

"Those are a big part of it, but Asher warned me, and of course, there was Ian's warning." Her father seemed surprised. "Ian warned you about Zarium today?"

"No, it was the night of the dance."

"About that." Alara sat up in the chair. "I asked Ian to say that to you that night. And though you haven't brought it up, I had Zarium plant the note that appeared in the pocket of your dress. I was hoping you would be suspicious about Zarium if the statue fell and the note was in your pocket. I caused the statue to fall, using my object-manipulation power."

Alara stood up. "What? Why?"

"I wanted you to choose Zarium, and I knew that if you believed he was involved in something, you would be more likely to choose him."

"I don't understand why you wanted me to choose him. How did you know he could be trusted? I want to trust him, but everything is confusing. How do you know he isn't just pretending to be on the good side?"

"You can't be certain anyone is truly on the same side as you, not even me," Teron said. "Anyone can be a traitor. However, sometimes we have to go with our gut feeling."

"And your gut feeling tells you Zarium is good?" Alara asked

"Yes." Her father licked his lips.

"That isn't good enough."

Her father rubbed his face and looked at her mother, who nodded. "Alara, we're moving this conversation into the Red Room," her father said with a serious tone.

Alara followed them in. When she got there, she remained standing. "Take a seat, Alara."

"Why?"

"Because some things are better received while sitting."

She stared at him and abruptly sat. Her mother sat across the table from her. Her father paced. "Seven years ago, there were groups of people who sought to take over and were openly rebelling and causing problems, and we knew we had to do something. At the time, I had an advisor, but more importantly, he was my friend. He was loyal, and I knew I could trust him."

"I remember there being talk of things in my classes."

Her father nodded. "Yes, we tried to shield you from much of this because you were so young. The problems got worse, and we prepared ourselves to go to battle and planned a surprise attack. We thought we had the upper hand, but there were traitors who leaked out important information."

"Your friend?" Alara asked.

"No, he was as good as I believed he was, but there were others who weren't. We had received information that they were meeting at a particular place, and we hurried to the spot and waited for them. However, they knew we were there, and they surrounded and attacked us. They bound us with ropes and magic and took us before their evil leader. Using dark magic, they were able to disable our powers."

Alara sat in astonishment. Her father had been through far more than she understood. No wonder he didn't want to do things without thinking through them first. "Well, obviously, you got out of this situation."

"The evil people laughed," he continued. "If they killed me, they had a plan to marry your mother and take over the kingdom. With no one left to stop him, the evil leader began chanting, and a dark force appeared around him. It grew larger and thicker, and I was sure that I would soon be dead. He pointed right at me, and the darkness shot toward me. Unexpectedly, I felt a shove and watched as my best friend fell limp to the ground. He sacrificed himself, knowing it was the only way to save the kingdom."

Alara's eyes widened. "Why weren't they still able to kill you though? You had no powers."

"You see, Alara, there is one thing stronger than any magic." He paused. Alara leaned forward as he said, "Love. And there is no greater love than when one gives his or her life so that another might live. The darkness was strong, but the light is always stronger. As soon as my friend was killed, the rest of us were able to use our powers again, and we overpowered those with the dark magic."

"That's amazing." Alara paused, looking at her father with wonder. "But," she slowly added, "what happened to those who possessed the dark magic?"

Her father rubbed his arm. "Many of them were captured and put to death on the spot. However, not everyone was captured; there were two men who escaped. We knew we wouldn't be able to find them. But Nori knew someone named Skye from where she grew up who had a rare power—the boundary-creation power, that could keep a person from going past physical boundaries that he set up. He took a piece of their clothing and was able to set up boundaries that wouldn't allow them to enter into our kingdom."

"What happened to the families of the traitors?" Alara asked.

Her father intertwined his fingers. "That was the hard part. Some of them had wives and children. They were all told that there had been a battle and their husbands and fathers had died, but that evil had been conquered. It was nearly impossible to know how much their families knew and if their families had been affected by the evil. For a time, things were safe and all returned to normal."

"Who was your friend who died?" Alara asked.

Her father was silent for a moment before putting a hand on top of Alara's hand. "My friend was Havid, Zarium's father." Alara gasped.

"But if he did so much good, why do some people still think that he was evil?"

"Because of the dark magic that was around his body."

Alara tilted her head. "That can happen whether the person was using dark magic or killed by it though."

"It can, but people in high positions of power have many enemies, and those enemies don't play fair. It wasn't hard for rumors to get started."

"Why didn't Tannah fight the rumors and clear their good name?" Alara put her hands on top of her head. "Why couldn't you have cleared his name and fixed the problem?"

Teron sat down next to Alara. "She did come to me to find out what would be the best course of action . . . I told her it would be best if she let it go and lived a quiet, simple life away from public scrutiny. I gave her a large compensation to help until Zarium could provide for them."

Alara shook her head. "I don't understand why you would do this." She looked at her mother, but she said nothing.

Her father took a deep breath. "Because there's more to the story."

"More?" Alara stood up.

"I don't know how to tell you this, but one of the traitors was Kursek, Zarium's—"

"Brother," Alara finished his sentence.

"I knew that if Tannah was fighting things, it was more likely that one of the people from our side would accidentally let that slip. People who were on the evil side wouldn't say anything against their own, so we were safe that way. It was better if everything was forgotten and not spoken about. If people found out about Kursek, there would have been a lot more problems for Tannah and Zarium."

Alara stared at the ground. "Does Zarium know about Kursek?"

"No, I never told him or Tannah. I couldn't stand to break Tannah's heart more than it already was."

Alara nodded and leaned forward. "Who was the other traitor?"

"I think it would be best not to reveal that," her mother said.

"But why?"

"Because very few people knew who the other one was. Havid and the two of us were the only ones. Again, it would be best the fewer people who knew. Maybe someday in the future, we will tell you."

Alara sat down. She folded her arms and rubbed them with her hands while looking at her parents, trying to process the information and understand how something like that could really happen. As the shock wore off, she unfolded her arms, clasped her hands together, and leaned forward. "You still don't know that Zarium wasn't affected by the dark magic, though."

Teron put his hand on top of hers. "I've used Zarium to do many assignments, and I have reason to believe that he is good."

Alara sat pondering that. "So," she began, "you think it's okay for me to continue to see Zarium? That is, if he will forgive me and agree to it."

Her mother jumped in. "Did you let Zarium know you were still interested in seeing him again?"

Alara rolled her eyes. "Yes, Mother, I mentioned that I'd like to see him in the future."

"Did he say anything about that?" Her mother questioned further.

"He didn't get the chance to because my annoying brother, Ian, chose that exact moment to open the door and interrupt us, and Zarium left."

"It's about time my daughter is annoyed at people interrupting her time with suitors rather than with the suitors themselves." Her mother winked.

Alara gave her a look. "Don't get too used to it. I still haven't changed my mind about marriage."

***

When Zarium returned home, he was greeted by his mom, who got a cup of tea for him and set it on the table. She sat down. "All right, I know something was bothering you earlier, so out with it." He took the cup and sat down. How could he explain all this?

He started by telling her about what happened in Durik a couple of days earlier and his and Alara's interaction when he discovered her traveling alone without her parents knowing. He also told her about earlier that day and how Alara all but accused him of being influenced by and potentially using dark magic. "I don't know," he sighed. "It seems like this was doomed from the very beginning. Everyone seems to want to keep us apart and keeps filling her head with things that make her question anything she thinks about me."

"Does this mean you won't be seeing her again?" Tannah pressed the cup to her mouth.

"She mentioned earlier that she'd like to see me again."

"But . . ."

"But I worry that she's only acting interested and wants to see me because she is still suspicious. So far, she hasn't seen me because she wanted to. Her main purpose was to get our three *meetings* over with so she could go on a spying adventure. What if this isn't any different?"

"If you don't try, you will never know. You'll have to decide if the risk is worth the potential reward."

Zarium took a sip and breathed out slowly. "How did you get to be so wise?"

"Practice."

He half smiled. "I suppose."

Later that night, when Zarium went to his bedroom, he picked up a small wood box from on top of his bureau, opened it, and pulled out the locket he had picked up in the forest weeks before. He hadn't figured out how to get it to her yet because he didn't want her to ask questions about how he got it. No one knew he had been in the forest that day.

He put the locket back in the box and thought about what his mom had said about Alara. She was right. Alara may never like him, but if he didn't even try, it was a guarantee he wouldn't win her over, so he might as well try.

Chapter 19

The next day, Zarium transported to Vashka early in the morning before the sun came up. He spent an hour walking around town thinking about the situation with Alara. He wanted to talk to Alara, but at the same time, he didn't. He noticed the vibrant orange and pink of the sunrise as he walked. Surely, that had to be a sign of a great day and lots of luck.

He walked closer and closer to the castle and entered the castle gates. Soon, he was standing at the door, still wondering if this was a mistake and if he should turn around and leave. He opened the doors and walked inside.

He saw Corah standing in the hall pushing the button for the light repeatedly.

"Good morning. Is something wrong?" Zarium asked.

"Our light isn't working correctly. All the lights were done last year; they should be good for several more years to come."

Alara ran into the hallway. "Mother, something is wrong with my powers."

"What do you mean?" Corah asked.

"My invisibility is acting strange. One minute I can stay invisible, and the next it comes and goes, or only part of me goes invisible. Watch." Alara proceeded to go invisible. Sure enough, Zarium could still see her hand. It was some time before the rest of her appeared again. "See what I mean."

"I wonder if something has happened to Nori. We should go check on her," Corah said.

"I'll do that and come back to let you know what I find," Zarium said, as he quickly ran to the door. He stepped outside, and thought of Nori's house. He ended up in town. He thought of the castle but found himself standing in another section of town. He started to panic. Finally, on the third attempt, he was at the castle gate again.

Zarium decided his best option was to go by foot to Nori's house. As he ran, his heart pumped hard, more from fear than from the running. He didn't stop until he got to Nori's house. Then he saw something that made him stop and frantically look around the area of the house. *The guard is missing.*

Zarium drew his sword and approached the house cautiously. He opened the door and called out to Nori. He walked inside, where he saw the furniture turned upside down and one of the chairs broken. The kitchen had every cupboard door and drawer opened, with the contents thrown on the floor. Shattered glass was strewn on the countertops and floor. He ran into her bedroom and saw that someone had gone through each bureau drawer and taken the covers off the bed.

Zarium ran back outside and, without thinking, used his place-transport power. He found himself standing in a group of trees on the edge of the Klant Forest between Vashka and Durik. *Great, of all the luck.* He was about to try transporting again when he heard Claud's voice. Zarium hid behind a large tree, searching for Claud, when he spotted a group walking away from him, going deeper into the forest.

He followed them, keeping a safe distance, so they wouldn't hear him. As he walked deeper into the forest, the ground became covered in grass, roots, and vines. It was oddly quiet. He listened but didn't even hear a bird singing.

When the group of people stopped, Zarium noticed other people who were already waiting. He counted twenty-five people. Zarium moved closer, hoping he'd be able to hear what they were saying. He got down on his hands and knees and crawled through the vines. He saw a group of bushes that would hide him perfectly not more than ten feet from the group. He inched his way closer and closer.

Suddenly, Zarium felt something touch his skin. He turned to look and saw vines wrapping around his legs. Before he could react, he found himself lifted into the air. The vines slithered until they covered from his neck to his heels. A group of people turned toward him.

"Zarium," Claud said. "What are you doing here?"

Zarium swallowed and cleared his throat. "I was walking through the forest when this tree attacked me."

Claud made a motion with his hands, and the tree lowered Zarium closer to the ground. "You were just casually walking?"

"Not exactly." Zarium racked his brain for an excuse. "I heard you on the edge of the forest tell some people you were going to discuss some ideas for the kingdom, and I was curious. You know from our discussions that I've been concerned about what is going on."

Claud said nothing as he made several circles around Zarium, rubbing his chin. "How do I know you aren't spying on us?"

"And why would I want to spy on you?" Zarium said, struggling to take a deep breath as Claud tightened the vines again.

Claud moved closer. "Maybe because my father put you up to it."

"He didn't. He doesn't even know I'm here." Zarium felt lightheaded but remained calm.

Claud smiled, though his jaw tightened, and Zarium swore the vines tightened as Claud's jaw did, making it difficult to talk. "If you . . . will loosen the vines . . . I will tell you . . . everything." Zarium was relieved when the vines loosened around his torso, though he noticed they tightened around his arms and legs.

"Now, spill it," Claud said.

Zarium licked his lips. "Look, there are things I want, and I believe you can help me get them."

Claud made a motion with his hands, and the tree dropped him to the ground. The others laughed as he landed. Zarium tightened his hands for a moment but relaxed them and slowly stood up. He rubbed his thigh where he landed.

"All right." Claud rubbed his chin. "I'm willing to consider this, but why should I trust you?"

Zarium fumbled in his pockets and pulled out the flyn bark that Corah had given him to convince Claud that he was on his side. He saw Claud smile. Zarium held it out to Claud. "I will give you this as a symbol of my loyalty."

Claud took it and examined it as if he expected it to be some sort of trick. Finally, he took the bark and slapped Zarium on the back. "I know how badly you've wanted one of these. I'm impressed you'd give it to me."

Asher came up beside him. "I still don't think we should trust him."

"Maybe you should prove you are on our side," Claud said. Zarium gulped. Claud turned back to the others. "What do you think? Should we have a test for our friend?"

The men threw their hands into the air and began to chant, "Test. Test. Test."

Claud walked around Zarium a couple of times. "Let's see, what could we have you do?"

Asher snapped his fingers. "I hear the king has the immobilization power. According to Claud, the power is transferred to one of the rings he wears. We could really use this power."

Zarium felt a sinking feeling in his stomach. "You want me to figure out how to steal the king's ring? Does he ever take it off?"

"Not very often," Claud laughed, "so you'll have to get it off and replace it with another ring that looks similar so he won't suspect anything. You have two days to figure out how you are going to do this."

"Where will we meet?"

Claud snarled, "Don't worry, I'll find you, and when I do, you better have the ring."

Zarium confidently replied, "Okay, you have a deal. I have a problem though."

"We're listening," Claud said.

"My powers don't work properly because Nori, whose dragons gave me my powers, is missing. All this will be a lot easier if I could use them."

Claud eyed him. "You went to Nori for your powers instead of someone in your own city?"

Zarium didn't want to let them know he had greater connections to Nori and that she was his aunt, so he made up a story. "My mother knew her from when they were younger in school."

Claud was quiet before replying, "All right, here's what we will do. The faram you speak of isn't dead. We ruffled her up a bit, hoping she'd start cooperating with us. But she refused to give us the words to get into her dragons. However, I have an idea that will help all of us. We still need my family to believe you're on their side. I don't want them to suspect anything. From now on, you will not speak up on our behalf in meetings. Act like we don't even like each other."

Zarium nodded, and Claud continued, "I will tell you where the faram is so you can get her back to her own house and heal her so that all your powers will go back to normal." Zarium's head shot up. Claud laughed. "Yes, I know you have the gift of healing, and I suspect it will come in handy at some point."

"Depending on how bad of shape she's in, I won't be able to heal her. I can only heal minor injuries."

Claud smirked. "Somehow you got the flyn bark you gave me. I'm sure you can figure out how to get another one." Zarium listened closely as Claud told him the location of Nori. When Zarium turned to leave, Claud called out, "And Zarium." Zarium turned around. "I don't want you spying on us or being secretive around us. Is that understood?"

"Yes." Zarium walked back through the trees and vines and didn't stop until he hit a group of shops, where he paused and took a couple of deep breaths. His heart was beating fast, and his legs were still shaking. He ran to some nearby stables and paid a man to borrow a horse. He had to find Nori.

Chapter 20

Alara paced as her mother told her father what had happened and how Zarium had left to go to Nori's house. Alara bit her nails until her mother told her to stop. "I can't help it." She bit one more nail before sitting on her hands. "Zarium has been gone for fifteen minutes already."

"He wouldn't have been able to use his transportation power. Besides, depending on how Nori was doing, he may have been delayed talking to her," her mother replied.

"We ordered the stable boys to ready some horses for us and the guards," her father said. "As soon as they are ready," he looked at Alara, "the two of us will go with the guards."

When word came from one of the servants that the horses were saddled, Alara and her father went to the stables. There were already five other guards waiting on their horses. Her father explained the plan. "Three guards will ride in front and two in back. When we get there, the front three guards will go in first and check the conditions and let us know if it is safe for the rest of us to go in."

He handed Alara a sword. "In case you need it." Alara took it and climbed on her horse. She placed the sword in front of her on the saddle, realizing the gravity of the situation. Her parents didn't usually allow her to carry a sword because they told her it wasn't appropriate for a princess to go into battle.

Alara's father, not wanting to alarm any of the town members who may see them, told the three guards in front to move the horses at a canter rather than a gallop. When they got there, the three guards went in first. Soon, they returned and told them that Nori wasn't there. Alara jumped off her horse and ran in and checked each room. When her father entered, she ran to him. "What are we going to do?"

"I don't know, but we should head back to the castle. Hopefully, Zarium will return soon, and we can make a plan from there."

Alara's father told two of the guards to stand outside Nori's house and to send one of them if they received any news about Nori. Then he, the other three guards, and Alara walked back to their horses and rode to the castle. Outside the castle gates was a small group of people who didn't look happy. Alara was grateful they had guards with them. As they got closer, one of the people shouted out, "Why don't our powers work?"

The guards held the people back and prevented them from getting any closer Alara and her father or to the castle wall. Alara's father said nothing as he rode past them. Alara looked at his face. He had a stoic expression as he looked straight ahead. Though he was putting on a brave front, she could tell he was worried because he kept cracking his knuckles, something he only did when he was really stressed. Alara chewed her nails. Alara and her father tied up the horses at the nearest tree and instructed one of the guards to tell the stable workers to leave them saddled.

Once inside, they met with Alara's mother in the White Room. They told her about the conditions at Nori's house. Alara's mother left the room and called to the nearest servant and asked her to get a group of six or seven servants to go clean Nori's house, including taking some chairs over and sheets to make the bed.

As Alara's mother was about to reenter the White Room, Alara's father asked her if she knew what was going on outside. Her mother walked back out to the nearest window. Alara joined her. At least fifty people were now gathered. Her mother called one of the servants and dictated a message telling the people to gather at the balcony on the east side of the castle in one hour.

In the White Room, Alara and her parents discussed what to say to the people. "We should probably just tell them Nori has been taken, and we are working on finding her," Alara's father said.

"I agree," Alara's mother said. "I also think that we need to remind them that even if we don't find Nori, things will be okay because the dragons will choose a new faram and all will go on as it should. Nori has been a faram for a really long time. Isn't it almost forty years? Many of the people in Vashka have never experienced a moment where their powers didn't work as a faram was being replaced."

When it was time, a group of guards walked out with them to the balcony where hundreds of people were waiting. Alara's mother explained Nori was temporarily missing and that they were awaiting more information.

"How long will it take?" A woman shouted out.

"We don't know," Alara's mother said. "Hopefully, it won't take longer than a week."

"What if you don't find her?" A man asked.

"Then the dragons will choose a new faram and all of your powers will go back to normal, again, most likely within a week."

More people shouted out questions, but Alara's mother said, "That is all the questions we have time for now. We will update you when we have more information." Alara and her parents turned and walked back into the castle while guards began breaking up the crowd. Alara looked one last time at the group of people and wished there was something she could do to help them, something she could do to help Nori. She hoped Zarium discovered something soon and returned. She checked her timekeeper. It had been over two hours, and still Zarium hadn't returned.

***

Zarium found the group of five rocks that were taller than a house a couple of miles west of the forest where Claud told him to go, but he didn't see Nori anywhere. He frantically ran toward some bushes, but she wasn't there. He searched behind some trees that were nearby, but he saw nothing.

He shouted out her name and listened, but there was no reply. *Remain calm.* He began walking in a circle around the area, looking for her. Finally, he found a shoe. Nori had to be there. He walked a few more feet and found her bag. He clenched his fists. It was a good thing Claud wasn't there at that moment.

He walked farther. He saw something poking out from behind some bushes. He got closer. It was Nori's hand. He checked for a pulse. It was weak, but at least she had one. Her hair was matted to her head, and she was bleeding from a gash over her right eyebrow. Her lip was swollen and bleeding where a tooth had punctured it. He gently touched her bruised and swollen left eye. "Oh, Nori."

Zarium lifted her off the ground and laid her across his horse. He pulled himself into the saddle and lifted her onto his lap. He rode carefully to Nori's house to make sure Nori didn't get bumped too much.

The first thing he saw as he headed down the path to Nori's house were two guards. He called out to them, and they helped him lift Nori off the horse and take her into the house. Zarium was surprised to see chairs in the living room and her bed made, with the mess around it cleaned up. They laid Nori on her bed, and Zarium told one of the guards to go tell the king and queen that he had found Nori.

Zarium didn't see, hear, or feel anything different with his powers. He hoped having Nori in her house would revive his power. Only one way to know. He reached beneath his clothes and pulled out a chain with a piece of metal with the words, "Greatness is not found in our circumstances but in our choices. Choose to be great," engraved on it. It was what the king had given him after his father's death. He fingered it for a moment, thinking of his father and the choices he had made. He put the chain back under his shirt.

He felt each of her limbs, noticing that her right shoulder was dislocated. He wondered how many of her organs had been affected. When she gained consciousness, he would ask her about any pain she had in places he couldn't see.

***

Alara and her parents were inside the Blue Room discussing what to do if the worst-case scenario happened, and they couldn't find Nori. A servant walked into the White Room and told them that Zarium had found Nori and that she was back in her house.

Alara and her father ran to the stables with some guards, where they mounted their horses. They were glad that the people who had been gathered outside the castle wall were now gone.

Alara felt like this was the longest it had ever taken her to get to Nori's. When she got there, she jumped off her horse and ran past the guard. She entered the house and went straight to Nori's room. She was shocked to see Nori so badly injured. She stood beside her bed and asked Zarium, "Will she be okay?"

Teron entered as Zarium said, "I don't know. I've been trying to use my healing powers, but I don't know if it will be enough. Unless I can get a flyn bark . . ."

Teron reached into his cloak, pulled out a piece of bark, and handed it to Zarium. "Perhaps this will help."

Zarium took it and lifted his shirt enough to put the bark over his necklace. "Thank you."

Teron nodded. "And Zarium. You can keep the bark as a reward for your faithfulness."

Alara was shocked that her father would let Zarium have it. Did her parents really trust Zarium that much?

"Thank you. Can I have someone do me a favor?"

"Yes," Teron said.

"Could you have a messenger let my mom know that I'm okay and let her know what happened with Nori?"

Teron stepped outside and returned a few minutes later. "Someone should be there within an hour," Teron said to Zarium.

Alara and her father stayed for the next couple of hours, but besides healing a few small wounds, there wasn't a noticeable difference in Nori's condition. Eventually, Zarium encouraged them to go back to the castle and told them he'd let them know if there were any changes.

Chapter 21

The next morning, Zarium was awakened as he heard a low groan. He sat up on the mat he had slept on the night before. In the darkness, he was confused about where he was. He heard the noise again and became fully awake, remembering what had happened to Nori. He jumped up and turned on a lamp. Soon, Nori made little movements with her hands and head, and her eyes fluttered and opened. The muscles in her neck contracted, but she was too weak to lift her head.

Zarium stroked her head. "Nori, you've been injured. Just lie still." He pressed on different parts of her body and watched to see if she flinched in pain. "Do you remember anything that happened?"

"No," Nori whispered. Then she closed her eyes again.

He ran outside in the dark and let the guards know that Nori was awake and to tell the royal family. Thirty minutes later, Alara and Teron arrived. They both had bags under their eyes and didn't look like they had slept much. Zarium glanced at his time keeper and realized it was only four thirty in the morning.

Zarium led them into Nori's room. "She has a lot of bruising, some broken bones, and probably a concussion," Zarium said. "All these are things that will heal. The bone in her one leg is broken really badly and will take more time to heal. I don't think she has any internal injuries, though I'm not positive."

Alara yawned. Zarium could see Alara's pajamas hanging below her dress and realized she had put her dress on over her pajamas. Her hair was thrown up in a bun, but there was hair falling out of it. He smiled. Even when she was a mess, she was still beautiful.

Once inside the room, Zarium stepped back and allowed the two of them to step closer to Nori. "She opened her eyes briefly earlier," Zarium said, "but she fell asleep again."

Teron and Alara watched her for a few minutes before Teron said. "I need to go back and report all of this to Corah."

"At this hour?" Zarium asked.

"She's awake," Teron said. "And she will want to know as soon as possible."

Zarium had an idea. "I need to talk to Corah. What if you two stayed here for a couple of minutes and kept an eye on Nori, and I go talk to Corah?"

"That would be fine," Teron said.

Alara looked away from Nori and made eye contact with Zarium. "Thank you for everything you've done."

"No problem. I'm glad to help. I will return soon." Zarium decided to try his place-transport power. His power got him there, mostly. It put him on the far side and almost a mile away from the entrance of the castle. He tried again, and it put him a little farther away. Finally, on the third time, it put him about fifty feet from the castle wall entrance. He walked to the entrance of the gate, through the path, and up the stairs to the door.

A servant let him in and told him to wait while he got the queen. When Corah got there, she led him to the White Room and closed the door. Zarium waited until the queen sat down, and he sat as well.

"You have news about Nori, I presume."

"Yes, Nori is badly injured, but she is doing okay. She woke up and talked to me."

"Do you think she will make a full recovery?"

"In time. I wanted to talk to you about something else too though. I met with Claud yesterday and gave him the flyn bark that you gave me weeks ago to give to him."

Corah nodded her head slowly. "I see. Did you put a tracker on it?" Zarium nodded. "Good, let us know if you find out anything useful about Claud or anyone else."

"I will." Zarium was about to leave when he remembered something else. "Claud wants me to pretend like I don't like him in meetings as a way to trick you and others."

Corah was deep in thought, and Zarium asked if there was anything else. "If I know Claud, and I think I do, he won't let you go on for long before he gives you assignments."

Zarium's hands went clammy. He didn't want them to know he already had an assignment and that it was to steal the king's ring. Giving a piece of flyn bark to Claud was one thing, but there was no way the king would give up one of his powers for nefarious purposes.

"Things could get risky," Corah said.

"I know. I'm willing to take the risk."

"I figured you would say that. Remember that it is essential they believe you are one of them, so do what they ask you to do within reason. However, I don't want you getting yourself into a situation that you can't get out of."

Zarium nodded that he understood and left the room. He walked outside, where he transported back to Nori's house. He was thinking of asking the king if he could return to Camden to get his mom. There was a knock at the door, and Alara answered.

Zarium looked up. "Mom, how did you get here?" He asked, surprised. She walked toward Nori's bedroom. "King Teron had a messenger come tell me where you were. I borrowed one of the neighbor's horses and came." Tannah sat next to Nori in a chair by her bed and stroked her hair. Zarium saw Alara's raised eyebrows and said, "Nori is my father's sister, making her my aunt." Alara formed an "O" with her lips but said nothing.

Zarium sat down on the other side of Nori and worked on healing her further. Since his transporting powers were still having problems, he figured the healing ability also wasn't working perfectly yet either. That would explain why Nori's eye was still puffy. He felt her head. It was hot. He asked his mom to get a cold washcloth and put it on her head.

His mom got up and returned a few minutes later with a towel and laid it across Nori's head. "Nori woke up for a few minutes while you were at the castle, but she almost immediately fell back to sleep," Alara said.

"Okay." Zarium saw her worried expression and tried to reassure her. "She should continue to get stronger and wake up for longer periods of time."

He thought about a plan to steal the ring. It became clear, he'd need an invisibility power, and he would have to steal it too. He knew two people who had one—Nori and Alara. He figured Nori would be an easier option. Now, he needed to be alone with her. He told Teron that he could go back to the castle. When he left, Zarium turned to his mom. "I haven't had anything to eat since yesterday. Would you mind going and getting something for me?"

She smiled. "I can do that."

Zarium looked at Alara. "Perhaps you'd like to go too. Get a little exercise. Surely, you could use a break to walk around for a few minutes."

"I don't know . . . maybe," Alara said.

Tannah took a hold of Alara's arm. "Zarium is right. It would do you some good to get some fresh air."

"Well, I'm not supposed to go anywhere without Zarium or my father being close by since they both have the thought-scrambler power."

Zarium pulled the tooth with the thought-scrambler power out of his pocket and handed it to her. "You can take this and return it when you're done. I'll be fine here. Just make sure you go invisible as well."

Alara agreed, and soon she and Tannah were gone. Zarium turned his attention back to Nori. He debated for a moment if he should take her invisibility power, but what other option did he have? Even if she did wake up, she wouldn't be able to get out of bed for a few days, so she wouldn't need her invisibility power. He knew she had transferred it to a rock she carried in a secret pocket that had small clasps sewn into the seam of her dress. He had to act fast before they came back.

He carefully opened the clasps, reached inside her pocket, pulled it out, and slipped it into his pocket. Now, he had six powers, but Alara would have the thought-scrambler power for a little while, so he could keep the rest of them still on him.

About forty-five minutes later, Alara and Zarium's mom returned. She handed him some chicken on bread. Even though he was hungry, it was difficult to eat because he was so nervous. He had to force each bite.

Alara started to hand him the tooth back. "Oh, I almost forgot."

Zarium waved dismissively. "You can keep it for now. I have some things I need to do, and I'm going to leave here for a couple of hours."

Alara eyed him. "What kind of things?"

"Things I can't tell you about at this time that are part of my responsibilities."

"Like—"

"We'll be fine here. We'll see you later," his mother hurriedly said.

Zarium stuffed the last bite of food in his mouth and transported home.

***

Alara drummed her fingers on her face. She wished she could follow Zarium. She was interrupted by Tannah, who said, "Would you like to help me make some bone broth for Nori?"

Alara nodded and went to the kitchen. Tannah and Alara talked about many topics over the next few hours. Tannah was easy to talk to, and Alara enjoyed her company. After a while, Tannah ventured to ask, "What do you think about Zarium?"

Surprised by the question, Alara blushed and stammered, "I . . . uh . . . he's really nice."

"But . . . ?" While Alara debated how to answer the question, Tannah said, "I used to worry about whether Zarium would be affected by the dark magic he came in contact with." Alara ducked her head. Tannah laughed. "Zarium told me about your concerns. The fact that he's often away doing secret business probably doesn't help. However, I believe he has a good heart."

Alara mused, "I've noticed that too." She blushed again.

Tannah couldn't help herself, "And he's good-looking." She nudged Alara.

Alara turned her head. She had definitely noticed that, despite trying hard not to. They took the bone broth they had made off the stove and gently shook Nori's shoulders until she woke up. "How are you feeling?" Alara asked.

"Okay," Nori said in a raspy, weak voice.

Tannah dipped a spoon into the broth. "Could you drink some broth?" Nori nodded. Alara helped her sit up and positioned a pillow behind her back, and Tannah slowly spooned the soup into Nori's mouth.

***

When Zarium got back to his house, he went to his mother's room. Years before, his dad and Teron had matching rings. His father had given one to Teron as a gift. When his father died, his mother took the ring off and kept it. When they first moved into the house, he had seen it sitting on the bureau, but later it was gone. He figured she moved it to a safe spot within the room.

His dad and Teron were about the same size, so with a little bit of luck, the ring would fit Teron. He could make the switch and hopefully, Teron wouldn't notice that he had the wrong ring.

He started with her bureau, thinking that seemed like a good place to put the ring. He was right and found it in the last drawer he checked. It was inside a black wooden box. He picked up the box and took it to the kitchen. As he opened the box again, the ring shimmered in the light. It was a gold ring with a square red ruby in the center. A metal piece of two swords crossing each other was attached to the top of the stone.

The ring represented friendship, loyalty, and sacrifice. Zarium almost didn't dare touch it, afraid the very act he was about to carry out would cause it to crumble into a pile of dust. Was he going too far? The deceit, stealing, lying, and worst of all, aiding evil. Would Teron do the same thing if he were in his shoes? Would his father?

Zarium had a bigger problem though. How was he going to get into the castle at midnight? The doors to the castle would be locked that late at night, and there was no way a guard was going to let him in without a really good excuse.

He also had never been in the king's bedroom before. Actually, he had never been anywhere except the ballroom, the sword room, and the front area with the meeting rooms and foyer. He stood in front of the ring. His hand hovered above the ring before he grabbed it and shoved it into a brown leather pouch he had hung around his neck for the purpose of keeping the ring safe. He slid the pouch under his shirt.

He walked outside and transported to Nori's. He was pleasantly surprised when he ended up at Nori's. *She must be doing better.* He walked in the door and saw his mom and Alara sitting in the living room talking.

"We woke Nori up while you were gone and gave her some broth," Tannah said. "There haven't been any problems since, so we think she was able to handle it. Hopefully that means she didn't have any serious internal injuries."

"Did she say anything when she woke up?" Zarium asked, walking into Nori's room.

"Not much," Tannah replied. "It took a lot of energy for her to drink some of the broth, and she went right to sleep when we finished."

He sat down next to Nori's bed and felt her head again. "Her head is still hot. Maybe we could put another cold towel on her." Tannah nodded and headed to the kitchen.

A minute later, Zarium heard someone walk into the room, and he turned, expecting his mother, but it was Alara. She bent over and put the towel on Nori's head.

"Thank you," Zarium said. He figured she'd leave, but she stayed.

Tannah entered the room. "I'm going to go outside for some fresh air." Zarium raised an eyebrow, knowing his mom was just trying to let him and Alara be alone.

As soon as Tannah left, Alara said, "Look, I know I'm not your favorite person right now, but I was wondering if you wanted to do something." Alara looked at the floor and swallowed hard. "We could go on another date now that Nori is feeling better. It would be good for us to get a break and have fun."

Zarium was guarded but hopeful. "I guess you're hoping you can go somewhere besides here and the castle and still be safe."

"I was more interested in getting to spend time with *you*."

Zarium's heart skipped a beat, but he didn't want to appear too eager. "I'll think about it."

"Oh . . . um . . . okay." Alara wound a piece of her dress around her fingers. "That's fine."

Zarium smiled to himself, knowing it was probably the first time a man didn't give in to all her wishes. "I think I'll join my mom for some fresh air." He got up, leaving her in the room with Nori.

***

Alara was surprised when she heard Nori whisper, "You two sure make things difficult."

Alara sighed. "Yeah, I'm good at messing things up with him."

"Want to talk?"

"I don't want to bother you with my problems," Alara replied.

"I'm not good for much right now, but my ears work." Nori took a breath before continuing. "And I have plenty of time to listen." Alara hesitated only for a few seconds before everything from their last date to what had happened since with Zarium tumbled out in a heap of words. When she finished, she waited to see what Nori would say. Nori sat thinking for a long time before replying, "Is there anything you can do about any of this?"

Alara was stumped. Most of it was out of her control. "I'd take different actions depending on whether Zarium is really trustworthy."

"Are you getting any closer to the truth by stressing about it?" Nori coughed, and Alara grabbed her some water and angled her head so she could drink some. Alara put the glass on the bureau.

Alara sat back down and sighed. "No."

"Inaction will only make you more confused. You're overthinking it," Nori chastised her while still smiling.

"Because I don't want to make the wrong decision."

"If you do nothing, it will be the wrong decision. If it were me, I'd choose to believe Zarium and do more with him. At least, I'd get more enjoyment out of the experience." Nori winked.

Alara blushed. It was true; it would be more enjoyable. Besides, she would know sooner if he was good because she'd be with him more. It made sense, but she didn't want to fall for Zarium and have her heart shattered. But then again, she supposed a shattered heart was a small sacrifice for the lives of thousands of people.

"But you have to be all in," Nori said. "If you keep going back and forth, you won't get the answers you want. It has to be all or nothing."

Alara considered that and was about to say something else when she noticed Nori's eyelids drooping. She patted Nori's hand and whispered, "Thank you, friend."

Alara took a book out of Nori's bookshelf and read until Tannah and Zarium returned. She told them that Nori had woken up and talked for a few minutes. Tannah felt Nori's head again. "Her head feels like the fever is lower than before." Tannah looked around. "It doesn't seem like there is much else we can do right now. I brought some cards with me. Would anyone like to play?"

Zarium grabbed some chairs and put them around the table. They played and talked into the evening. Alara looked for reasons to say something or compliment him on his game skills as they played. He was cordial to her, but she was discouraged that he didn't reciprocate.

A knock at the door brought a welcome surprise when Ian walked in. He had been gone on a trip when all of the problems had started. Alara stood up and hugged him. "I was worried about you when all of our powers weren't working. I'm glad you made it back."

"It took me a little longer to finish what I was supposed to do. Mother asked me to come and get you and bring you home for the evening."

"Okay," Alara remembered the fox tooth and handed it back to Zarium. "Thanks for letting me use it today. Have a good night."

Zarium nodded. "You as well." With nothing left to say, Alara followed Ian out the door and got on the horse she had tied to one of the trees on the side of the house earlier.

Chapter 22

At eleven thirty that night, after his mom fell asleep, Zarium crept into the kitchen, got on a chair, and put omps that had his person-transport power and his tracker power on top of a cupboard. There was only a couple of inches between the cupboard and the ceiling. A perfect spot. Now he could carry Teron's ring on him and still use his powers. Zarium crept outside. He let the guard know that he needed to check on some things and would be back later. Before transporting, he made himself invisible. He didn't want anyone to know he had been anywhere near the castle that day.

Zarium walked around the castle, hoping for some inspiration about how to get in. He walked around to the back of the castle and looked up. There were windows, but the windows had bars, and he couldn't squish in between them. He put his hands on the wall, but there wasn't anywhere he could grip to just climb up the wall.

The guard who walked around the top of the castle came to his side. Zarium stood still and waited until the guard moved to another part of the roof. He took out some rope he had brought with him and threw it toward the window. Time after time, the rope came back down. After several tries, he finally got it to connect with one of the bars on a window. He carefully pushed the rope until it started coming back down on the other side of the bar, and he could grab the other half.

He climbed until he got to the window ledge. Now it was going to be tricky. The roof was about seven feet higher than where he was. He would have to wait until he was sure the guard was on the opposite side from him. He timed how long it took the guard to get around and how much time he spent when he could see him on his side. When the guard left, he waited until he was sure the guard wouldn't hear him. Then he jumped and caught the edge of the roof and pulled himself up.

Knowing there was a window under him, he assumed there was also a room. He took the flyn bark out of his pocket and placed it over a metal bracelet. He reached behind his back and pictured a blanket. He placed the blanket on the ground and envisioned a door. Quickly, he removed the blanket to reveal a . . . he frowned. There was nothing there but the roof. He tried again, this time reaching behind his back while picturing a door, and as he brought his hand out, there was a small door that could fit in the palm of his hand. He sighed. *Seriously! I don't have time for this.*

He wondered if it would be possible to connect the small door to the castle somehow. He took the small door and placed it where he wanted, but when he opened it, it didn't open into a hole, but rather into the hard surface of the roof. He put the small door in his pocket.

The guard moved, and Zarium repositioned himself to be as far from where the guard was as possible. Zarium stopped and thought about the powers he had. He had a piece of flyn bark that could enhance powers. *How can I use them to solve this problem? Think, Zarium, think . . . I can transport, but only in locations without solid walls, floors, and ceilings . . . but what if . . .* He smiled—it was a long shot, but maybe it could work.

He took out his knife that had his place-transport power and put the bark over it, pictured one of the rooms of the castle, and . . . It hadn't worked, and he found himself thrust mercilessly against the roof of the castle. *Why didn't the dragons give me the ability to go through walls?*

He saw the guard turn around. He had heard the sound of Zarium hitting the roof. The guard moved in Zarium's direction. Zarium slowly stood up and moved a few feet over. The guard walked around the perimeter of the roof and went back to one spot to stand again.

Zarium sat down on the roof, discouraged, knowing there would be bigger problems than sneaking into the castle if he didn't get that ring to Claud. Zarium debated talking to the king and came up with mini speeches he could tell the king without giving away his true purpose. He paced. Then he heard a sound from the tower on the one side, and soon what looked like a solid wall opened up and a guard came on the roof.

The other guard walked toward the tower. Zarium quickly put himself just behind the guard as he headed into the castle. Once inside, the door closed behind them. It caught Zarium's shoe, and there was a slight delay in the door closing. *Would the guard notice?* The guard turned around. Zarium took a step to his left. The guard ran his hand down the door. When he was satisfied that it was shut, he turned back the other way and pushed on the wall. The wall opened up to a set of stairs.

Zarium examined the door that led to the roof. It was obvious that you could only open it from the inside since it opened out and there weren't any handles on the outside. He waited for several minutes before gently pushing on the door on the other side of the room. He listened for any noise before walking down the stairway.

The last time he had felt this nervous was when he was younger, and he and Kursek would sneak snacks from the kitchen after they were supposed to be in bed. Those were fun times, and he missed them. He wished that this was as trivial as stealing food from his parents. But if he failed this time, instead of getting in trouble and having to stay inside, he'd face much graver consequences, especially from Claud.

At the bottom of the stairs, there was a hallway to the left and one to the right. He debated which one to take. He saw a guard round the corner from the right and head to the left. *I guess I'll go to the right.* As he walked down a hallway, he saw many doors but knew that none of them were what he was looking for because he knew that there were guards stationed outside the rooms of each of the royal family.

He went around a corner and saw a guard in front of a room. That had to be one of their rooms, but whose? He made a mental note of the location and kept walking to see if he could find other rooms with guards.

He came to some stairs and went down them. He again chose to go to the right, but after following it all the way to a dead end, he turned around and went back again.

He came to another set of stairs that went down. He was again led to another hallway with rooms. A couple of them had guards in front of them.

He saw a room that had a huge red double door with gold handles. There wasn't a guard though, so he kept walking. Soon, he saw the area of the castle that he was used to—the main foyer and the meeting rooms.

He went back to the first stairway he had come to and went the other way. Again, there were many doors but no guards. He had seen five guards standing in front of doors. But there should have been six. Was it possible no one guarded Jarius's door since he hadn't been around in months?

He walked back through where each of the guards was, looking for a hint that one of them was the king's bedroom, but they all looked pretty much the same. He came to the double doors with the gold handles again and decided to see what was inside. He pushed down on the door handle and gently pushed the door a little. He listened for any sounds and heard snoring. His pulse quickened. Surely, this was the right room. He opened the door a little more until it was wide enough to squeeze in. He closed the door quietly behind him and waited for his eyes to adjust to his surroundings.

The light from the full moon shone in from the window, making it easier to see. He saw a room fit for royalty—it was bigger than his whole house. In the center was a large bed with a beautifully carved frame. Off to one side, several feet away, was a bathtub. The walls were made of expensive stone that he'd never seen before and figured had been imported from another land. Above the bed was a painting of the royal couple on their wedding day. Convinced that this was the king and queen's room, he had only one goal—to get the ring and leave before anyone caught him.

He inched his way forward until he got to the bed. The people in the bed were definitely the king and queen. He went to the side with Teron. He saw one of the king's hands on top of the cover. *Darn, it's the wrong hand.* The hand he needed was under the covers toward the middle of the bed.

Zarium waited and waited and waited. Finally, the king rolled over in his sleep. His hand was still under the covers, but it was now closer to Zarium. *I can do this. No, I have to do this.* He waited some more and moved the covers a little bit. Then he moved them a bit more. He could see the king's wrists. He was so close. The king mumbled, moving slightly. Zarium wiped his brow.

At last, he pulled the cover down low enough to see the ring. He was glad to see it wasn't super tight. He carefully began pulling it off. All was going well until it got stuck on the knuckle. *I didn't come this far to fail now. Come on.* He gave it a quick, harder tug, and it went over the knuckle, but Teron moved again, and his hand moved too.

Zarium panicked because the ring fell off when Teron moved. *Can't I have a break here?* He carefully slid his hand under the covers and felt around. His finger found it. He pulled it out.

He pulled his dad's ring out of the leather pouch, but as he went to stick the ring on, Teron made a sound and moved his hand under his pillow. Zarium had no way of getting to his finger now. He made a decision to leave and not worry about the ring. He knew Claud would be mad, but he would be madder if Zarium got caught.

Zarium stood up and crept slowly toward the door. He opened it and listened for any noise. Convinced it was safe, he poked his head out. When he didn't see anything, he left the room and closed the door behind him. There was barely a perceptible click as it closed.

Zarium walked briskly down the hall and past a room with a guard. He walked through each hallway and up each staircase until he got to the room that led to the roof. He was about to open the door when he stopped. He couldn't walk out the same way he came, or the guard on the roof would hear him as he left.

He looked at his timekeeper—half past one o'clock. He waited, hoping that the guards would switch out before morning. A little while later, he heard someone coming up the stairs. He checked his timekeeper again—two o'clock.

He positioned himself in the corner opposite the wall with the door. Soon, he saw a guard. The guard walked to the door and pushed. Zarium waited until he stepped outside, where, just like last time, the guard held the door. Zarium quickly slipped out the door and moved several feet away from it. The guards switched places. Zarium watched the new guard walk around the perimeter. When he walked to the one side to scan the area, Zarium went to the opposite side and started his descent.

Zarium snuck back into Nori's house, where he saw his mom was asleep in one of the chairs in the living room. He went to Nori's room and put the rock back in her pocket. Then he grabbed the mat he had slept on the night before and soon fell asleep.

Chapter 23

The next morning, Zarium heard Nori. He stretched and got off the mat, rubbing his back. He stood up and yawned and then walked into Nori's room. She was awake and told him that she was hungry. He felt her head. Her fever was gone.

"What would you like for breakfast?"

"Some toast with peach jam."

"I'll get right on that."

He walked to the kitchen and got out the bread. Then he got out the pan and put it on the stove. When it was hot, he placed the bread on it and waited while it browned.

He put Nori's toast on a plate and went to her room. He helped Nori sit up in the bed, and he handed her the toast.

"How do you feel, Nori?" Zarium asked.

"Better than I did a few days ago."

"You're looking and sounding a lot better." Zarium looked at her arms and legs. "The bruising is gone now. If your leg hadn't been so seriously broken, it would have healed by now."

"I guess I'm just lucky to be alive."

"You are." He heard his mom stir. "Good morning," he called out.

Tannah stood up and walked toward him. "What are you doing this early in the morning?"

"Nori is actually hungry and wanted some toast with jam." He grinned.

He motioned for his mom to sit and asked her if there was anything he could get her. "I guess I wouldn't mind some toast and jam as well." Zarium nodded and walked back into the kitchen and put two more pieces of bread on the pan. As he cooked it, Tannah walked out into the kitchen and asked, "How long will it be before Nori is back to normal?"

Zarium shrugged. "Maybe a couple of days. She has made great progress. She went through a traumatic event, but she's going to be okay." Zarium flipped the toast. "Are you still wanting to go home this morning? I can go with you."

"That would be nice, but I think I'll get dressed and go to the marketplace before we head back. They have a better variety here than in Camden."

Zarium put jam on her toast and handed it to his mom. "Well, eat first and then you can go." He took a big bite of the other toast.

His mom finished eating, got dressed and left. Zarium heard Nori calling to him and went to her room. Nori told him to have a seat, so he did. She jumped right in. "Last night, I woke up. I felt my pocket for my rock, but it was gone. This morning it is back."

Zarium avoided eye contact. "Perhaps it was a dream."

"It didn't feel like a dream."

"You've been very sick, so I'm sure a lot of things have felt off."

She nodded and didn't prod him anymore. He hoped he was off the hook when she said, "I awoke when you were climbing into bed. I noticed my time-keeper said it was after two o'clock. Where did you go?"

He knew that if he told her that she dreamed that too, she'd ask him if he was in the house all night. He couldn't stand the questioning. "I couldn't sleep and went for a little walk. I thought it might help me to get some answers. When I came back, I slept really well." He saw the look Nori gave him and knew she didn't believe him.

He excused himself and went to the kitchen to clean up the dishes. His mom returned while he was putting the last thing away. "You show up when all the work's done I see," he teased.

"I guess I take after my kids." She laughed.

They were interrupted by Alara and Ian walking in the door. Zarium didn't get a single word out of his mouth before Ian said, "Our father's ring with his immobilization power is gone."

Zarium tried to look surprised. "How is it gone?"

"He had it on last night," Ian said. "But this morning, all of his other rings were on his hand, but that one was gone."

Zarium stumbled over his words. "Did they check the bed. Maybe it fell off and is in the covers somewhere."

"The servants checked the bed and scoured the room before we came here," Alara said. "Oh, and one more thing. My parents would like to see you."

Zarium felt nervous. "They want to see me? Now?"

"Yes, can you go?" Alara asked.

He told himself not to worry and that he was being paranoid. He looked at his mother. "I will take you back home when I return." She nodded, and Zarium hurried out the door and transported to the castle.

Once inside the castle, Zarium was led to the Yellow Room where Teron and Corah were waiting. He shut the door behind him. "I just heard from Ian and Alara that Teron is missing his ring with his immobilization power."

"Yes," Corah said. "We suspect there was dark magic involved."

"Why do you believe dark magic was involved?" Zarium asked.

"Because we have guards who stand right outside our bedroom door." Corah said, "How did anyone get past them? Even if they had invisibility powers, the guards would have seen the door open."

"That makes sense," Zarium said, but he knew there hadn't been any guards that night.

Teron cleared his throat. "Zarium, do you remember how I gave you a piece of flyn bark the other day to heal Nori?"

"Yes."

"When I gave it to you, I put a tracker on it." Zarium felt warm and wished he could escape through the door. He hoped the conversation wasn't going where he suspected it was going. "We know you were in the castle last night," Teron said

Zarium rubbed his hands on his pants. What was he going to tell them? He appealed to them with the only thing he could think of. "King Teron, you once trusted my father with your life, and he didn't let you down. I need you to trust me in that same way now. You have information you have kept hidden from Alara, for reasons she may not understand, and there are reasons why I can't explain this."

Zarium held contact as his eyes bore into him. He wondered what they were thinking. Their stoic expressions made them hard to read. Would this ruin everything?

Teron spoke, "Zarium, you may go. When you get to Nori's, tell Alara and Ian to come back."

Zarium shifted his lower jaw back and forth. Could he say anything to help his cause? He stood up, bowed. "Yes, Your Majesty."

Zarium walked slowly toward the front doors, feeling a huge weight. He transported to Nori's, walked in the door and told Alara and Ian that their parents needed to talk to them. When they left, he checked on Nori and asked her if she'd be okay for a few hours. She told him she would be fine and that if she needed anything, she would call a guard. Zarium went back out to the living room and told his mom they could go.

When Zarium and his mom returned safely to Camden, he remembered that it was the third day since he had given the gift to Claud. If he wanted to track him, he had to do it that day. Zarium first transported to Vashka. No matter where he went, he couldn't locate Claud. He began the journey of transporting to Zarothan. Since it was so far away, and he couldn't transport more than a distance of a few miles at a time, he stopped at several places along the way including Durik and checked to see if Claud was in any of those places.

Each place Zarium tried ended with him not finding Claud, and soon Zarium knew he would find him in Zarothan at Mt. Fraton. When he got to Zarothan, he stopped and tried to locate him, but he wasn't in the city. Finally, Zarium went to Mt. Fraton. He transported to a place in the forest that he had been to before.

He didn't have Nori's invisibility power, so he had to be careful that he didn't transport to the wrong spot and get seen by Claud or the others. Once at the spot in the forest, Zarium tried using the tracker, but there was nothing. He was going to have to get closer. He transported several hundred more yards closer to the mountain. *Still nothing. Where is he?*

Zarium felt the hairs on his arm stand up. He worried that he should have gotten the invisibility power. It would be a lot more comfortable at that moment. Zarium transported until he was at the front of the mountain. He found some tall bushes and lay on the ground. *Please work.* He thought of Claud. Then a picture formed in his mind.

Claud was there in a meeting. From the surroundings, they were inside the mountain. There were other people, many who Zarium didn't recognize, but then he recognized Asher, and a couple of castle guards. Claud was walking as he talked to the group which gave Zarium a greater view of the area. While he couldn't hear what they were talking about, he could take guesses.

Then Claud walked over to a spot that had a metal cage. Someone was in it. *Just a little closer.* Claud stopped. *No, keep walking over there.* Then Claud walked closer and put his hand on the cage. There were two people in it. He recognized Jarius, and then he saw the Prince of Faskin. Zarium could tell that Claud was talking to them. How he wished he had super hearing.

Claud walked near another cage that had a few more people in it. Zarium didn't recognize them but thought they could be farams. Then he saw the dozens of cages with dragons.

Zarium stopped focusing on Claud. He had to get back to the castle and let the king and queen know what he had seen.

When Zarium got to the castle gates, he entered and went up the stairs to the door of the castle. Once inside, he asked to see the king and queen.

A servant led him to the Red Room and told him to have a seat. Zarium hadn't waited long when Teron and Corah entered. Before they could say anything, Zarium stood up and blurted out, "Claud is definitely one of the main people involved in the Magic Robber group, and their numbers are getting larger. What I saw in the forest the other day was a small group, but when I tracked him to Mt. Fraton today, there were at least a hundred people."

Teron walked closer to Zarium. "Did you see more than just a meeting?"

Zarium nodded. "Yes, I saw Jarius—"

"He was alive?" Corah asked.

"Yes, and Shem, the Prince of Faskin, was in the cage with him. Then I saw more cages with dragons in them."

"Thank you," Corah said. "If you find out more, let us know."

Chapter 24

The next morning, Zarium transported to Nori's house and walked inside. He was happy to see that Nori was sitting up in bed. She had picked up the book Alara had been reading the day before and was reading it herself. "I bet you're starting to get bored being stuck in here, huh?"

"Hmph, I hate not being able to do what I want." Nori pointed to the bookcase. "Could you grab me that piece of paper and pencil from off the top of the bookcase?"

He grabbed it, and she started to write a list. "I need you to go to the marketplace and buy some things."

She made the list and handed it to him, and he left to get the items she wanted. It took him nearly an hour to find everything on her list, and he had stopped three times to ask someone what an item even was.

He decided to walk back to Nori's and enjoy the nice sunshine. As he walked, he heard his name. He searched the area but didn't see anyone. "Over here," he heard a voice say. Zarium looked toward a group of trees, and there he saw Claud.

Claud wasn't as happy as Zarium assumed he'd be. "You messed up. You weren't supposed to take the ring. You were supposed to replace it."

"I tried, but Teron moved and I couldn't reach his hand. I was lucky just to get out of there."

Claud nodded. "All right, where's the ring?" Zarium reached into his pocket and handed it to Claud. Zarium turned to leave. "Not so fast. I want to make sure this is really the ring. Start walking away from me, and let's see if I can stop you." It took a couple of practices, but eventually, Claud stopped him easily.

"We have a couple more assignments for you to prove your loyalty," Claud said. "Meet me in two days in Durik, on the south side of town by the Golden War Horse Statue."

Zarium nodded and turned to leave. Claud called out to him, "Wait, I promised to get you more powers to help with things. I *always* keep my promises." Claud handed him two things: a piece of string and a rock. "These come from people who got powers from other farams. The string contains a nature's doorway power and will allow you to go through walls if they are purely natural, like a mountain, and the rock will allow you to go invisible."

"Thank you," Zarium said.

"Oh, one more thing. Make sure you practice with these and get good at using them. I made sure that none of the farams who gave people these powers are on our list to do anything to in the near future. These powers should work for a long while." With that, Claud disappeared.

Zarium continued his walk to Nori's. When he got inside, he said, "I'm back."

"You can leave the bags on the counter."

As Zarium put the bags on the counter, he remembered that Claud had given him two powers. That meant he had six powers on him. He thought about his powers. He decided to keep the omps with his powers: invisibility, place-transport, tracker, object-creation, and thought-scrambler. He put the string on top of the cupboard next to the rock with his person-transport power. Then he went into Nori's room. "Do you need anything else before I leave?" Zarium asked Nori.

"Yes, I'm not able to check on the dragons. I wonder if you might do that."

"I'd be happy to help you. Do you need help getting to the other room?"

"No, I want to have you use my power, so you can open their land and check on them."

Zarium's eyes widened. He hadn't planned on this turn of events. He could see where this could go bad really fast. He debated. What if someone else found out he knew how to get in and could use that against him, or what if something happened to the dragons and he was the one people blamed? "Nori, I don't think that is a good idea."

"Why not?" She furrowed her eyebrows. "It isn't like I'm asking you to start taking care of them from now on. I just want you to make sure everything is okay." She shrugged. "I've trusted you with my life, so I should be able to trust you with my dragons."

He sighed and rubbed his temples. "Okay, I will do it on one condition." He waited until he had her attention. "You can't tell anyone that you told me the words to say." Nori started to nod in agreement when Zarium said, "I mean it; you can't tell anyone no matter what."

She nodded her head. "Okay, I promise." She told him that in the kitchen was a metal pot with a wooden handle. She asked him to go get it. Zarium walked over and looked at her wall. There were three pots that would fit the description. He grabbed one of them and returned to her room, and asked her if that was what she wanted.

"No, it is the biggest one." Zarium walked back to the kitchen and grabbed the biggest one. As he handed it to her, she said, "Put it on your head?"

He bit his upper lip and scratched the side of his head. "My head?"

"Yes, it has my dragon-realm power. At least for now. I trade them out every couple of weeks which makes it harder for anyone to get access to my power."

"You've got to be kidding. Can't I hold it in my hands?"

"No, you will need your hands in a minute. Now, humor me and put it on." Zarium stuck it on and shook his head. "Do I look as stupid as I feel?"

"Yes," she laughed. "Now, go to my closet shelf." He walked over to her closet. "Do you see a yellow faded box?"

"Yes." He pulled the box down and opened it. Inside was a big sheep horn.

"You'll need that to call the dragons after you open up the land."

"Are you sure your dragons are going to trust me? What if they don't like me?"

"Everything will be fine as long as you have the sheep horn. Remember, there are thirty-four of them, so make sure they're all there. Before we start, go lock the door and come back in here."

He left and locked the door. When he came back, she motioned for him to go closer to her. "Lean in, so I can whisper the words you need to say to open and close the land." She gave him instructions on how to say them and what actions to do.

When she was done explaining, he told her the instructions and performed the actions to make sure he had them right. Then she shooed him into the other room. He stood there, wondering if this was a bad idea, but he began spinning and inaudibly whispered the words. Nothing happened. "Nori, it didn't work." He took a breath in.

"That's because you haven't done it before. Don't worry, you will get it. Try again."

He did it again, and this time, he watched as a light started glowing and grew bigger and bigger until he could see a land covered in plants and dragons all around him. He hadn't seen the land of the dragons since he had received his magic powers. He stared in amazement. *Wow!*

He stepped into the scene and took a few steps forward when he noticed that all the dragons were running away and hiding behind trees or rocks. He put the sheep horn to his mouth and blew. The dragons poked their heads out and looked at him. He blew the horn again and waited. One tiny dragon with three eyes crept slowly toward Zarium.

Zarium stooped down and put his hand in front of him. The dragon sniffed it and moved closer and closer until it was touching Zarium's hand. Zarium gently patted its head. Then Zarium stood up and blew the horn again. This time, several more dragons went forward, forming a line a few feet in front of Zarium. There couldn't be more than twenty-five. He blew it one more time, and another large group came out from behind some rocks.

He counted them and said the words to close the land and found himself in Nori's house again. He went to Nori's room. "Everything was good, and all thirty-four dragons are accounted for. Do you need anything else?"

"No, that was the main thing on my mind."

"Well, if you're good, I have a couple of things I'd like to do right now."

"You go ahead and do whatever you need to."

Zarium left Nori's house and transported to the castle. He entered the gates and went inside, where he asked a servant if Alara was available.

A few minutes later, she walked quickly toward him. "Is Nori okay?"

"Nori's great. I think she'll make a full recovery and be back to her normal self within a week."

Relief washed over Alara's face, and she smiled. "I'm so glad to hear that. Thank you for everything you have done."

"It was nothing. I'm glad I could help."

"It was something to Nori . . ." She reached out her hand and touched Zarium's arm while gazing intently. "And to *me*."

Zarium stuffed his hands in his pockets. "So, I want to apologize for the other morning when I was cold toward you."

"It's okay, I deserved it."

He shrugged. "Whether you deserved it or not, I would like to do something with you sometime."

Alara smiled. "Like a date?"

Zarium could barely contain his excitement. "Yes, a date. Would tomorrow work for you?"

"I'd like that," Alara said softly.

"How would three o'clock sound?"

"I'll be ready . . . maybe this time I could plan something for you?"

"That would be great." He flashed her his biggest smile. He awkwardly stood for a moment before saying, "Well, I probably should go, but I'll see you tomorrow." He turned and opened the door to the castle and walked outside. As he closed it, he turned and saw Alara still standing there watching him. He gave one last wave and closed the door. He did a fist pump and smiled. Life was good.

Chapter 25

When Zarium returned home that evening, he saw his mother sitting at the table, going through a box. He sat down next to her and peered inside. He smiled. It was some of the letters his father had written to her. He wondered what had prompted her to get this out.

"I bet you're missing him a lot right now," Zarium prodded.

"I always miss him, but today I wish he were here to counsel with. I wish he could reassure me that everything would be okay."

Zarium studied his mother's face. She had a few more lines, and she looked tired. He knew it was hard on her to lose a husband and son. His eyebrows furrowed, and he wondered if she would lose one more. He put his hand on her arm. "Everything's going to be okay."

Tannah tried to smile. "I worry. I can feel it building again."

"What is 'it'?" he questioned.

"The tension. I know there are things going on that I'm not privy to, but it doesn't mean I can't feel the change. It was like this before your father left that last time."

Zarium didn't know how to comfort her. She continued looking through the box. Zarium watched her. "If you don't mind, I'd love to hear some of these letters."

Tannah looked into his eyes before nodding and pulling out a letter.

The next morning, Zarium put on a nice pair of pants and a red shirt that his mom always told him made him look handsome. He spent a little longer on his hair, making sure it was all perfect. When he walked out into the living room, his mom whistled. "Someone looks extra nice today. Is this for Alara?"

He blushed. "Yes, we have a date this afternoon."

"You're calling them dates instead of meetings now." She raised her eyebrows a couple of times.

"Yeah. I think things are a lot better. I guess we'll see what happens." Zarium bent down and put on his shoes. "I was thinking about some of those letters you read me last night. I was wondering . . . how did Father find the courage to do what he did? How did he keep from being afraid?"

"Zarium," she spoke softly, "Courage isn't something you need to find. True courage isn't the absence of fear but rather the strength to do what is right in the face of fear. It isn't defined by one moment but rather by the seemingly insignificant daily actions that make up who you are. Then, when the time comes that you need courage, it will already be a part of you."

As Zarium contemplated that, there was a knock at the door. It was one of the castle messengers with a message for him. He read the letter. "It is a letter from the king and queen requesting I come to a meeting at noon."

At the castle, a servant led Zarium into the Red Room. Only Teron and Ian were there. He was told to have a seat and shortly, Levon also entered and sat down. The king stood up and shut the door. Teron walked to the chair he had been sitting in, but he didn't sit. He put his hands on the table and leaned in close. "I am wondering what you have found out from Claud and Asher? Have you had any meetings with all of you and him?" No one spoke. The king's eyes widened. "You don't know about each other?" He rubbed his chin. "Interesting."

"I have neither confirmed nor denied that I'm meeting with them," Levon replied. "Is there a reason why you are suspicious of any of us?"

Zarium could feel his face getting warmer. He fought to keep any expression from his face. Teron continued watching the three of them. He sat down. "Okay, let's try this again. I have reason to believe that all three of you have intentionally met with Claud and Asher at least once."

Zarium wondered why the king was doing this. Why would Teron blow his secret? He thought back to the meetings and all that had happened. He had seen Levon in a meeting with Claud and Asher, so that wasn't surprising. But Ian was always so outspoken against Claud in leadership meetings. Was it possible one of them was a traitor? Or did the king suspect him?

Teron spoke, and Zarium shifted his focus back to him. "I also have reason to believe that he has given all three of you tasks to complete and that all three of you will do these. However, if I'm not mistaken, none of you are actually on Claud's side. You're only pretending."

The silence was deafening. Zarium saw Teron look at him and nod. Zarium slowly inhaled before speaking. "King Teron, I will confirm that what you have said is true concerning me. But I cannot tell you everything that has been spoken between Claud and me."

Teron acknowledged that he'd heard Zarium but didn't take his gaze off his two sons. Levon said, "Ditto to what Zarium said."

Finally, Ian whispered, "The same with me."

"That's all I wanted to know," Teron said, "and more importantly, I wanted the three of you to know about the other two. There is strength in numbers. Remember that. Besides, too many secrets lead to problems. I hope this meeting helps there to be less problems." He looked at each of them and puffed out his chest. "I am proud of each of you. I know how difficult this must be. You are dismissed."

Zarium let out a breath of air, only then aware of how tight the muscles in his jaw and neck were. He stood up and walked stiffly out the door. Levon walked briskly past and whispered to Zarium and Ian, "Follow me." Zarium nodded his head and hoped the king wasn't wrong in his assumptions.

Zarium followed Levon to a part of the castle he hadn't been in. They stopped at a room and went inside. Once inside, Levon stood in front of the wall and pushed on pieces of the wall. He gave the right side of the wall a hard shove, and the wall moved in like a door, revealing a room behind it.

Zarium held back as Levon and Ian walked through. Soon, Levon poked his head through the opening and motioned for Zarium to come. Zarium stuck his head inside a small empty room and looked around before stepping inside.

Once Zarium was inside, Levon motioned to a tunnel in the wall. "Now we're going to crawl through here." Zarium wanted to protest, but he followed behind them. Zarium's list of grievances was growing as they crawled through the space. He was rehearsing in his mind exactly what he'd say when he was interrupted by a crunching sound and something wet on his hand. *Great.* If they didn't need to be quiet, he had a few choice words he would've liked to say.

At last, they came to an opening. As Zarium climbed out, he wiped his hands on the wall, smearing a mix of blood and guts on them. Levon placed a heavy brick lid over the opening of the hole. Ian smiled at Zarium and motioned with his hand, "I see you found a friend in there."

"Very funny," Zarium said. He looked down at his pants. *So much for putting on nice pants for my date.* "Now what?" Zarium cast his eyes over the small, dark, cold room they were in. It couldn't hold more than eight people standing up. "What is this? Some secret room?"

Levon turned on the light. "Yeah, there are a lot of rooms that are hidden in the castle."

Zarium's mind was spinning. "What if someone else has the same idea, and they show up here too?"

Ian and Levon smiled at each other. "Well, this room wouldn't be all that cool if it didn't have multiple entries," Levon said. "We can take another exit out if we need to."

Zarium conceded. "Okay, but let's make this quick."

Levon spoke, "We are going to tell each other what extra powers we have and what Claud has asked us to do."

Zarium refused to be the first one to speak. So much was on the line. Finally, Ian broke the silence. "I can go invisible and have supervision . . . I have to steal a dragon."

Zarium's eye shifted. He took a deep breath in and let it out slowly. "I can go through purely natural-made walls and go invisible." He turned to Ian. "I can help you steal a dragon." Ian jerked slightly but otherwise remained still.

All eyes were on Zarium. He paused, digging at the ground with his foot. "Nothing, and I mean nothing, better leave this room."

"Weren't we already operating under this assumption?" Levon asked.

"Okay, fine. I stole King Teron's ring and gave the power to Claud."

Both of them turned toward him. He raised his hands. "Oh, come on. Don't pretend like you won't be doing things that are just as bad."

"Okay," Ian said, "Levon, what about you?"

"I have an invisibility power and a sleeping power." Levon hesitated and closed his eyes. "Also, I have to kidnap Zarium's mom."

Zarium opened his mouth and rubbed his face with his hands. His mom? What was he supposed to do with that? It dawned on him how well Claud planned this out. "Really?" He paced before saying, "Okay, I have a plan. We will steal the dragon first, but only one."

"What if we get caught?" Levon asked.

"I don't think that's an option," Ian said.

"He's right," Zarium said. "If we get caught, we'll be on our own and in a lot of trouble."

"So, how do we get a dragon?" Ian asked

Zarium smiled. "Meet me at that blacksmith shop by Nori's tonight at midnight."

Chapter 26

By the time Zarium finished doing all the things he hadn't planned for that day, it was nearly time for his date with Alara. He sat in one of the chairs in the sitting room and waited.

He stood as Alara entered. "You look beautiful."

Alara blushed. "Thanks, have you had a tour of the castle before?"

"No. Is that what we are going to do today?"

Alara nodded. "Come." She smiled and beckoned him to follow. She led him through a narrow hallway and down some stairs he had never seen before. She was happily talking about the next place she was going to show him and how she was sure he would love it. As they walked, he slipped his hand into hers. He thought he heard a slight pause in her words, but she recovered and kept going, not even acknowledging that anything had happened.

They entered a door that led to the biggest kitchen Zarium had seen. When they had lived in a larger house, they had a big kitchen, but it was nothing compared to this. "Wow!" Zarium said. "There are three stoves, not to mention . . ." He quickly counted. "Ten sinks and look at all those pots and pans! You could fit half the market in here." He put his hand on one of the surfaces. It was perfectly clean.

Alara laughed. "Not quite." She tugged at his hand and led him past four people preparing and cooking food and out of the kitchen to another hallway.

Zarium asked, "What is your favorite part about being a princess?"

She tilted her head to one side. "A few weeks ago, I'd have told you that nothing about it is appealing, but I've been having a change of heart." She paused as they went up some more steps. Zarium recognized where they were as soon as he saw the red double doors. Alara pointed to the left. "My parents' room."

Zarium nodded but felt guilty even looking at it. Alara continued, "Now I'm seeing that there are benefits to being a princess and future queen."

"Such as?"

"Such as the ability to affect and influence things for the better."

Zarium squeezed her hand. "You're going to make a great queen."

"I guess we'll see. I've still got a lot to learn."

As they walked past a guard, she pointed to a door. "And this is my bedroom." She didn't open the door but rushed right past it. She led him down another hallway. There was a large mural that was at least twenty feet long and ten feet high. He remembered it being in this hallway when he broke in to steal the king's ring, but he had been in such a hurry that night, he hadn't really paid attention to any details.

He stopped and looked at it. It depicted people and dragons helping each other fight an enemy. *Interesting.* She stopped about midway through the mural and turned around and faced the wall on the opposite side of the hallway. "This is the coolest part of the whole castle."

Zarium looked at the empty wall in front of him. Was he missing something? He raised an eyebrow. "Alara, this wall is nice, but it's just a wall. There isn't even a painting on it."

She let go of his hand as she walked a little to her left and pulled out one of the square stone blocks. She put her hand inside, and the wall moved. *They love their secret passageways here.* Zarium moved closer and saw another passage leading downstairs. It looked dark, and he wondered what could be lurking down there. "Are we going down there?"

"What are you chicken?" Alara flapped her hands and made chicken sounds.

If only she knew. "No, of course not." She grabbed his hand and led him down the stairs. Every few feet, she'd push a button, and a light would come on. "Does this part of the castle ever get used?" Zarium asked.

"No, hardly anyone even knows about it. Hundreds of years ago, when the castle was first built, it wasn't as big as it is now, so this was the main living area of the castle. In time, the castle was enlarged, and this was mostly forgotten. I may be the only person who uses it."

They came to the end of the stairs and walked down another hallway. Zarium noticed there were rooms every so often, but Alara wasn't saying anything about them. "Where do all these doors lead?"

"Mostly to spare bedrooms, though, there is one further up that is another kitchen."

"Oh. Or maybe a dungeon. It's creepy enough down here to be the dungeon. It's all dark and smells musty. I wouldn't be surprised if we saw bones."

She ignored his comment and continued leading him through the hall and up a small set of stairs, where there was a room. She opened the door, but she stopped and faced Zarium. "The other day, I told you that I'm going to trust you and be all in. This is just one way I want to show you that I believe in you."

Zarium felt a thrill of excitement. He really was winning her over. He wanted to just take and hug her but thought that might be overdoing it. Instead, he calmly said, "That means a lot to me."

She turned and walked in the room. As Zarium followed, he looked around. It was a big space with some paintings and statues of people, animals, and dragons. "Is this a storage area?"

"It's kind of become that, but it's more than that."

She went to the very back of the room, pulled on the stone block, twisted it and pulled, revealing another secret room. Once inside, Zarium saw that there were soft chairs, a table, and a box. He lifted the lid to the box and smiled. "Your secret stash of snacks, huh?"

"Well, sometimes I can be down here for quite a while. I need something to eat and drink."

"What do you use this room for?" He stood in the doorway, examining the door.

"I mostly come down here to relax and have time to myself." She plopped down into one of the chairs and closed her eyes.

"Do your parents know you come down here?" He sat down in another chair. "I have a hard time picturing your mother approving of you being here."

"Yes, silly. Nothing gets past my mother," she scoffed slightly.

"What about your brothers? Do they ever come down here?" He sat on the other chair and bounced. It was actually comfortable.

"I don't know. I only come down once in a while, and I haven't run into any of them in years. When we were kids, we played down here all the time. To be honest, I forgot about it for a while. I only rediscovered it in the last year or so."

"So, is this like your 'special' spot?"

"Special spot?" Alara questioned.

"You know the place you go that helps you rejuvenate."

"I guess so." She cleared her throat, and Zarium waited for her to speak. Alara rummaged behind the chair Zarium was sitting in and produced some papers with markings all over them. "These are my evidence papers." She put the papers on the table and spread them out.

"Your what?" Zarium said, standing and walking to the table.

Alara pointed at one part. "Well, I have names of people and suspicious things that involve them."

Zarium saw his name with a list next to it, explaining all the reasons she suspected him. *She sure has a lot of evidence against me. No wonder she hasn't trusted me.* "That is quite the evidence you are gathering. I see you have plenty on me, yet you are still down here in a creepy dungeon-like part of the castle with me."

"I told you. I have reason to believe that I can trust you, and I'm trying to do that. Shhh," Alara said, suddenly, moving toward the wall closest to the hallway. She put her ear to the wall.

At first, all Zarium could hear were muffled voices. The voices got closer and closer. Zarium looked at the wall where they had come in. It was shut, but still he worried that somehow someone would know they were there.

They listened and soon heard the voice of Asher. "I'd feel better about him if we could tap into his thoughts and know that he's really on our side."

"Obviously, he has the thought-scrambler power," Claud said.

"And why do you think he feels the need to scramble thoughts?" Asher countered. "Perhaps it is to trick us."

"Oh, come on. We all use this ability. Isn't it obvious that he can't have my father knowing what he's thinking? Don't worry about him. I have a plan to make sure he's on our side."

Alara looked at Zarium, but he just shrugged. He knew they were talking about him and was relieved that they didn't say his name. "We need to act quickly and prepare for battle in the next few days before your parents have time to gather more strength," a third person said. Zarium felt light-headed and moved to a chair to sit down.

Alara gave him a look and moved next to him. She waited until the voices were no longer heard and put a firm hand on Zarium's arm. "What is it? What's wrong?"

Zarium shook his head. It was a voice he hadn't heard in years. "It can't be . . . but it is. But why would he be with Claud and Asher? It doesn't make sense." Alara stared at him in confusion. "One of the people . . ." He gulped and choked out, ". . . was Kursek."

"But he was banished," Alara said, looking confused. "He shouldn't be able to get inside the kingdom, let alone in here."

Zarium felt sick and confused. He stood up. "What do you mean Kursek was banished?"

Alara's eyes shifted back and forth. She shook her head. "I um . . . I said something I shouldn't have."

Zarium stared her down. "Well, you can't unsay it, so you might as well tell me what you are talking about."

In a whisper, Alara told him about the conversation she had with her father a few days before. Zarium said nothing for several seconds. He ran his hands through his hair. "This can't be. How could . . . I don't . . . does my mom know?"

Alara shook her head and tapped her fingers together. "I-I don't think so. I believe my father kept it a secret."

Zarium paced. "Kursek was part of the group that helped kill my dad. How could he? He should have . . ." Zarium pounded his fist into the wall.

"I'm sorry, and I can't even imagine how hard this must be, but if you are certain that was Kursek's voice, we need to tell my parents as soon as possible. What if there are others in here? What if they do something to my parents?"

"I know my brother's voice. It's Kursek."

Alara motioned for Zarium to follow her. They went through the hidden door and listened to make sure they didn't hear any voices in the storage room. Alara opened that door and listened some more. When they were sure it was safe, they exited the room and ran through the halls and up the stairs. It was all Zarium could do to keep up with her. When she got to the top, she stopped. Zarium nearly ran into her. "Why did you stop?" He whispered.

She elbowed him. "I'm listening to see if we hear any other voices before entering the main part of the castle."

***

When Alara was sure there was no one in the hallway, she opened up the secret passage, and they left. Alara led Zarium back to her bedroom. She pushed Zarium inside and followed after him, locking the door behind her. She got ahead of Zarium.

"Well, this sure is turning out to be the most interesting date I've ever been on."

She turned and gave him a look. "We're going to the closet."

"The closet? Oooh, I can honestly say I've never had a date in a closet before."

She lightly smacked him. "Okay, enough of that. At least we're safe. Or safer than we were." Alara ran to her closet and threw boxes out all over the floor. "Aghh, I hate that my mother was right. She always said that someday I would wish I were a cleaner person. Someday is today."

When she got most of the boxes out of her closet, she motioned for Zarium to come. She pushed on the wall and it opened. She got satisfaction out of watching Zarium's mouth fall open. "Life is better with secret rooms." Alara stepped through the door, motioning for Zarium to follow.

Once through the closet, Alara focused on having her parents meet her in the Blue Room. She hoped her mother was close enough to receive her thoughts. Zarium and Alara ran through a short hallway and turned a corner, where there was a door. When they opened it, Alara sighed with relief. Standing before her were both her parents. Zarium and Alara stepped into the Blue Room. "What is so urgent?" Her mother asked, the alarm evident in her voice.

Alara quickly rehearsed what had happened. She watched her parents give each other a shocked look. They turned to Zarium. "Are you sure?" Teron asked.

Zarium squared his shoulders and nodded. Alara could see her parents passing the pencil back and forth, discussing something in their thoughts. It frustrated her. *I thought they were going to let me take a bigger role in things.* She held her tongue and reminded herself that they were all on the same side.

Finally, her mother spoke, "I'm going to call an emergency meeting with the Great Five for tomorrow afternoon."

Alara panicked. "You aren't going to tell them about today, are you?"

"No," her mother replied. "I'm going to tell them that one of the banished traitors is back and see what the council thinks would be best. I want to make sure we are the ones calling the shots, not them. We have to make the first move, but we can't make it too soon."

Chapter 27

That evening, Zarium went to the blacksmith shop by Nori's house and waited for Levon and Ian. Levon and Ian arrived together a few minutes later. "All right," Ian whispered. "What's the plan?"

"Do you and Claud have a meeting place tonight?" Zarium asked.

"Yes, we were both in the castle earlier, where he gave me the directions for the handoff in Durik tonight."

"Okay." Zarium turned to Levon. "I need you to give me your sleeping power."

Levon reached into his pocket and started to pull out a timekeeper that had the power on it. He had it almost out when he stopped. "How do I know you won't put us to sleep?"

"You don't," Zarium said, "so I guess you'll have to take a chance. It's what we've been doing with you."

Levon handed the timekeeper to Zarium. "For it to work, you have to be looking at the face of who or what you are singing to. You also need to be within a short distance of the person. Whatever you do, don't attach the flyn bark to it, or you could put all of us to sleep."

Zarium nodded and turned to Ian. "After I put her to sleep, I will let you in. I will open the dragon realm, and you will steal the dragon."

Ian puffed out his cheeks. "Are the dragons going to let me take one of them?"

"I don't know. I've never stolen a dragon before," Zarium chuckled, "but I bet we find out quickly."

Ian put his hands up. "Hold on. Could the dragons eat me?"

Levon nudged him in the ribs. "You'll be the first to know."

"Well," Zarium said, "if nothing else, it will be an adventure, and on the bright side, I can do some healing." Zarium sat down and told the others to be quiet while he figured it out. He looked up at the stars. Some people believed that the stars were made from dragons who had died. *Dragons.* Others believed that people used to have the power to put the stars into the heavens. Or that maybe the dragons did it themselves using their own magic. *That's it!* He jumped up. "I have an idea. Let's see if dragons can be affected by their own magic."

Everyone agreed it was worth a try. They reviewed the plan to make sure everyone knew what to do. Zarium told them to go invisible and that he'd put the guard to sleep and motion when it was safe for them to come.

Zarium walked toward the guard who was standing in front of the house and put him to sleep. The guard slumped to the ground. Zarium motioned to the other two.

Zarium knocked on the door and waited. "Who is it?" Nori asked.

"It's me, Zarium."

Nori opened the door, standing in her pajamas. "I'm about to go to sleep. Can this wait until tomorrow?"

"I need some quick advice about a couple of things." He saw her hesitate. "I promise. I'll be quick, and you can even lie in your bed while I talk to you."

"Okay," Nori said. Zarium entered and closed the door. He waited for her to lie down and then put her to sleep. He went to the front door and let Levon and Ian in. He whispered for them to stand by the wall and not move until he had put one of the dragons to sleep.

He grabbed the pan and put it on his head. Ian and Levon raised their eyebrows. "I swear this is how it works," Zarium whispered. He began moving his hands and twirling around the room, whispering certain words until a large area opened up in front of them.

A lot of the dragons were either hiding or preoccupied doing something. He needed to get one of them by itself, but how? He smiled as the same small dragon who had come up to him when he had counted the dragons for Nori came up to him again. He patted his head, and soon the little dragon fell asleep. *It worked!*

He motioned for Ian to come over. "You can pick up this dragon. I would, but it isn't my responsibility to steal, so I'm not doing it." Ian bent down and picked up the dragon as Zarium said, "I don't know what powers it has, but it's small, so I figured that would be easier than the one that looks like it's ten feet tall."

Ian took the dragon. "Thanks, I think. What happens if this dragon wakes up while I'm carrying it?"

"That is motivation for you to be as quick as possible," Zarium said, closing the land of the dragons. Afterward, he pulled out his knife and handed it to Ian. "Here's my place-transport power."

Levon stepped forward and motioned to Zarium. "Perhaps you should give him my timekeeper so he can put it back to sleep in case it wakes up."

Zarium nodded and handed Ian Levon's timekeeper as well. Ian took them. "Do you want me to meet you two back here in the morning?"

"Well, we should probably wait here until the guard wakes up to make sure nothing else happens tonight. Besides, I'd rather get my power back tonight," Zarium said. "If you don't return in the next three hours, I'm going to assume something happened to you. I'll wait back at the blacksmith shop."

"I'll wait with Zarium," Levon said.

Hours later and miles worth of pacing, Ian appeared. Zarium breathed a sigh of relief. Ian went to him and put the knife in his hand and the time keeper in Levon's hand. "Everything went well with the dragon?" Zarium asked.

"Yes," Ian said.

"What are we going to do next?" Levon asked. "Are we going to tell my mother and father?"

"No," Zarium shook his head. "We can't tell them we stole a dragon. No way would anyone be okay with doing this. If they knew, they would have made us think of something else. You guys can't say anything to anyone. Now let's all go home and get some sleep."

Chapter 28

The next afternoon, Zarium arrived at the Grand Council Room early and was the first one there. He thought about what had happened over the last couple of days, what he had heard Claud say about him when he and Alara were in the secret room, and about the meeting he would have with Claud that night. He wondered what Claud meant when he said he had a plan to make sure he was on their side.

Zarium heard Corah speak and was startled to see a full room. Corah explained that Teron's power had been stolen a couple of nights ago. Chatter filled the air. Corah interrupted them. "This isn't all." It went silent, and she explained, "One of our Faram's dragons was stolen last night. I wish those were the only problems, but we also found out yesterday that one of the traitors who was banished years ago has been able to breach the kingdom's boundary. Also, some of their plans were overheard, and now we know they are planning an attack."

Zarium expected the people in the room to break out in chatter again, but this time it remained silent for several seconds before someone spoke. "What has been done to make sure they aren't infiltrating the castle as we speak?" The King of Shara asked.

Corah spoke again. "As soon as we found out, we sent a message to a man named Skye, who helped with the boundaries years ago. We were able to get a piece of clothing from the traitor we know about, and Skye was able to use his boundary-creation power to reestablish the boundaries. He had already left the castle, so Skye was able to secure the entire castle, including each meeting room."

"What do you need us to do to help prepare for this battle?" King Exor asked.

Corah sighed. "We need more soldiers who can go to battle and provisions for all the soldiers."

"You can count on us," King Exor said. The leaders of Shara, Kova, and Clim promised to send more men and provisions as well.

After the meeting, Zarium was approached by Alara, who said, "I was wondering if you'd like to go for a walk?"

"I'd love to, but I have to go somewhere else first, but I'll return in like twenty minutes."

Alara turned and left, but before Zarium could leave, Teron called out to him and asked him to stay for a moment. "Let's go to the White Room and talk for a minute."

Zarium left the room and went to the White Room. Once inside, Teron didn't waste any time on pleasantries. "Zarium, it's time to put our plans in motion. You must listen to me and do everything I say exactly as I say it." Zarium nodded. "Give me your word, Zarium."

Zarium hesitated, but only for a moment. "I give you my word."

Teron explained the plan. It was well thought out, but it didn't leave room for error. Zarium rubbed his chin. "How do you know this will work?"

"Because we know what Claud wants, and as long as Claud gets that or at least thinks he is getting it, things should go smoothly."

"I understand." Zarium shifted in his chair and leaned forward. "But will it be enough? What if things don't go as planned?" Zarium tapped his left temple. "Is Alara going to get hurt?"

Teron hung his head for several seconds before raising it and looking Zarium in the eye. "There is always a risk, but this has to be done. As long as the others believe they are getting what they want, things will go as planned. And Zarium . . ."

They looked at each other before Zarium said, "I know if all else fails, there must be a . . ." His words trailed off. He couldn't say it. The king patted him on the back and nodded. Zarium's thoughts raced. *Sacrifice.*

Zarium headed out of the castle and went to the one place he dreaded most—Nori's. He knocked on the door and waited for Nori to open it. She invited him in and they sat down in the chairs in the living room.

Zarium immediately asked, "How are you doing?"

"I'm okay. I'm a little slow, but most of the pain has left."

"I'm so glad to hear that." He moved closer and touched her leg. "It feels a lot better." He looked down at the ground. "I'm really wondering how you are doing because today, in the meeting, it was announced that one of your dragons is missing."

Nori looked at him until he felt uncomfortable. "Yes. I don't suppose you know anything about it."

Zarium put his hands in front of him defensively. "I can honestly say I didn't steal your dragon."

"But perhaps you helped?" Nori asked, not taking her eyes off his face.

Zarium took her hands in his. "You trusted me enough to tell me how to enter in the first place. Maybe you can trust me now."

"I didn't tell anyone that I had given you the knowledge to get in, so I guess that says something."

Relief rushed over Zarium. "Thank you. You won't regret this."

***

Alara was ready and waiting in the main foyer when Zarium returned. They went outside and Zarium said, "Would you like to go to the eatery that's not too far from here?"

"That would be great. I'm famished."

They walked to a small eatery and ordered some corn and a piece of chicken for each of them and sat down in one of the chairs to eat. They ate a few bites before Alara brought up the meeting. "It was a little surprising that Nori had a dragon stolen during the night, don't you think?"

"Yeah, we're probably lucky that there weren't more stolen." Zarium took a bite of his chicken.

Alara finished the corn she was eating before saying, "Yeah, I find that part a little strange, and it makes me wonder why."

"Perhaps they didn't have time to take more," Zarium said, as he finished his chicken and wiped his hands on a napkin.

Alara picked up her chicken and stood up. "This whole thing makes me nervous. I need to walk, so maybe we can finish eating as we walk." Zarium picked up his corn and followed her.

Alara brought up all the strange events of the last couple of days and tried to watch Zarium's face to see if he knew more than he was saying. She was about to ask about the short meeting he had with her father after the security meeting, but she caught sight of Berica and Levon walking. She snuck up beside them and put her hands over Berica's eyes. Berica guessed right away that it was Alara.

"What are you two doing?" Alara asked.

Both of them awkwardly fumbled for words and went red. Finally, Levon spoke, "Berica and I have been out shopping, and I was about to take her to her house."

Alara turned to Zarium. "Would it be all right if I talked to Berica for a little while?"

"Of course," Zarium said.

"Is it okay if I steal her for a little bit?" Alara asked Levon.

Levon let go of Berica's hand. "Yeah, I wouldn't want to interrupt girl time."

Alara looked at Zarium and Levon, "Perhaps you two could walk us back to the castle?"

Levon grabbed Berica's hand again and Zarium walked beside Alara. At the castle, Alara clumsily hugged Zarium at the door and avoided Berica's eyes. She let her parents know she was home and was going to talk with Berica.

When Alara got Berica alone, she pinned her up against the wall and smiled. "All right, you two were awfully awkward back there when I asked you what you were doing." Berica blushed three different shades. Alara grabbed Berica's hand but didn't see a ring. "Come one. What's going on?"

Berica hesitated before saying, "Promise not to say a word to anyone?" Alara nodded. "Levon and I were shopping today in the marketplace when one of the jewelers lured us into his shop. Levon encouraged me to try some rings on and see if I liked any of them, but he didn't buy one. We haven't even been talking about marriage, but on the way back to my house, he brought up the topic and asked how I would feel about owning one of those rings. You interrupted us shortly after that."

Alara shrieked with excitement. "I have been waiting for this day."

"Well, he still has to buy the ring."

Alara bounced on her toes. "At least I have some hope now."

Alara and Berica talked until it was time for Berica to go home for the evening. Alara walked her to the front door and said goodbye. Alara went to her room, where she heard a noise outside her window. She opened the curtain and peered out. A group of soldiers with uniforms from another land had just arrived. She saw her father and several guards go out to greet and welcome them.

Chapter 29

Zarium returned home and spent the evening with his mom. He couldn't shake the feeling that things were going to get very tricky for him. He was unsettled about his meeting with Claud. When it was time to go to bed, he went in but didn't go to sleep. He didn't want his mom to worry about what he was doing; he had to keep his late-night trip a secret. He lay on his bed until it was time to go, then he climbed out his window and transported to Durik to the Golden War Horse Statue where he agreed to meet Claud.

He jumped when he heard his name. "Zarium, how good to see you tonight," Claud hissed. "Follow me." Zarium followed Claud down the road and through some trees. They walked right through the middle of some bushes with thorns. Zarium's leg caught on a branch. When he pulled away, a piece of his pants and flesh were torn.

Claud beckoned to him, encouraging him forward. "Don't worry, a little blood won't hurt you."

Zarium nodded and quickly healed the spot before continuing on. Finally, there was an opening where they stopped. Zarium reached down to pick off some of the leaves that had attached to his leg. Claud walked up to him until he was mere inches from him.

Claud lifted his shirt slightly, pulled on the handle of a knife with a six inch blade, and brought it up to eye level with Zarium. Zarium's eyes widened and his heart pounded. Claud rubbed his finger on the tip, and a small cut and blood appeared. "I had it sharpened just for you."

Zarium felt dizzy. He forced himself to stay in the spot. "What do you mean?" Zarium asked, straining to keep his voice strong and steady.

"Tonight, you make the blood oath."

Zarium swallowed. Panic like he'd never felt before filled every muscle of his body. He had to keep a clear head and think through this. The blood oath involved pricking a finger and signing a contract with blood. Besides, doing something evil or coming in contact with a dead body that had dark magic around it, this was another way that a person could easily get access to dark magic. If one broke the oath, though, that person would die.

Zarium stared at the knife, the metal shimmering in the moonlight.

***

Alara was awakened by hard knocking. She groggily looked toward the window. It was still dark. She checked her timekeeper. It was after midnight. *What in the world could be going on?* She got up and went to her door, asking who was there. Her parents and Levon answered. She cautiously opened the door.

Levon spoke first. "Alara, Berica is missing from her home. She didn't go home tonight. You're the last person who saw her."

Alara wiped her eyes. "Wh-what do you mean?"

"Her mother contacted me and she isn't at home." Levon turned to leave.

Alara shivered and rubbed her arms. Just then, a guard brought a message to them. It was for Levon. Levon began reading it out loud but stopped. His eyes rapidly scanned the page. He let out a yell. "What's wrong?" their father asked. "What does the note say."

Levon shook his head. "I can't tell you, if I tell anyone the contents of this letter and they find out, they will kill Berica."

"Who are 'they'?" Their mother demanded.

"I can't tell you that either. I'm sorry, but I must go." Levon ran down the hallway.

Alara turned to her parents. "What are we going to do? Maybe we should follow him."

"No, the risk is too great," her father whispered. "I'm sure the message contained more for Levon."

"What if it is a trap for him?" Alara asked. Her father wrapped his arms around the two of them. Alara wiped away several tears. What would happen to Berica?

***

Zarium held the knife, racking his brain for a plan. He brought his finger up to the blade. Claud yelled. "Do it. Now!"

Suddenly, Claud's head turned sharply—a rustling in the bushes. He motioned to Zarium to be quiet. Zarium lowered the knife.

They crouched down and waited. Asher came into the clearing on a black horse. Zarium's stomach churned. Someone was laid over the front of the saddle in front of Asher. Asher climbed off his horse and approached them. "Berica believed I was Levon. She came willingly and never suspected anything until it was too late. She never saw me as me either," Asher said.

"Great work," Claud laughed, slapping Asher on the back.

Zarium asked as casually as he could, "What are you going to do with her?"

"Leverage. I have a feeling Levon will do whatever we ask if it means she will be safe."

"Put her with the others," Claud said.

Asher nodded and smiled at Zarium. It was the first approving look Zarium had ever received from Asher. Asher put his feet in the stirrups of the saddle and rode away.

Claud turned back to Zarium. "Either you take the blood oath, or you won't live to see another sunrise."

Zarium nodded. He reached his hand forward and touched the end of the knife. Blood ran down his hand. Claud handed him a piece of paper with a contract written on it. Zarium signed his name. Claud rolled up the paper and stuck it in his pocket. Claud put his hand out, and when Zarium grasped it, Claud gave it one firm pump up and down. "This may turn out to be the best decision you've ever made."

Chapter 30

The next morning, a messenger arrived with a message for Zarium. Zarium thanked him and closed the door. He turned to his mom, who was preparing breakfast, and said, "The king and queen have requested that I come to a meeting right now."

"I don't have all of breakfast ready, but here, take this." His mother handed him an egg on a piece of bread. He grabbed it and took a bite before slipping on his shoes and transporting to the castle.

At the castle, he was taken into the Red Room where Ian, Corah, and Teron were already sitting. He sat down quickly and waited.

Teron didn't waste any time. "Berica has been kidnapped." Zarium hoped that his look of surprise seemed genuine.

"And where is Levon?" Zarium asked cautiously.

Teron dropped his eyes. "I don't know. He refused to give any details, and he left the castle last night, and we haven't seen him since." Teron shuffled some papers around. "Also, anyone who has the ability to track people through gifts or move things with their minds has lost these powers because of Nori's stolen dragon." Zarium made a mental note that he didn't need to keep that power on him anymore. Now, he only had to shuffle six of them.

Corah looked toward Zarium. "Tomorrow, we want you to take Alara out to the countryside about a mile east of the Tykee Forest."

Zarium gripped the table. "Do you think that is wise, all things considered?" Zarium looked between Corah and Teron.

"We have discussed it, and we have a plan," Corah spoke with absolution.

Zarium was taken back by the finality of the decision. "Okay, I could prepare a picnic. Alara told me that she used to do this and loved it."

"That would be nice." Corah smiled.

"Also, when this meeting is over, we want you to leave your thought-scrambler power here and think about taking Alara to the spot we discussed at eleven o'clock tomorrow."

"You want them to know that we are there?" Zarium opened his mouth and closed it. He opened it again. "You're having us walk into a trap?" Zarium tapped his hand on the table. "A *lot* could go wrong. Are you sure this is worth the risk?"

"I know," Teron took a deep breath, "but Ian and I will be there, though invisible, making sure that if anything goes wrong, you won't be alone. If something does happen, Ian will stay with you, and I will come back to the palace and bring the guards."

"Just when I think that you can't possibly ask me to do anything more absurd . . ." Zarium looked at the king and queen, but their faces were set. He knew his place. "I will do this."

Zarium handed them the fox tooth and left the room. He asked the nearest servant to get Alara. When she came, he said, "I was thinking that maybe tomorrow we could do something special."

Alara rolled her eyes up and tapped her jaw, acting like it was a hard decision. "For you, I think I could arrange it." She flashed him a smile. "What are we going to do?"

"Well, that's the special part. It's going to be a surprise. I'll pick you up at eleven and make sure you are hungry enough to eat."

Alara nodded. "Okay, I'll see you then."

Zarium waved and walked out of the castle. He looked forward to seeing Alara, and he was enjoying her flirting, but he wished he didn't have to see her in a situation that could put her in danger.

After Zarium left the castle, he walked around town thinking about his plans with Alara. He thought about going a mile to the east of the Tykee Forest and focused on a leaving time of eleven o'clock with the thought that they'd get to the picnic spot by eleven thirty. He thought about it over and over again. He hoped that Claud would receive his thoughts. Of course, Zarium wouldn't know unless Claud tried something on the picnic. Satisfied that he had done all he could, he went back to the castle and asked to have a quick meeting with Teron in the White Room.

When Teron entered, Zarium said, "I did what you asked. I still don't like it, but I did it. I guess we'll see how tomorrow goes."

Teron handed Zarium the fox tooth. "Thank you. Trust that we know things you don't and have a purpose for this."

Zarium took the tooth. "I'm trying."

That evening, Zarium helped his mom weed some of the flowers in her garden. As they worked, he told her that he was going to go on another date with Alara the next day.

"What are you going to do for this date?" She tugged on a stubborn weed.

"I'm going to take her on a picnic. I brought home one of the carriages from the castle stables and was thinking that maybe we could decorate it tomorrow morning."

"I'd love to help with that." She stood up, wiped her hands on her apron, and walked toward the house. "Let me grab some stuff that would help."

Zarium quickly stood up and followed her into the house. She went to her room and pulled out a couple of boxes and handed them to Zarium. "Put those in the living room, so we can easily grab them in the morning." Zarium sat them in the living room and told her he was going to get ready for bed. He had a big day ahead of him, and he wanted to be rested, so he could be fully alert and on the watch for anything suspicious on the picnic.

The next morning, Zarium woke up early but discovered that his mother was still awake before him. He picked up the boxes in the living room and took them outside by the carriage. On his way back in, his mom came out the door and handed him some scissors. "Go around back and cut some fresh flowers."

He walked around back and started cutting a variety of flowers—yellow, purple, pink, and orange. He took them to his mom and helped decorate the carriage with ribbon and flowers. Lastly, his mom put some blankets on the seats and a couple of extra ones in the back.

When they were done, Zarium walked around the carriage. "This looks a lot better than I could have done on my own."

"Some things need a woman's touch . . . like most things in a man's life."

He smiled and kissed her on the cheek. "Duly noted." He climbed inside, and she handed him a basket that she had prepared earlier that morning, filled with rolls, fried chicken, and some fruit.

Zarium transported to the castle and went inside. Alara and her parents were sitting in the main foyer waiting for him. Zarium bowed as he entered the room. He pulled out some flowers he had behind his back. "Flowers for two lovely ladies." He handed one bouquet to Corah and one to Alara.

"Thank you, Zarium," Corah said with a nod.

Alara smiled. "I love them."

"You are responding much better this time than when I gave you flowers at the dance," Zarium teased.

"Yeah, well, I like you a little more than I did then." She winked. "So, what are we doing today?"

"Follow me." He reached out and took her hand. "Queen Corah and King Teron, you can also come see."

All of them went outside where they saw the beautiful carriage pulled by two white horses. He turned to Alara. "I want to take you for a picnic, but first we need to travel there." Alara handed her flowers to Corah, who then handed Alara the feather with her place-transport power. Alara was surprised, but Corah explained it would be safer this way.

"But is it safe for me to be away from the castle?" Alara asked.

"We will be out in the middle of nowhere, so we shouldn't come across any people," Zarium said.

Zarium took her hand and helped her into the carriage. He climbed into the seat next to her. He flicked the reins, and the horses moved forward. As soon as they got out of town, Zarium turned the horses to a dirt path that went through the middle of a field adorned with beautiful flowers and a few trees, and overhead was the sound of birds singing. If it were an ordinary day, everything would have been absolutely perfect.

As Zarium drove the carriage, he was content to just listen to Alara talk because it allowed him to focus more on their surroundings. He hoped she didn't notice that he was preoccupied. "It must have been nice growing up without having to do housework."

Alara crinkled her nose. "I didn't get off that easily. When I was younger, my mother made us do housework, and I hated it. She made us iron our own clothes, make our beds, clean, and even clear our own dishes from the table and wash them. It wasn't until the last few years that she finally allowed the servants to clear the table and wash the dishes. Now, I realize that there is satisfaction that comes from working hard and accomplishing something. When I took care of Nori, it was hard work doing the cooking and cleaning things up, but I enjoyed being able to help her."

"Did you have to do any of the outside work?"

"The only thing I did outside was sometimes help water some of the flowers. I never had to weed or help prune anything because Mother said it wasn't appropriate for a princess to have dirt in her nails or scratches on her skin. You can imagine her disappointment when I still got dirty or had scratches on my skin." Alara shrugged.

Zarium looked upward. "I can imagine. What about your brothers?"

"My brothers did have to do a lot of those things. We also learned to saddle our own horses and brush them down. To this day, some of my brothers take care of their own horses rather than having the stable boys do it."

"I guess it is probably important for all of you to be independent and not have to rely on someone else to do everything."

"That is the point. My parents didn't want us to become adults who didn't understand how the world worked."

Zarium nodded. "That makes sense. I remember back on one of our earlier dates, you mentioned that you had some interesting pets. Care to elaborate?"

Alara's eyes lit up and a corner of her mouth lifted. "We often brought things in from outside that we found. I tried keeping a couple of frogs in my bureau until one of the servants was changing the sheets on my bed and heard a croaking sound. Jarius also tried having a pet rat. He had it for quite a while before it got out of a wire cage he made for it and ended up in my parents' room. Sadly, the rat didn't make it, and no one actually told my parents that it was his pet." She raised a finger and shook it. "I think if they had let us have a dog or cat or something, maybe we wouldn't have kept trying to keep wild pets."

Zarium gave a lopsided grin. "I don't think it would have helped. We had a dog when I was younger, and we still tried to have a pet snake and a skunk."

Alara held her nose. "A skunk?"

"Yes, I was seven, and I tried catching it. Tried is as far as I got because I didn't get close enough to touch it before it sprayed me. My parents threw away my clothes, and I had to take several baths. I couldn't go to school for a few days because I stunk so bad." Alara laughed until she had tears coming down her cheeks. He pretended to give her a stern look. "I'm glad you find it funny."

Alara wiped her tears. "Even I was smart enough to never touch a skunk." She laughed some more.

"Yeah, I know. Not my brightest moment." Zarium looked around him and stopped the carriage. "This looks like a good spot to stop and eat." He jumped out of the carriage and helped Alara down. He got the blanket and basket out of the carriage and set them up on the grass.

She looked at the setup and smiled. She put her hand over his, "I'm glad I get to be on this date with you. Thank you for this. You recreated one of my favorite memories."

"Yes, you seemed so happy when you told me about going on picnics, and I wanted you to feel that again."

She surprised him when she threw her arms around his neck. She quickly released him and sat down on the blanket. Zarium smiled. "Apparently, I need to do things like this more often."

Alara batted her eyelashes. "I wouldn't be opposed to that."

Zarium couldn't have been more excited, but he couldn't get too drawn in. Today, he was first and foremost on an assignment from the king and queen. Zarium took a bite of his roll and scanned his surroundings.

"Is there something wrong?" Alara looked out over the field as well. "You have seemed a little nervous today, and you've been looking around a lot ever since we got off the main road."

Zarium moved his arms behind him and leaned back on them. "I'm just taking in all this beauty." He turned his attention to Alara. "I'm always amazed at how you're so comfortable with who you are, and you know what you want. It's one of the things I love about you."

Alara squeaked out a thank you and awkwardly reached for some more fruit. Zarium leaned forward and looked around. Then his head jerked, and his eyes widened. Zarium spoke quietly and quickly, "Someone is watching us. I can feel it. We need to get back to the castle immediately."

"What about our stuff?"

"Leave it; it doesn't matter."

Suddenly, three men who Zarium didn't recognize appeared out of nowhere with swords in hand. Alara screamed as they made their way closer.

Chapter 31

"Alara, go back to the castle. Now!" Alara heard Zarium scream. Alara thought about the castle, but nothing happened; she was stuck where she was standing. Someone was forcing her to stay where she was.

Ian appeared as one of the men grabbed Alara's hand. Alara used her other hand to punch his nose. His eyes watered, and he grabbed his nose. He let go of her hand for just a moment. Ian grabbed a rock and hit the man on the head, knocking him to the ground. Ian pulled out a sword and attacked one of the men who were after Zarium.

Zarium shouted his earlier command to Alara as the man Ian had hit over the head reached out for him. He grabbed the man and flipped him. When he hit the ground, Zarium pressed a knife against the man's throat. He rolled him over and tied his hands and feet, so he couldn't move. To make sure the man couldn't use a power to get away, he hit him again on the head with the hilt of the knife and knocked him out.

Zarium ran toward Ian who had two men attacking him. Before Zarium could get there, one of the men lunged toward Ian, thrusting a sword at him. Ian jumped, but the sword got him, and he fell to the ground. Zarium grabbed the man around the neck and squeezed until the man slumped to the ground.

"Alara—"

"I still can't move," Alara cried out.

The last man attacked Zarium. As the man ran toward him, Zarium thought of a rope and brought it out from behind him. Zarium threw the rope toward the man, causing him to fall. He stepped on the man's hand causing him to release his sword. Then he tied him up as well.

Alara still couldn't move though. Zarium turned back to the three men. "Which one of you is preventing Alara from moving?"

Alara noticed a small movement. She screamed, "Zarium, it's him." The man stood and ran toward Alara.

Zarium ran as hard as he could. Alara knew Zarium had to get to the man before he touched her, or he could use dark magic to transport her somewhere else against her will, and all would be lost. The man was reaching for Alara. Zarium jumped. Before he reached the man, Alara disappeared.

***

"Noooo," Zarium screamed. He landed on the man and held him down. The rope had been loosened. Zarium pulled it tight. "Where is she?" Zarium demanded, shaking the man by the shirt.

Then Alara appeared. Zarium stood and wrapped his arms around Alara. "When I thought he had caused you to disappear . . ."

"I went invisible, so that maybe he wouldn't actually grab me. Sorry, I was trying to help."

"It was brilliant. You did a great job. It just scared me."

Zarium heard a shout and looked over his shoulder. A group of five soldiers had just transported there.

Zarium yelled out to them. "Ian has been hurt." He pointed. "You two take Ian back to the castle." He pointed to the other three. "And you three, make sure these three men don't have any magic powers on them."

When the magic of all three men had been taken, Alara and Zarium transported to the castle. They quickly found out where Ian was and went to the room. Zarium ran to Ian while Teron and Corah hugged Alara. "Were you hurt?" Corah asked Alara. Alara shook her head.

Teron and Corah walked to Zarium who had his hand placed over Ian's heart. "Is he going to be all right?" Teron asked.

"The knife went into his heart. I'm not sure how deep the wound is. I will do my best. This kind of wound will take longer to heal." Zarium felt an intense pressure. He started sweating. His father's death flashed through his mind. He had to save Ian. "I'm doing everything I can."

After what seemed like forever, though only half an hour later, a guard walked in. "We have an update for you. We know who attacked them. All three of them were using shapeshifting powers to look like someone else, which is why we didn't recognize them. Two of them were castle guards."

Zarium noticed that Teron didn't seem surprised. "What about the third?" Teron asked.

"Maybe we should talk out in the hall," the guard replied.

Teron shook his head. "No, whoever it was, you can say it here."

The guard shot a glance toward Zarium, and in that moment, Zarium knew his world would never be the same. "It is Kursek. He's also the one who stabbed Ian."

Zarium said nothing. What could he say? His face went red, partially from embarrassment and partially from anger. How could Kursek do this to the family? He felt Alara squeeze his hand. He couldn't face her right now. Zarium took a deep breath and focused on Ian. Healing would come better if he were thinking positively.

The guard continued, "I ordered the two guards to be executed, but we weren't sure what to do with Kursek."

Zarium kept his eyes down. "Execute him too. You can't risk him escaping again."

Neither Teron nor the guard moved, and Zarium answered the unspoken question. "I don't want to see him. I have nothing to say to him. Seeing how little he cares will only make it harder." Out of the corner of his eye, he saw Teron nod to the guard. Zarium felt Teron's hand on his shoulder. He blinked back the tears welling up in his eyes. "If it's all right with you, I'll let my . . . mom know." He choked on those last words, knowing he was about to dash all his mom's hopes.

"Okay," Teron whispered. Teron motioned to Alara and the two of them left.

***

Once the door closed, Alara immediately spoke up. "We have to do something. I'm not going to sit by and wait anymore. We know nothing about Jarius or if he's even alive. Berica is gone, and we have no idea where she is or if she's okay. Levon has left, and now this has happened to Ian. How much longer can we possibly wait?" She folded her arms.

"Alara, this isn't up for debate," her father said. "It is too dangerous."

"No. What's dangerous is sitting around waiting for them to pick us off one by one." She shook her finger on each word for emphasis.

"I have enough on my mind. I don't need this right now." With that, her father walked into a room and closed the door.

Alara was more frustrated than she had been in a while. She wanted to go for a walk but knew it was too dangerous. She went to the nearest window. She saw more soldiers arriving. This was the fifth group of soldiers she had seen in the last couple of days.

***

A couple of hours later, Zarium was relieved to see Ian stir. Corah spoke Ian's name. His eyes fluttered and opened but closed again. "He's getting stronger." Zarium wiped some sweat from his forehead. "If he makes it through the night, he'll live."

Teron returned. Zarium stared at the king until he made eye contact. Teron nodded, confirming what Zarium already knew—Kursek was dead.

All Zarium could think about was his mom. At least Kursek couldn't hurt anyone else in the family. He thought of Levon and how he was supposed to kidnap his mom. Where was Levon? Was he still going to kidnap her? So many unanswered questions.

Teron cleared his throat. "I've been thinking . . ." Corah and Zarium looked at him. "Zarium, I know this is a hard time for you, and you have a lot on your mind, but—"

"It's fine. If you need me to do something, just ask. I didn't just promise to serve you when it was easy."

Teron moved closer. "I want you to try to reach Claud and get him to meet you somewhere so you can talk." Zarium nodded. "It is possible he won't know about Ian or the guards being there," Teron said. "I want you to act like you were surprised that they showed up and that in order to move Claud's plan forward, you couldn't fight them off."

"Of course. Also, can you send a messenger to my mom, telling her I won't be home tonight? It would be best if I stayed here in case. I'll tell her about Kursek tomorrow."

The next morning, Zarium woke up in a guest room and checked on Ian. He put his hand over Ian's heart and thought about it being healed. Corah, who had had servants move a bed into Ian's room for her to sleep on, also woke up. "Is he . . . ?"

"He's going to make it, but he's very weak. I'm going to go meet with Claud now, but I'll be back in a little while."

Zarium went to the large rock close to the forest. He had been sending his thoughts to Claud to meet him there since the night before. He hoped that Claud had been close enough to receive them. He hadn't waited long when Claud showed up. Claud walked up to him. "All right, what happened yesterday? I sent men out to kidnap Alara on your little picnic, but none of my men returned."

"Well, when your men appeared, it so happened that the king had a couple of men following us using invisibility. Your father has kept a tighter rein on Alara and has resorted to having her followed at all times. When they appeared, there wasn't much I could do, since I couldn't fight against the king, or else it would have ruined your plan."

"Do you know what happened to my men?"

"I don't," Zarium lied, keeping eye contact.

Claud walked closer to Zarium, staring him down. He clenched his jaw, and Zarium felt like he couldn't breathe as a wave of dizziness overcame him and he knelt to the ground. Claud knelt next to him. "I can make life miserable for you if you don't do everything I say."

Zarium nodded. Claud stood back up and snapped his fingers. Zarium took a deep breath, desperate for the air. Claud pounded his fist into his other hand. I want Alara. We are ready to fight; it is now or never. We need to take them by surprise. Here is what you are going to do. Alara has wanted to go on a spying adventure for some time. Talk to her about it and get her to beg my parents. She has done everything they asked. Also, I need you to tell my father that you are laying a trap for me and get him to follow."

"I will arrange to make it happen." Zarium transported back to the castle and requested an audience with the king and queen. When he was told they were busy, he told the guard to tell them that it was an emergency. A few minutes later, Teron and Corah appeared and ushered Zarium into another room.

Zarium told them of his meeting with Claud and what the plan was. "He expects me to start traveling with Alara in two days. What do you want me to do?"

The king and queen stood silent, passing the queen's pencil back and forth. When they were done Teron said, "We will make him think that his plan is being carried out, but it will really be our plan. Alara has wanted to go to Zarothan for some time now. We will tell her that we want the two of you to go and check on some conditions there. She will be delighted to go. When Claud crosses your path, act like you were always on his side and that you betrayed Alara." Zarium's face dropped.

Teron softened his voice. "Zarium, I know this is hard, but it's the only way this can work. Alara has to believe you betrayed her because Claud and the others must see you as one of them. We can't risk them taking you prisoner. Alara won't be able to fake being surprised or angry at you. We need this to be genuine."

"I know." Zarium looked at Corah. Her head was down, and he knew that she was sick with worry and that she even hated parts of their plan. But Zarium knew she understood, like he did, that some things had to be done, even risky, hard things.

Teron put his hand on Zarium's shoulder, "Follow me." The three of them walked out into the main foyer. They asked a servant to summon Alara.

When Alara entered, she ran to her parents and begged again. "I know the two of you don't want me to go to Zarothan because you're worried about my safety, but I feel like this is something I can and need to do. I've made a list of all the pros and cons. Look at the good reasons to go. We can rescue Jarius and Berica. Surely, their lives alone are worth this risk."

Alara handed them the paper; she pointed to another section. "I've also written down a list of things that could go wrong with possible solutions. Some are simple and others are more complex." She stopped and examined her parents' faces.

"Alara, you have done all the conditions that we required to go on a spying mission," her mother said, "and we are keeping our side of the bargain. With the recent events with Ian, we feel that we need certain information as soon as possible. We need to know exactly where the Magic Robbers are, so we can have a surprise attack on them. The day after tomorrow, you and Zarium will depart for Zarothan."

Alara smiled and hugged them both. "Thank you! I won't let you down."

She went to Zarium and hugged him. "Isn't this exciting? We get to go on an adventure together."

Zarium faked a smile. "Yeah, I'm so excited for you. I know this is what you've always wanted." He shot a look toward Corah and Teron. Again, he'd have to keep the truth from her. With as hard as that was, nothing was going to be as hard as his next task. He told Alara and her parents goodbye and transported home.

Chapter 32

Zarium walked slowly through the gate. Each step was difficult as if someone had fastened weights to each of his legs. Flowers lined the walkway. He kicked one of them. How dare they look so cheerful and happy. A life was ended, and now a heart would be broken. When he walked in, his mom was washing dishes. She turned at the sound of the door closing. Zarium turned away and slowly took off his shoes.

She stopped washing the dishes. "Something is wrong." She walked into the room and stood before him. "What is it?" Zarium took a deep breath and closed his eyes. When he opened them, there were tears. His mom grabbed him by the shoulders. "Did something happen to Alara?" He shook his head. "Nori?" He shook his head again.

He watched as the only other option dawned on her. She took a step back. "It's Kursek, isn't it?" She put her hands over her mouth. Zarium slowly nodded. She started to drop. Zarium caught her and slowly lowered her to the ground.

He held her as she sobbed. It wasn't fair. She shouldn't have to go through this much. After several minutes, she asked him for the story. It pained him to explain to his mother what had happened. To lose a son was bad enough, but to lose a son because he was a traitor, who was probably partially responsible for his father's death, was almost unbearable.

After what seemed like forever, his mom wiped her eyes and asked, "So, what happens next?"

"His body has been prepared for burial. We can go see him today or tomorrow."

His mom nodded. "I'd like to go today."

"Of course. I'll go ask the neighbor if we can borrow his horses."

When they got to the castle, Zarium helped his mom off her horse and walked beside her up the path to the castle and finally to the stairs. He opened the door. Once inside, a servant got the king and queen for him.

Soon, Teron, Corah, and Alara came. Teron took Zarium's mother's hand. "I'm sorry. I wish . . ." A tear trickled down her face. "It isn't your fault."

Alara gave Zarium and his mother a hug. "I'm sorry for your loss."

Corah wrapped an arm around Zarium's mom. "We truly are sorry." Corah led them down a hallway to a set of stairs that went down to the room Kursek was in. The room was a plain gray stone for the walls and floor. There were no decorations or rugs.

Zarium couldn't help but think how the room was depressing, fitting the mood perfectly. At the front of the room sat a coffin on a simple brown wooden table. Zarium stopped and leaned against the wall. He still didn't want to see his brother, if he could even be called that anymore. His mother turned to him. "Will you go up with me?"

He stared into her eyes. This was the last thing he wanted to do, but if she wanted it, he would oblige her. He nodded and took her outstretched hand and walked to the front with her.

At first, he looked straight ahead at the wall, but eventually he glanced down at the body. His mother was gently caressing Kursek's hands.

Zarium studied Kursek's face. He had filled out more since Zarium had last seen him. He had a lot more muscle, and his face was chiseled. Zarium looked away. He heard his mom mumble something he couldn't quite hear. She took one last look before turning to Zarium. "I'm ready to go now."

As they walked toward the back of the room, Teron said, "We will have some men go to Camden tomorrow and bury him there." She nodded that she understood but said nothing. She turned and looked one more time toward the front of the room before walking out the door.

As Zarium walked past Alara, she took his hand briefly and squeezed it. He gave her a half smile. They walked up the staircase, down the hall, and outside to their horses. As they rode, Zarium thought about how there would be no fancy funeral or special honors.

When they got home, his mom sat in a chair and leaned back. Zarium sat in a chair across from her and thought about things. He was surprised when he heard Kursek's name.

"Kursek was always the one to lighten any situation. Remember how he would tell jokes?" His mother smiled.

Zarium swallowed. "Yeah, and he liked to play little pranks, too. Sometimes he would sneak into my room at night and wait until I got into bed and then pound on the walls."

Her eyes glistened. "How about the time he took the snakes to school?"

Zarium laughed. "Well, actually, that was awesome. The teacher was so scared, she cancelled school, and we all got to go home early. Only Kursek and I didn't go home. We went swimming in the river instead."

"Of course you did," his mom said, chuckling. "So many good memories." She bit her lower lip. Zarium stood and walked to where she sat. He put a hand on her shoulder and gently rubbed it as she softly cried. She reached her hand up and put it over his hand. "At least we still have each other."

Chapter 33

The next day, Zarium went to Vashka to prepare a few things. First, he stopped by Nori's. She answered the door and let him in. He looked toward the cupboards. "I left some omps on top of your cupboards. I just need to retrieve them now."

"You have more than five?"

"Yes, in the last couple of weeks, I've been given more to help with various assignments, so I couldn't carry them all on me."

He pulled a chair over, stood on top of it, and grabbed the items. He left the omp for tracking people up there because it wouldn't do him any good, since that power was gone until Nori's dragon was returned. He stepped down from the chair and moved it back to where he got it from. "Nori, I don't know if you heard, but Alara and I and a few others will be going to Zarothan tomorrow."

Nori's head jerked, and her eyes narrowed. "I see."

"Do you have any great words of wisdom for me?"

"Magic is great, but using your brain is even better."

Zarium tilted his head slightly to the left. "I suppose that's true. Do you know something I don't?"

"I just know that sometimes the best weapon is having the wisdom to do what's best and at the right time."

"I'll keep that in mind. Well, I need to get going, but I'll see you in a few days or so." Zarium had to force out those last words. He hoped they were true.

Nori hugged him. "I'm holding you to that." She pulled away and looked into his eyes, "And I expect to see my dragon when you come back." She shook her finger at him.

Zarium licked his lips. "I'll have it." He smiled. "How do you always know so much?"

"Because I use my brain." She gave one hard nod and told Zarium goodbye.

Zarium left and walked to the castle. The first thing he did was visit Ian. Ian looked a lot better than he had a few days before. Zarium sat beside him and did some more healing. Ian woke up and whispered his name. "What?" Zarium leaned in closer.

"Alara," Ian hoarsely whispered.

Zarium moved closer. "What about Alara?"

"Take care of her."

"I will. I promise."

Ian shut his eyes. After a few minutes, Zarium left to see if he could talk to the king and queen. They met with him in the Black Room. "I just stopped by to see if there are any last-minute things you need me to do," Zarium said.

"No," Teron said. "You can go home and spend time with your mother."

"Okay, thank you. Before I go, I'm wondering one thing. What does Alara know?"

"She knows that she is going to Zarothan, where she is going to search and see if she can find Jarius, Berica, the dragons, or get any information from anyone in the city who might know anything," Corah said, looking at the table. "She doesn't know that we are going into battle."

Zarium shook his head. "Okay, I guess that's good enough. Is it okay if I leave a power with you? I currently have some that Claud gave me, and I can't carry them all on me at one time, so I need someone to take one of them. I will get it back from you tomorrow and just leave one of them in a bag in the wagon."

"Yeah, that would be fine," Corah said. Zarium handed them the string with the ability to go through natural walls. He bowed and told them he'd see them in the morning. Before he left, he asked one of the servants to get Alara and have her go to the main foyer. He went in and sat on the couch and waited. He leaned over with his elbow on his legs and his head resting on his hands, thinking.

He looked up as Alara entered. "I was told you need me," she said.

"Yeah, I just wanted to see if you needed me to do anything before tomorrow. I'm about to head home."

"Just one thing."

"What's that?"

She walked toward him, went up on her tiptoes, and kissed him on the cheek. "I'll see you tomorrow." She took a couple of steps back.

Zarium looked into her eyes and brushed a stray hair from her face. "Until tomorrow." He walked back a couple of steps, keeping eye contact before turning around and leaving.

Zarium spent the evening with his mom. They went for a walk, and as they walked, one thought weighed heaviest on Zarium's mind. There was one part of the plan that he knew still had to play out. He thought about preventing it, but he knew it had to happen.

He went through dozens of scenarios, racking his brain for a solution, wanting a way to keep her safe. He hoped that as long as he played his part well, his mom would be safe.

"Zarium, did you hear what I said?"

"Oh, sorry, I was just thinking of something else. What did you say? I'm listening."

"When all of this is over, we should go on a short trip and leave our worries behind us. We could go to Hant and visit my sister, Shiram."

"That would be fun. I haven't seen them since I was like twenty." Zarium was glad that she was remaining optimistic and planning for the future. They bought a fruit tart from one of the shops and ate it as they walked. Zarium ordered what he always did—strawberry. "Maybe," Zarium said, "we could ride a tarock to see Aunt Shiram. That would be something different and fun."

"I haven't been on a tarock since before you got your magic."

"Well, it's set then. I'll contact Huxley when I get back." *If I come back*, he thought as one word flashed through his mind. *Sacrifice.*

Tannah slowed down until she stopped walking. Zarium stopped too and looked at her. "What's wrong?" He asked.

"You are going to come back, right?" Tannah asked, the worry written on her face.

"I hope so." He bent down and picked up a rock off the ground and threw it. "I can't guarantee anything, but if things go according to King Teron's plan, I will make it home."

Tannah resumed walking. "Hmm." She paused before asking, "What does Alara think about you going?"

"Well, actually, she will be going with me."

Tannah turned her head toward Zarium, the surprise evident on her face. "A little odd that the king and queen are letting Alara go to Zarothan at a time like this. That they'd send her into battle."

"Yes. I can't give you the details about this. I'm sorry." He knew she wouldn't ask any more questions. She knew how things worked with the kingdom's secrets.

When Zarium retired to his room for the night, he got the box with Alara's locket. He decided he would take it with him. Maybe he could give it to her at some point. He went to bed, but sleep didn't come easily for Zarium. He lay awake worrying about all the things that could go wrong. Mostly, he worried about what would happen to his mom and Alara. After hours of tossing and turning, he got up and went out to the kitchen. He was surprised when his mother joined him a few minutes later.

"Couldn't sleep?" Tannah asked.

"No." Zarium continued stirring his tea with a spoon.

Tannah wrapped her arms around him. "Your father would be so proud of you, as am I."

"Thank you. I still don't know if I have it in me to do what I have to, if I have enough courage."

Tannah cupped his face. "You're your father's son. Of course, you have enough courage."

"I think a lot of it has to do with who my mom is too."

"Maybe a little." She smiled. "Just remember to do what's right and everything else will be fine."

He pulled away and looked down. "Sometimes the lines between right and wrong are blurred. What if I don't know what the right thing is?"

"If what you do will save the kingdom, then it is the right thing. And no one is perfect. You'll probably make mistakes, but as long as you stay focused and do your best, you'll make the right decisions when it's important."

Zarium thought about the decisions that would have to be made. How would he balance devotion to the king with perceived devotion to Claud?

Chapter 34

Alara woke up the next morning excited for the day. She quickly brushed through her hair and put it up in a tail. *Finally, I get to go on an adventure.* She hopped out of bed and looked at the bags she had packed the night before. She wondered if a week's worth of clothes would be enough or if she'd need more. She examined her list and checked each item off—soap, shoes, a brush, and snacks. She checked her timekeeper. It was almost time.

She looked at her bracelet with her invisibility power, and her heart ached for Berica. She wondered if she was safe or scared. Alara knew she had to succeed. Now was her chance to be the heroine she'd always wanted to be. Her heart beat a little faster. She took a deep breath and picked up her bags. She walked to Ian's room. He was awake, reading a book. "Don't you have anything else to do?" She teased him.

"Very funny."

She put her bags down, walked closer to Ian, and gave him a hug. "Behave yourself while I'm gone, and I'll see you in a week or so."

"Okay," he smiled. She turned to leave when he said, "Alara." She turned back around. His eyes bore into hers. "I think the reason the dragons only gave you one power is because you are amazing enough the way you are."

Alara wiped her eye. "Thanks."

She picked up her bags and walked through the castle, running her hands along the walls. Her mother hated it when she did that as a kid, but she wasn't a child anymore. She moved her hand and walked down the stairs to the main foyer. As she rounded the corner, her parents were already there waiting.

Her mother walked to her and embraced her. "Don't worry; you'll be fine. You have everything you need. Stay invisible as much as you can so that no one knows you are with Zarium." She handed Alara her pencil. "You'll need this so Zarium can talk to you without looking like he's talking to himself." She released her, and Alara started walking toward her father, when suddenly her mother grabbed her again. "Trust Zarium," she whispered in her ear. Alara looked deep into her mother's eyes before nodding.

Zarium walked in and stood in the doorway. Alara acknowledged him and walked toward her father. "Thank you for letting me go."

Her father nodded and hugged her. She noticed he held her a little longer than she was expecting. When he released her, she picked up her bags and walked to Zarium. He took the bags with one hand and put his other arm around her back, and they walked toward the door. She went invisible.

They went down the stairs to the wagon that was waiting for them. Zarium urged the horses forward, and soon they were traveling through the city. Alara was quiet, thinking about everything. As happy as she was to be allowed to go on this adventure, she still felt it was odd that they really let her go. She felt a nudge from Zarium as he said, *"Must have a lot on your mind, huh?"*

"Yeah, I guess so."

"I packed plenty of food, not to mention your parents loaded some as well, so you should have almost anything you need. If ever you need to stop, let me know, and we will stop." Zarium waited for a reply and said, *"Alara, I can't see your head; you will have to speak out loud."*

"Oh, right. Yes, I understand."

***

As evening time approached, Zarium stopped the horses and pulled a good hundred and fifty feet off the road through a little path into some trees in the middle of the forest, so they could set up camp for the night. The forest was all they would see until they reached Zarothan. He told Alara she could go visible because no one would find them where they were.

He handed some items to Alara from the wagon and pointed to a clearing and asked her to set them over there. Then he gathered some wood and built a small fire, so they could cook some of the food. He gave some eggs and a pan to Alara and asked her if she could crack the eggs into the pan. He told her that he'd just talk out loud since they should be safe this far out in the middle of nowhere.

He took out his knife and began cutting up some potatoes. "I see you didn't trust me with the cutting," she chuckled, cracking the first egg.

"We can't have you cut your finger off," he joked back.

"Of course, it wouldn't be that big of a deal because I know this man who could heal it."

"Do you now?" Zarium wiggled his eyebrows. "I bet he's really handsome and charming."

"Eh, he's passable." Alara laughed.

"Passable. Come on. I'm offended." He waved the knife he was holding at her. "Maybe I won't give you any dinner."

"Okay, maybe you're more than passable." She handed him the pan with four eggs cracked into it. He took it and put the potatoes into it. "Tonight and tomorrow morning are the only times we will get a warm meal." He put the potatoes into the pan. "The rest of the time, it will be dried fruit and meat."

Zarium got out a small bag he'd prepared for her that had some food, paper, and bandages in it. He handed it to Alara. "Keep this on you at all times, so you'll have something just in case we get separated. Also, if we were to get separated, make sure you drop the pencil, so I can pick it up. This way you could send me thoughts, so I could find you again."

Alara eyed him before asking, "Zarium, do you know something I don't about all this?"

"I mean, I am pretty smart, so maybe I know more than you."

She laughed. "That isn't what I meant. What I mean is, do you believe we will get separated?"

"I don't know exactly how things will go, and I want to be prepared for the worst-case scenario."

He thought about the worst-case scenario. He had some very good ideas of how that would turn out, but he couldn't tell Alara any of that. He had to follow the plan. For a while, neither of them said anything.

He picked up a stick and broke it. *The plan. What a joke.* The hope or the guess would more appropriately describe it. No one really knew how any of this would turn out.

He threw the stick on the fire and took the lids off the pans and scooped some potatoes and eggs onto plates for Alara and him. He opened up a sack and brought out two rolls that his mom had made. He handed one plate to Alara. He thought of his mom. What was she doing right now? Would she be safe? By now, Levon should have kidnapped her. He figured it was a precaution similar to why they kidnapped Berica. They wanted leverage.

He shook his head. He couldn't think about that right now. He took a bite of food. He was glad Alara didn't ask anymore questions about what was going to happen.

When Zarium had finished eating, he started putting away the things they had gotten out for dinner. He got out their blankets and pillows. He cleared the stuff out of the wagon and made Alara's bed. Then he pulled out a couple of blankets and lay them on the ground next to the wagon. When he finished, he sat down on a log by the fire. He rubbed his neck. "It's funny how much has changed in the last month."

Alara looked up. "Are you referring to something particular?"

"Well, there was the dance, when you weren't even a little bit impressed by me."

Alara plucked a plant close to her and picked off the petals. "About that, I was a little more impressed than I let on. That was why I didn't respond very well."

Zarium raised his eyebrows. "When you like someone, you treat them as if you don't?"

"Remember, I didn't want someone to ruin my plans. I've always wanted to go on adventures, and you were a threat to what I wanted. Really, I thought you were pretty handsome, and nice, and a good dancer, but I wasn't going to admit that." Alara blushed. "It's getting late. Maybe we should go to sleep, since we have along day ahead of us tomorrow." Alara stood up and walked toward the wagon.

Zarium grinned and stood up. "You know, you can go on adventures and still have a little romance." He shrugged. "I mean, isn't that what's happening now?"

Alara climbed into the wagon and lay down. "Good night, Zarium."

Zarium walked to his bed, lay down, and smiled. He put his hands behind his head and thought about how good things were at that moment.

The next morning, Zarium awoke early. He knew they'd be traveling late that night and needed to get to Zarothan and get into their places to await Alara's father. They ate and packed up their things.

Alara got into the wagon and waited for Zarium to climb up. When he got in, he just sat there. "What's wrong?" Alara asked.

Zarium turned to her. "I don't know what will happen today or tomorrow or the next day, but I do know I can't go into these days without you knowing how I feel today. I know for you this was just an obligation, but for me, it was so much more."

She put her finger to his lips. "I know. I really like you, Zarium, and I hope everything goes well for the next few days. Hopefully, we can have more dates when this is done."

He chuckled. "Or meetings. I mean, both are pretty great as long as you are there." He cleared his throat. "In case I never get the chance again." He leaned in and kissed her gently.

When he pulled away, she looked into his eyes for a moment and smiled before going invisible. "I'm sure you will get the chance again. I can make sure of that," she said, putting her arm around his.

He steered the horses in the direction of the main road. "I'll count on it." He wondered if he could really count on anything. There were too many other players in this game and too many traitors. It was hard to know who to trust and who not to trust. He hoped the players he was counting on would come through and that things would turn out according to the right plan.

As time wore on, the mountains of Zarothan became more noticeable, with Mt. Fraton looming high above the landscape. This was the last leg of the journey. He occasionally scanned the trees and tried to pay special attention to anything that seemed out of the ordinary.

Hours before they reached the forest, while it was still light, Zarium heard a rustling sound coming from the forest. He looked around but didn't see anyone. He glanced at his timekeeper. It was about the right time. He groaned within himself. It was too late to reconsider. He put a protective hand around Alara as the sound of another stick snapped.

"Zarium," Alara whispered. "Did you hear that?"

"Yeah, I did." He grabbed Alara's hand.

Suddenly, a group of four men and one woman appeared and surrounded the wagon. Zarium squeezed Alara's hand. *"Be still and trust me."*

"Zarium, how good to see you here," Asher said. "We were beginning to wonder if you got lost on the way."

He couldn't hesitate. "No, but it is a long ride and breaks were needed."

"Yes, well, you have done well. Alara, you might as well appear; we know you are here," Asher called out.

"Alara, it's okay; you can appear," Zarium calmly said. Alara went visible.

"Zarium, I was hesitant to trust you," Claud said, "but you have proven yourself. You have delivered her to us. Now prepare for the rest of the plan."

Alara turned to jump off the wagon. She came to a forced halt and was lifted into the air. She cried out, "What is happening?"

Claud laughed and answered. "This is a power I recently got because Zarium stole our father's ring."

"You betrayed me," Alara shouted at Zarium. "You betrayed my father and the kingdom. No. I trusted you. My parents trusted you." Her voice cracked. "Your mother trusted you! How could you?" She tightened her fists.

Zarium saw the pencil clutched tightly in her hand. He focused on only allowing Alara to receive his thoughts and scrambling them for everyone else. Something he had been practicing with Corah. He hoped she would drop it. *"Alara, drop the pencil. I need you to trust me one more time."* She looked at him, her eyes piercing his conscience. What was that look—anger, sadness—no, it was disappointment. Zarium looked at her hand and repeated the thought. When he was about to give up hope, the pencil dropped. Zarium felt some relief.

***

As the pencil dropped, Alara watched as Zarium casually picked it up. She was more confused than ever. Her mother's words rang in her head. *Trust Zarium.* What if her mother was wrong? The only reason she dropped the pencil was because she figured that either way, she'd lose it.

She clenched her fists and kicked her legs in the air. She turned her attention to Claud as he approached her. "How could you?"

"Alara, I should be the one to rule. I want to rule. You don't even see it as a privilege. I've talked to Mother and Father many times about this, but they won't change the law. Maybe this will help them to see things my way. They will do almost anything for you. Besides, if they don't, there could be an 'accident,' and, as the oldest son, the crown would fall to me anyway. They can do this the easy way or the hard way."

"But why?" Alara held back tears. She wouldn't let him see her cry.

"This power is much stronger than the powers the dragons give us. Don't you see what this could mean for us as rulers? No one would ever come up against the royal family. We would be unstoppable." Claud spread his arms out. "We could gain other kingdoms, and in time we would control everything." He tightened his hands into a fist.

"When we were kids, you were interested in helping people and being kind. What happened, Claud?" Alara said, trying to buy herself time.

"Dark magic is enticing."

"What made you want it?"

Claud rubbed his chin. "You mean you don't know." He laughed. "Well, this is interesting. I was exposed the same way Zarium was—through someone else. Over time, I found the dark magic to be intriguing and then desirable."

"Who were you in close contact with?" Alara asked.

"The same person you were, Alara. Though you didn't spend as much time with him because of how much younger you were." Her mind raced. What was he talking about? Who had she been in close contact with?

"Remember Uncle Roark?" Claud asked.

Alara nodded. Uncle Roark had in another city, but he had visited them a lot during a certain time period. Now, Alara realized it was around the same time her father had fought the battle. Her uncle had supposedly come to help her father with the battle that day. All that Alara knew was that he had never returned. Her father's words hit her full force. *We didn't know if their families would be affected or not. Only time would tell. The traitors were banished.*

"He was with Father that day too," Claud said. "He was good at pretending. Father thought he could trust him, but he had other plans. He was going to kill Father and then marry Mother. If it had worked out, we wouldn't be having this discussion now because we would have grown up with all of this being normal."

"So now what are you going to do with me?"

"For now, you will be kept in a safe place while we wait for Father to decide what he will do. His choices will determine much of yours, his, and Mother's future. Zarium has already played his part well, and I'm sure he will continue to do so."

Alara watched as Asher and Claud slapped Zarium on the back. "Good job, now it is your job to go prepare for the king." Zarium nodded. Claud turned back to Alara one last time before she was taken away. "Don't go thinking that Zarium will somehow save you. He took a blood oath, swearing allegiance to the dark magic and our cause. He's one of us."

Alara felt like she had been punched. Claud told them to take her bracelet. Alara felt colder and noticed the sun had gone behind some thick clouds, taking with it the last ray of hope she had.

A woman grabbed Alara's hand. Alara felt something hit her hand, and the scenery changed.

Chapter 35

Zarium knew what time King Teron was supposed to leave and went to the approximate spot he and his soldiers should have gotten to, and sure enough, he found them. He pulled his horse into a walk next to the king's horse. Teron looked at him, and Zarium nodded. They all knew what that meant—there was no going back now; this had to work.

"Zarium, can you find out where Alara is?"

"I have some guesses where they may be keeping her, and I have the pencil. I'm hoping she will let me receive her thoughts. I don't know, though." He hung his head. "I imagine I'm not her favorite person right now."

Just then, Corah appeared. "What are you doing here?" Teron asked, his face going red. "You're supposed to be hidden away safely, where I don't have to worry about you."

"I couldn't stand by while everyone I love is going to an uncertain future. Nori and I had a good talk, and she gave me her invisibility power. I have been following closely behind this entire time."

"So, you heard every conversation?" Zarium asked. Corah nodded. Zarium smiled weakly. "I know where your daughter gets her determination from . . . and why she's so stubborn." He smiled a little bigger.

"You do understand that everything has to go as planned?" Teron gave her a look that said it wasn't negotiable.

"I know." Corah matched his gaze

Zarium interrupted them. "I'm going to go talk to Claud and then find Alara."

***

Alara found herself in a dark, damp area, tied up with thick rope, lying on top of a large rock. She couldn't move her arms, legs, or head. She was frustrated, and disappointed, and depressed, and heartbroken, but she knew she couldn't give up. She had to get out and warn her parents.

She heard footsteps and tensed up. Asher came into view. "Princess." He spat out. "All hail the princess."

Alara refused to speak; she wouldn't give him the pleasure of making her angry. He put his face inches from hers and stroked the side of her head. If she could have pulled away, she would have. Asher whispered, "I told your brother that you are much too pretty to let die and that even if you didn't willingly join us, I could break your spirit." Alara clenched her jaw and narrowed her eyes, fighting the urge to tell Asher what she thought of him. Asher's head jerked, and he stood up. "I have to go, but don't worry. I'll be back."

Alara assumed he had received a mental message from Claud or someone else. She had to figure out how to get out of there before Asher came back. She tried moving, but it was like something had her completely held fast. Besides ropes, she figured someone used dark magic to ensure she wouldn't get away.

"Aghhh," she screamed out.

Then Alara heard her name from a voice that made her heart soar. "Tannah, is that you?"

"Yes, Alara, it's me."

Alara felt a mix of relief and sadness. Relief that she wasn't alone, but sadness that Tannah was stuck here too. "Are you tied up too?"

"Yes."

Alara's blood was boiling. "How long have you been in here?"

"They came and got me shortly after Zarium left yesterday."

Zarium. Alara frowned. Then she clenched her teeth. Zarium. Just hearing his name made her want to throw something. She wondered if his mother knew he'd betrayed both of them.

Alara's thoughts turned to Zarium. How could he do this to her? How could he kiss her one minute and betray her the next? Was he just pretending to be on Claud's side? Her parents trusted him, but then again, her father had been betrayed by other people he thought he could trust before.

"Surely Zarium will find and help us," Tannah said

"I hope you're right," Alara said. Tannah had no idea how much she hoped.

The guard who stood outside the entrance to their area entered. "That's enough out of you two." He picked up Alara and moved her to a flat rock farther away from Tannah. The guard used a power that made them groggy. Alara felt her eyes growing heavy and fought to keep them open. She looked forward and saw a waterfall forty or so feet away from her. Though she didn't know whether it would help or not, she thought hard about letting Zarium receive her last thought before her eyes closed: *waterfall.*

***

Zarium transported to the mountain and asked where Claud was. When Claud showed up, Zarium said, "I've done as you asked, and they are in position. By tomorrow morning, they should be exactly where you want them, and you can get the jump on them."

"Good work, Zarium. I knew I could count on you, but just in case you are planning on bailing, I have something that may persuade you."

"What do you mean?"

"We made sure you wouldn't want to change your mind or sides."

Asher laughed, "We knew your mother would be your weak spot. So far, you have played your part well, and your mother is safe."

Zarium fought the panic that welled up inside him and took a slow breath. He knew this was going to happen, but it was still different knowing it had really happened. "I won't let you down."

Asher licked his lips and sneered, "Nothing can be put above the allegiance of the kingdom that soon will be ours."

"I understand all that."

"No, no, I don't think you do." Asher smiled a wicked smile. "You see, unless your mother and Alara join us, they will have to be killed."

Zarium let it fully sink in but kept his facial expression the same. He wanted to punch Asher, but he knew it wouldn't help anyone if he got chained up. "You're right. I hadn't thought about that, but I can see how that would be necessary."

"I'm surprised. I was sure this would be the part where you'd go weak on us," Asher said.

"Nothing is more important than making sure the plan works," Zarium replied.

"Your brother would be impressed. He wondered if you were too soft."

"My brother is here?" Zarium asked, trying to seem like he knew nothing about what had happened.

"No," Claud angrily said. "He was one of the men who got captured the other day. I can see the king kept that secret from you. You'd be amazed at how many secrets my father has kept from you."

Zarium swore. "I can't say I'm really surprised. Well, if he does anything to Kursek, King Teron will answer to me."

Claud nudged Zarium. "We better not find out you are planning an escape for your mother." Claud gripped Zarium's shoulder, digging his thumb in. "If you do anything contrary to the plan, I will kill both of you."

Zarium flinched. "Don't worry. Everything will go as planned." Claud loosened the grip. "I will go and prepare for the next part," Zarium said, glad for an excuse to get away from them.

Zarium went invisible and transported to another part of the mountain. He left his wagon at the base in the middle of some thick trees. He stared at the omps in the wagon. He chose five—thought-scrambler, place-transport, nature's doorway, invisibility, and healing—and hoped they were the right ones for what he needed to do.

He entered one of the main openings. From his several visits to the mountain before, he knew that inside was an intricate design of natural tunnels and openings.

There were seven main areas that he remembered from before. Each of them was big enough to keep a few people in. There were other smaller openings barely big enough for one or two people to be crammed into. He hoped that wherever Alara and his mom were that at least they were somewhat comfortable.

All of a sudden, Zarium received a thought, "*Waterfall.*" It was a message from Alara. Zarium thought back to the last month when he had been exploring the mountains. He had seen a waterfall. It was small and inside the mountain. It had a passageway to the side of it that opened into a big room. He was grateful that Claud had given him nature's doorway power so that he could use his place-transport power to get through the caves and tunnels more quickly.

He pictured the waterfall in his head and the area he remembered it being around, hoping he had the right one. To his relief, he found himself standing in a big room where he saw his mother. His first inclination was to run to her; however, he realized that it could be a trick or that there could be someone else guarding them who was invisible.

He went over to his mother and stood close by for some time, observing her. After a few minutes, he was satisfied that it was his mother. He started to move closer when he heard a noise. He couldn't see the person, but he had heard that voice before—first the forest and now here. If it wouldn't ruin everything, he'd pound the traitorous servant's face in.

He had nowhere to go but took a few steps back, so he wouldn't be directly in the way if he came over to where his mother was. The guard walked around another spot a couple of times. Zarium realized that Alara was over there. Then the guard walked to where Zarium's mom was. Zarium backed up some more. The guard paced in front of her a couple of times.

Without warning, the servant thrust his hand in Zarium's direction. Zarium ducked. Did he suspect he was there? Zarium didn't dare stand back up. Finally, the man left, and Zarium knelt beside his mother and loosened the ropes enough to make sure they didn't dig into her skin. He gently kissed her cheek. "I promise I'll get you out of here." Zarium crept carefully over to Alara.

***

"Pst."

Alara heard a voice and groggily groaned, trying to turn her head, but then she remembered that wherever she was, she couldn't move. She thought back to how she got there. If there was one thing that Alara prided herself on, it was that she was independent and could take care of herself. Yet, somehow, here she was in need of being rescued. She wondered if the day could get any worse.

"It's me," Zarium whispered.

The day got worse. Suddenly, the past day's events came tumbling through her pain-filled head like a stampede of wild animals. "You little—"

Zarium put his hand over her mouth. "Shhh. Asher or Claud will find out I'm here if you aren't quiet."

"Is there a difference between you and them?" Alara spat out.

"I know you're mad, and I understand why, but I need you to trust me now, and I need you to do exactly what I say."

"The last time you said that, things didn't go so well."

He loosened the ropes that were around her wrists and ankles. "I know, but I'm hoping this time will be different. I loosened the ropes, so you will be comfortable, but don't take them off. If you get caught, it won't be good."

"Why should I trust *you*?" Her eyes flashed with anger.

"What other options do you have?" He gave her a half smile. "And at least if you have to work with someone, you got me, who wants nothing more than to see you happy."Alara glared at him. "You think I'm happy right now?"

"No, but ultimately you will be happy that you trust me."

"Let's say I agree to believe you. What is your plan?" She avoided eye contact.

"For now, I need you to stay in here, but I promise that I'll be back, and when I return, I need you to give me a sign that it's safe for me to come in. It's important you pretend to be asleep if anyone comes, until you know it's me." He bent down and picked up a small rock, which he handed to her. "When I come back, I will throw a rock over there. I have the pencil, so I can receive your thoughts. I need you to think 'safe', so I know it's okay for me to come in. Do you understand?" She nodded. He grabbed her shoulders with an intensity that surprised her. "You have to force yourself to stay awake. I can't take a chance that someone will sneak in here while I'm gone."

"Okay."

"I have to go."

Alara watched as he disappeared. She had no problem staying awake. She went over all the events of the last week in her head. She was more confused than ever. Should she really trust Zarium, or was he just using her to get to her father?

Chapter 36

Zarium saw Teron's army and reappeared. As he did, Teron said, "Please tell me there is some good news."

"There is. I found Alara and my mom."

"Are they okay?" Corah asked.

"They are," Zarium said. "They've been keeping them both asleep."

Zarium motioned for the king and queen to come closer and whispered, "I have a plan. I need one of the men who is about the same size as Alara or someone who has a power that would make them appear about the same size, so I can have him switch places with her. Also, see if someone has the ability to go invisible and to place-transport."

Teron searched among his men until someone was found who could switch places with Alara. Teron handed two omps with the powers of invisibility and place-transport to the man. Zarium motioned for Corah and Teron to step a few feet away and lowered his voice even more. "This is the last time you two will see me before tomorrow. Remember that no matter what happens, you can't get there too early. You have to trust me. It's imperative that you don't get to your places until I say so. If you get there too early, there will be nothing set up to help you at all, and everyone's life will be in danger. No matter what you hear or what happens, you have to wait until the right moment." He looked at Teron. "Also, I need you to have the power to read minds, so we can communicate. Find someone among the soldiers who can lend you the power." Teron nodded.

Zarium touched the shoulder of the soldier going with him, and they transported to the front of the cave. He was about to give him the next directions when it dawned on him that while he had the power to go through walls, the other man could only place-transport when nothing was physically obstructing him, so it was going to take longer than planned to get back to Alara.

Then it got even longer. The shortest way to Alara was to go through a large open area; however, Claud and the group were having a meeting there. Zarium debated trying to walk through there but knew it was too risky, even if they were invisible.

Zarium was unfamiliar with the way they went and took three wrong turns. *Agh!* This wasn't supposed to take this long. He took a breath and cleared his mind as he came to another fork. *Which one?*

He chose the one on the right. They were walking longer than he thought they should have. He was about to turn around when he went around a corner and found the room. He slowly and carefully walked toward the opening of the room. His eyes scanned the room, looking for any movement or anything that seemed different from before. He didn't see any immediate threats, so he threw his rock and waited.

"Safe." He sure hoped it was from Alara and not someone who found out about their plan. He walked slowly and carefully into the room.

He was relieved when Alara was still there and awake. He untied her the rest of the way and quickly explained the plan to her. He motioned to the soldier, who went to them and gave Alara the place-transport and the invisibility power. Alara gave her riding cloak to the man, and he put it on and covered his head with the hood. He lay down, and Zarium loosely tied the ropes around his wrists and ankles.

Zarium looked back at his mom, wanting to speak to her one more time, wishing he could rescue her too. He walked over by her and watched her sleeping. He knelt and whispered, "I love you."

He stood back up. He knew he couldn't put anything above the plan. He walked to Alara and told her to follow him. Alara did as she was told. Zarium tried to remember the way he got in so he could get out, but he got lost a couple of more times, and he was sure that Alara was enjoying his discomfort. Finally, they got out of the cave. Zarium walked a few feet from the mountain. About eight feet up, he saw an edge and what looked like a crevice.

"What are you doing?" Alara whispered.

"I'm looking to see if the spot up there is big enough for you to hide in for the night and get some sleep."

She sighed. "You do realize I've been sleeping for the last couple of hours."

He grabbed a rock with his hands and pulled himself up, placing his foot on another rock. "I know, but you'll want to be well-rested for tomorrow."

"Why, what's tomorrow?"

He found another hand and foot hold and pulled himself again. "Do you have to ask so many questions? It's annoying." Zarium kept climbing. He got to the crevice and poked his head in. "This will work." He climbed back down and told Alara to go visible and that he'd help give her a boost up.

"Why do I have to stay in there. I'm not doing anything until you give me some details." Alara jutted out her chin.

"I'm sorry, but I'm in a hurry, and I don't want you to know too much because it could be used against you if you were caught again." She gave him a look. He looked upward. "Okay, the man you switched places with is one of the soldiers in the kingdom. I've been in communication with your father. He's on his way here with some soldiers for a battle that will happen tomorrow after dawn. Now, please climb into the hole up there."

Alara put her foot in his hand but turned back around. "Well, why can't I go see my father?" Alara asked, still standing on his hands.

Zarium shifted his grip. "Because it's important to the plan that we do things this way."

"Whose plan—Claud's or my father's?"

Zarium groaned. He didn't have the energy for this. He gave a hard push and waited for her to pull herself the rest of the way. "A little of both. I need you to stay here until it is time for you to reveal yourself."

"How will I know when it's time?"

"Because I will send someone to get you. In the meantime, I don't want anyone to know you escaped. Your safety means everything to me. Please do what you're supposed to."

"Okay," she whispered.

Zarium turned to leave when he remembered the locket. He pulled it carefully out of his pocket. "I can't explain how I got this right now, but I have your locket. I know it doesn't have any great powers in it, but I thought maybe you'd want it back. Maybe it will bring you good luck." He wondered if she would be mad, but her eyes softened and she smiled. He tossed the locket toward her.

"Thank you. This means more to me than you know."

"Well, I believe in you, whether you have any other powers or not. Now, could you please stay invisible?"

"For you, I'll try."

Zarium shook his head. There was no controlling Alara.

Zarium transported back to the inside of the mountain to the place where Claud and the Magic Robbers were meeting. As he walked in, everyone in the room grew quiet. Zarium cleared his throat. "Everything is ready for tomorrow."

Claud invited him to come to the middle of the room. Zarium hesitated for only a second before walking confidently to the front. Claud put a hand on his shoulder. "Zarium has done his part in ensuring that the kingdom will soon be ours." The cheers were deafening. Zarium couldn't believe how many people were in the room. He tensed as his eyes fell on someone he hadn't expected but wasn't completely surprised about. Their eyes locked for a split second, and Zarium hoped Levon was truly carrying out Teron's plan.

After the meeting, Claud told everyone to get some sleep and sealed all entryways so that no one could get in or out. Zarium felt like the walls were crushing in on him. How would he get to Alara again? This wasn't supposed to happen. He watched Levon go to a spot close to the far wall to lie down. As far as Zarium knew, it wasn't part of the plan for Levon to be there. Again, Zarium wondered if everything was going to be okay.

Zarium waited a while before creeping over to Levon. He shook Levon a couple of times. He leaned down and whispered, "I know you're awake, so let's get this over with."

Levon rolled over. "Do you want to get us both in trouble?"

"No, I want to know what you're doing here," Zarium whispered.

"I had to come. Claud ordered it."

"Does your father know?"

Levon hesitated before saying, "No."

"Why are you doing this?" Zarium asked in frustration.

"Because Claud will kill Berica if I don't."

Zarium didn't want to be the bearer of bad news but knew this had to be said. "You do realize that even if you do everything Claud asks, he could still kill Berica?"

"Leave me alone," Levon replied. "It isn't like you're perfect . . . taking the blood oath. Really?"

Zarium opened his mouth to explain but stopped himself. He crawled away, knowing that if this conversation kept going, he'd get them both in trouble.

***

Alara stayed in her hiding spot for a while, trying to sleep, but how was she supposed to sleep when her insides felt like an entire mountain had fallen on her? She knew Zarium had told her to stay there, but she couldn't shake the feeling that she needed to find the others. She hesitated. The feeling nagged at her again.

She curled her necklace around her finger, contemplating what she could do to help. She didn't need special powers to help the kingdom's cause, just the element of surprise and maybe a little patience. A smile spread across her face, remembering when Nori told her that she needed to cultivate that as a virtue. She could do this. She was the future queen, and she had what it took to save the kingdom.

She took a deep breath, mustered all her courage, and climbed out of the hole before she could change her mind. It was dark, so she couldn't see where to put her foot. She felt around until she found a place for her foot to step and lowered herself down and felt for another spot. She thought she found one when she slipped and started sliding. She fell the remaining five feet down, scraping up her hand and one leg on the way down. A little blood instantly formed.

The first thought she had was that Zarium could fix it. *No, I don't need a man to be okay. I can do this.* She couldn't use the place-transport power that she still had from when she traded the soldier places because she had never been to Zarothan before and had no idea where to go. This would be one of those times when walking would be necessary. She remembered that Zarium or maybe Claud had said something about the front of the mountain. She could figure out how to get to the front.

She walked carefully around the side of the mountain. Soon, she saw the path that led from the mountain east toward Vashka. She breathed deeper, grateful that she had found the front. She looked around and listened to see if she heard any sounds. When she didn't hear anything, she kept moving. It was still dark, so she hoped she could find a spot to go before anyone woke up.

She walked away from the mountain and looked up, trying to find somewhere to go. It was too dark to see anything, so she walked back toward the mountain and looked for a spot where she could climb up. With a little light from the moon, she was able to find a spot on the left side that had a rocky path that went up. She started walking up it.

When she reached the top, she cautiously stepped up on top of a flat surface. She walked around the space, noticing that it was mostly a half circle and probably about two hundred feet big. As she walked toward the back of the space, she saw what looked like a cave.

She walked back to the ledge, looking to see if there was somewhere she could hide. Most of the ledge had a sharp drop to the ground. But on the far side of the front of the ledge was a dip that went down about four feet and had a pointed piece that jutted above the flat surface where she stood. She found a tight, uncomfortable spot and squished herself into it. She checked her wrist out of habit but remembered they had taken her timekeeper when they put her in the cave. All she could do was wait.

An hour later, she heard Asher, Claud, and other men and women whose voices she didn't recognize. She was glad she was invisible and tried not to think too much about where she was or what she was doing. She had to control her thoughts, or she knew she would be caught.

She could hear them talking, but she couldn't quite make out their words. She wanted to get closer, but she couldn't risk being heard. She waited for what seemed like forever, when she heard Claud say the name Levon. *Could there be more than one Levon?*

She peered over the top of the ledge. It wasn't just Levon she saw; there was Zarium too. Claud was going over some last-minute details and assignments. "Levon, you will be in charge of grabbing our father. Do you understand?"

"Yes," Levon replied quietly.

Alara felt numb. Was he just pretending to be on Claud's side? Would Levon join Claud just to save Berica?

Chapter 37

Zarium focused on only allowing Teron to receive his thoughts. *"Are you in place?"*

"Yes," Teron replied.

Zarium searched the space before him, but all he saw was the road and lots of trees, but he knew that somewhere, an army was sitting, ready to go visible. Claud snapped his fingers, and some men left and brought back a person who was tied up. They took off his hood. *Jarius.*

"Jarius, this is your last chance," Claud yelled, his fist in the air. "If you join us, you will be free. Otherwise, we will kill you."

Jarius calmly replied. "I won't join you."

Claud picked Jarius up with his power and threw him against the mountain. "Are you sure?"

"Zarium, is it time?" Teron asked.

"No. Wait."

"They're going to kill Jarius."

"Give me a second; I'm thinking."

Jarius shook his head and leaned on his one arm. Claud picked him up again. Jarius' arms and legs flailed as he was lifted higher and higher. Jarius fell with a loud thud.

"Zarium."

"Hold on."

Zarium fought the urge to run to Jarius and help him. Zarium looked at Levon. Levon stood facing forward, his jaw was tight.

Then the message came to Zarium's thoughts. The person he had sent to get Alara reported that she wasn't there. The plan hinged on Alara being in a certain spot. How would it work? What would he tell Teron?

***

Alara flinched each time Jarius was thrown. Rage coursed through her veins. Where was her father? Had Zarium lied about that too? Was anyone going to help? She saw a huge caravan round the corner with the biggest surprise of all—her mother in the lead. As they came closer, Claud shouted out a "welcome" to them.

Claud yelled to someone, and they went to Jarius, and both of them disappeared. Alara wondered what would happen to Jarius, but she remained invisible. She had one advantage over everyone—secrecy. She hoped her mother would be proud of her for sitting still and thinking things through rather than rushing into everything. Surely, this would prove she could be queen someday.

"Hello, Mother, and other notable people. I trust your journey went well." Claud said, each word laced with sarcasm.

"Claud, you don't have to do this," their mother shouted from a distance.

"Yes, I do." Claud stepped forward. "I was born to lead and be in power. If you would all try this power, you'd find it very desirable."

"How would you feel if you were a citizen of a land and the ruling family controlled every aspect of your life?" Their mother asked.

"Is that the best you got for me?" Claud laughed, and so did his followers. "It doesn't matter how I'd feel because it isn't the reality. The reality is that I'm going to rule with or without my family joining me. It's in everyone's best interest to join me. Or you can feel sorry for the others and end up in the same situation as them. It's your choice."

"This isn't the way it is supposed to be done." Their mother's voice turned to pleading. "I raised you better than this."

Claud pointed toward their mother and shouted, "I don't have time for this." Their mother yelled out as she was lifted into the air until she was floating several feet above the ground. She kicked her legs, but she was stuck.

Alara panicked. Would he dare throw their mother around like they had Jarius? Levon stepped forward. "Put her down gently, Claud."

"How dare you," Claud sneered. Claud snapped his fingers again, and someone went inside the opening of the cave and returned with Berica. She was tied up and had a piece of fabric in her mouth, keeping her from being able to speak. Her eyes moved wildly. Tears ran down Alara's face. "Have you forgotten? If you try to stop me, you'll never see her again," Claud yelled.

Levon put his hand up. "Okay, I'm sorry. Don't hurt her." He looked hopelessly at their mother. Berica was ushered back inside the cage. Alara noticed Zarium was focusing hard on something. Then a shout was heard, and her father appeared close to where her mother was.

Claud turned his attention to their father. "I wondered where you were. You think you can stop me? Or maybe you thought you could trick me." Claud dropped their mother several feet to the ground. "Welcome to the party—my coronation party." Alara's father and a couple of other men helped Alara's mother up. She brushed herself off as the Magic Robbers on the mountain ledge moved close together and began chanting in a circle. Alara saw Zarium and Levon move to the side.

***

Zarium nudged Levon. "Get down off this ledge and go stand next to your father like you are supposed to. You need to get there before this next part, or you may get pulled into the battle and unable to do your part of the plan."

"Okay," Levon said. "Good luck, Zarium."

"Wait," Zarium said. "Give me your invisibility power. Claud is already expecting you to go down there, so you won't need it. Before I go down, I'm going to see if I can rescue Berica."

Levon handed Zarium his omp. Zarium started to move when Levon said, "Zarium, I can still see you."

"What?" Then he remembered he had five powers on him. He couldn't take another one. He handed Levon the string with the nature's doorway power. "Here, take this, I'll get it back later." Levon took the string. "Now go," Zarium said.

Zarium heard people on the ledge start yelling out in pain. One of the people who had been chanting in the circle fell to the ground, followed by two more people a few seconds later. The Magic Robbers stopped moving, and all their swords came out as they began swinging them.

Zarium moved farther from the group toward the mouth of the cave. He crouched down behind a small rock at the entrance. He could see Berica. Now he had to get to her.

Teron's soldiers, who had been invisible, appeared, and soon, everyone from the circle was engaged in a fight. Teron's army had the advantage, and more Claud's men fell. Zarium had to move out of the way as two men, wielding swords, came at him. He turned and stuck out his foot to trip the one who was a Magic Robber. Teron's soldier stabbed him in the chest and turned just in time to fight another man.

More of Claud's group fell, and those who were guarding Berica rushed out to help. Zarium moved quickly toward Berica. She was moving her hands and feet, trying to get them loose. "Berica, it's me, Zarium. I'm going to get you out of here. Hold still." She stopped moving, and he took out his knife and cut the ropes. He removed the gag from her mouth. He took her hand and put an omp in it. "This is an invisibility power. Have you used it before?"

"Yes, I'm well practiced with Alara's. We used to play with each other's powers for fun."

"Good. Go invisible." He grasped her hand. "Don't let go. Just follow me." They moved out of the cave. Zarium could see that even though Teron's men had the advantage of surprise, Claud and his evil cohorts were beginning to win. The dark magic was proving more powerful.

Berica pulled Zarium's hand. He started to turn to her when he saw a person flying through the air, headed toward the wall behind them. Berica screamed as he pulled her toward him and threw her to the ground while putting himself as a shield over the top of her.

He heard someone else shout as one of Teron's men was thrown a few feet from them. Claud's side was gaining force. More of Teron's men were falling. Zarium had to get Berica and himself out of there fast. He helped Berica back up. "Run."

He saw the king's men start to retreat, climbing and jumping down off the ledge as fast as they could go. Claud's group ran after them, trying to get any of them they still could. When Berica got to the edge, Zarium helped her down and led her to a large tree. "Hide behind here and don't move," Zarium said.

Teron's men were all off the ledge of the mountain when one of Claud's men shouted, "Berica is gone."

Claud looked around. Levon was visible and standing in his spot. Zarium transported to where he was supposed to be right as Claud yelled out, "Where's Zarium. Did that fool—"

Zarium appeared. "I'm here," he shouted.

***

Alara wasn't sure if Zarium being in his spot was a good thing or a bad thing.

"Father, Mother," Claud sneered, pointing to the fallen soldiers, "Don't you see that you're no match for us. Do you really believe you have a chance?"

Claud gave a signal, and the Magic Robbers returned to their circle formation and walked slowly at first, but picked up speed with each round. They chanted louder and moved faster and faster. Alara watched as a thick darkness gathered around them until no one in the circle could be seen.

Alara's father ran toward the mountain, but it was like there was a force that stopped him from going past a certain point, and he was shocked when he hit it. He was flung backward several feet.

When Claud and the others stopped, they pointed toward the kingdom's army. A loud cracking sound pierced the air. Alara didn't understand what they were doing until people yelled in confusion that their powers were gone. Alara realized she was still invisible, though. *The rock protected me from the dark magic.*

"Now that none of you can stop me, I offer you one last chance to join me," Claud shouted.

Their father shouted back, "You will be defeated. You can't win everyone, and Alara is the rightful queen."

Claud nodded his head toward Asher. Asher disappeared and Claud continued taunting them. "Alara isn't going to be much help to you either. But depending on yours and her choices today, she may not have to die."

Asher appeared, panting. "She's gone. Alara is gone. I found a man in her place." "What?! Who was in charge of her? How could she disappear? I will not have my sister thwarting my plans. Find her!" He turned to Zarium, "Did you do something you shouldn't have?"

"I have no idea where Alara is," Zarium said. "Was my mother still there?"

Asher confirmed that Tannah was there. Claud shot Zarium a look, questioning him. "If I find out you've crossed me, you will die a very slow, torturous death."

Alara slowly climbed down from her hiding spot, stepping carefully to make sure she didn't slip and fall. On the ground, she moved toward her father and mother, barely even breathing, afraid they would hear. She walked past them and the rest of the army until she was at the back. Then she went visible, and walked through the soldiers toward the mountain until she was standing next to her father.

From the expression on the faces of Claud and the others, they were surprised. Claud clapped his hands. "Well done, Alara. What an entrance, and you're just who I was hoping to see. You haven't changed your mind, have you? Because if you haven't, I don't know what you are doing here. I already have your power, not that your one little power would have been any match for us," he laughed.

"If I did change my mind, what would you do with me?" Alara asked to buy herself time while trying to figure out what to do.

"I'd have you renounce your title, and you would have a position in my court. Alara, I'd give you all the power you could ever want. You'd never be stuck with only your one power." Alara acted like she was considering it. Claud spoke again. "Either way, you'd have to take a blood oath just like Zarium."

Alara saw the shock on her father's face. Clearly, he didn't know about Zarium and the blood oath. "The blood oath?" Her father looked at Zarium, clearly confused.

"The plan was never to preserve my life, Your Majesty," Zarium whispered.

Zarium is going to break the blood oath and give his life for me. The words of her father came back: *Nothing is stronger than when someone dies to save another.*

"So, what is it, Alara? What will you do?" Claud yelled.

"I will *never* join you," Alara yelled.

Claud lifted both his hands high above his head. The darkness that had surrounded him earlier engulfed his hands. He brought his hands down, pointing toward Alara. Alara heard someone shout, "No," and saw her father heading toward her from one side and Zarium from the other.

But Alara refused to let someone else die for her. She would make the sacrifice herself and save the kingdom. She didn't need magic to be courageous, and her sacrifice would be greater than any power she ever wanted. The darkness from Claud's hands was headed straight for her. She stepped forward, putting her hands in front of her as she did.

Chapter 38

Suddenly, a bright light came out from Alara's hands and surrounded her like a giant shield. It went out several feet on both sides of her. From behind her, she heard Zarium and her father crash into each other.

"What's that?" Claud shouted. "Where's it coming from?"

"It appears to be coming from Alara," Asher said.

"Impossible. What trick is she playing?" Over and over again, Claud tried using the dark magic to steal the magic from her, but it didn't work.

Alara stood there with her hands out, not sure what to do. "Would someone like to tell me what's going on?" She yelled over her shoulder.

"Your locket. It still had another power after all," her father said.

"How do I use it?" Alara asked

Her father shook his head. "I'm not sure. It's the ultimate protector. Dark magic won't pass through the shield as long as it is shining. If I remember right, you can control it and take away other people's power if that person is using their power to hurt you."

"Do I say certain words or do an action?" Her arms were feeling heavy, and she wasn't sure how long she could keep them in that position.

"I don't know," her father shook his head. "I've never seen it in action."

Claud and his followers ran into the mountain. Alara knew she needed to act fast. She thrust her hands forward, focusing on one of the people running away. The person was knocked to the ground. Alara wasn't sure how it worked, but she immediately tried again. Shortly after, four people were lying on the ground.

Alara and the group moved toward the mountain. The four lying on the ground were alive but without powers. A couple of the soldiers took them and tied them up.

Unfortunately, Claud and Asher got away. A group of soldiers ran in after them and others who had taken off, but it was too late, and they couldn't find any of them.

***

Levon ran to Zarium. "Where's Berica?"

Zarium pointed to a tree. "I told her to stay behind that tree right there."

Berica appeared, and Zarium watched as Levon ran to her. It only took a few seconds for Alara to see Berica and to run over there as well. Zarium gave them a moment before interrupting the reunion and asking Levon for the string back, so he could go through the mountain walls.

He transported to where he last saw his mom. He didn't see her anywhere. *No, they took her! They can't do this!* He dropped to his knees. "Zarium."

Zarium whipped his head toward a small opening in the wall of the cave and saw his mom step out. He ran to her and hugged her. "Thank goodness you're all right."

She pulled away. "Is the kingdom safe?"

"Yes, everything is going to be fine, and when I get you home, I'll tell you all about it." He helped her through the cave, grateful that it would be easier now that Claud and his men weren't taking up space in one of the rooms. They went around a couple of corners and exited right out the front. Zarium helped her down, where Corah and Alara rushed to her.

Zarium didn't see Teron anywhere. "Alara, where is your father?"

"He and a group of soldiers are looking to see if they can find Jarius anywhere."

"I'm going to go search too. Look after my mom until I get back." Zarium tried using his person-transport power, but over and over again, nothing happened. Jarius wasn't in close enough proximity, not even with the flyn bark.

After several more attempts, he transported to Teron. He found him as he was coming out of the cave in the front. "King Teron," he shouted.

Teron turned around and faced him. "You didn't find him either?"

"No, I'm sorry."

Teron tapped his chin. "I guess we'll let the others know."

When Teron and Zarium got off the ledge, Corah turned to them. The look on her face made it clear that she knew that they hadn't found him.

Zarium watched as the king, queen, and Alara hugged each other. Alara turned to Zarium. "You tried to save me. But you took the blood oath and you broke it. How are you still alive?"

"The night that Claud gave me the choice of death or the blood oath, Asher showed up with Berica, which distracted every—"

"Wait, you saw Berica after she was captured, and you didn't rescue her?" Alara asked surprised.

"I couldn't. It would have ruined the plan. However, as Claud turned his attention to Berica and Asher, I was able to combine a flyn bark with my power, and I made fake blood appear. When Claud turned back to me, I hid it with my other hand, pretended to prick my finger, and moved my hand so the blood appeared there. That is what I signed with. It wasn't my own blood. I never took the blood oath. It took me a couple of tries to make the fake blood appear, though, because I had never tried to produce anything like it."

Teron placed a hand on Zarium's shoulder. "I knew I could trust you."

"Well," Alara said, "what do we do now?"

"There are others who need to be rescued who are still trapped inside," Zarium said. "Also, there are dragons inside the mountain that we need to find and return them to their places as quickly as possible."

Corah proposed an idea. She told Zarium and Alara to go back to Vashka and find some servants or other people on the council who had the power to place-transport and come back so they could start transporting everyone faster. An hour later, they both appeared with more omps to transport others. They went back and forth until everyone was back in Vashka, including the people and dragons who were kidnapped.

Chapter 39

As soon as everyone had returned to Vashka, Zarium went to Nori's. When she opened the door, he held the dragon out.

"My dragon!" She said.

Zarium handed him over. "I told you everything would be okay."

Zarium watched her get the pan with her power to open Mirum. Without placing the pan on her head or twirling, Nori opened the realm of the dragons. She placed the dragon back inside and closed it up.

"Nori, why didn't you have to twirl and put the pan on your head while you did that?"

"I had to have something to entertain me when I couldn't get out of bed. I only told you to do that so I could laugh about what you must have looked like," Nori said, with a twinkle in her eye.

Zarium thought back to how Levon and Ian had seen him look like a fool. "All right, you got me good. I can't give you a lot of details now, but just so you know, a lot of people had their powers disabled during the battle, so they will be coming to you to get their powers back."

"Do you need your powers back?"

"No, I was one of the few who didn't lose them because Claud was only taking away the powers of those he believed were on the king's side. I would tell you all about this, but I really need to be heading back to the castle now."

"All right, but you better come visit me sometime."

Zarium promised he would and transported to the castle. He found Teron talking with some of the guards. He waited patiently until Teron turned to him. "What can I do for one of the best men I know?"

Zarium lowered his eyes. "I don't know about that but thank you. I was coming to see if you needed me to do anything."

Teron pointed to a group of people. "Why don't you help with keeping order among those waiting to have their powers reinstated."

Zarium turned and looked at the group. A few people were arguing over which of them deserved to get done that day and return home. "I see you only give me the hardest assignments." Teron laughed as he turned and walked away. Zarium headed toward the group.

***

Alara spent many days working with her parents and brothers to restore order and help assure people that everything was okay. Those who had powers taken away when the Magic Robbers did the chant were able to get them back immediately by going to the faram. The chant only disarmed the powers. For those who had their omps with powers stolen had to wait until it had been a month since that power had last been in their possession to get them back.

Leaders from other lands were contacted, and the people who had been kidnapped were returned. The king of Faskin was happy to see that his son was still alive; however, other people weren't as lucky. All the dragons were also returned to whichever faram they had been stolen from. It was a lot of work, but Alara was glad that things had turned out as good as they had.

After things slowed down, Alara's parents invited Zarium, Tannah, and Berica over to have dinner with them. Ian was still healing, but he was much stronger and able to attend.

As they sat around the table chatting, the servants brought in roasted pork, a mix of vegetables, and a salad. Before they started eating, Alara's mother stood up. "I'd like to make a toast." She paused before continuing. "A toast to the bravery of each of you, who acted in such a way that makes me proud to have you in my life."

The sound of glass clinking together filled the air. Alara watched her mother sit down, but she knew that Jarius's absence was harder on her than she would let anyone know. Alara wondered if he was still alive or if Claud had killed him.

Her thoughts were interrupted when Levon stood up, cleared his throat, and knelt in front of Berica and took her hands. "When you were gone, and I wasn't sure if I'd see you again, all I could think about was how important you were to me and how much I needed you." Alara held her breath as Levon reached into his pocket. "I went back to the jeweler later that day and bought this." He slipped a ring onto her finger. "Will you marry me?"

Berica squealed with delight, "Of course, I will marry you." She kissed him soundly.

Everyone at the table stood up and hugged the two of them. Alara hugged Levon. "It's about time."

"That's what we're all going to say about you."

Alara looked toward Zarium, who was busy talking to Ian. Alara shook her head. "I think we have plenty of time before we say that. I'm in no big hurry."

"Famous last words, huh?" Levon smiled.

She lightly punched him on the shoulder, "Don't be putting any ideas into his head."

Berica had just finished talking to someone else and turned to Alara. "I don't think he needs any help having the idea."

Alara shook her head. "That's enough of that." She wrapped her arms around Berica. "This is the best day ever."

The next morning, Alara went to visit Nori. Things had finally settled down at the castle, and the line that had been at Nori's with everyone wanting their powers reinstated had finally died down. Alara knocked on the door and waited. Nori's face lit up when she saw Alara standing there. Alara pulled Nori in and hugged her. "I have so many questions for you?"

"Come in, my dear, and make yourself at home." Alara sat down, and Nori said, "Now, you said you have questions. What can I do for you? Do you need your powers reinstated?"

"Well, yes, actually. My invisibility power was disabled." Nori started to stand. "But that isn't the only reason I have come."

Nori sat back down. "Oh, do you need advice? Maybe about Zarium?"

"I do need advice, but it isn't about Zarium. I'm here because when I was on the mountain, something unusual happened."

"What is it?" Nori asked, extending her hand to Alara.

"It seems I have another power."

Nori's eyes widened. "After all this time. Is it really possible?"

"Yes, and I'm not sure how to use it or even exactly what it is."

"Come, dear, tell me what you have."

Alara recalled how Zarium and her father tried to protect her, but explained that she jumped in front of them. "Then a light came from my hands that created a shield that extended outward, preventing anyone or even magic from getting to us."

Nori's eyes widened. "Could it be? After all this time."

"What?"

"It's the power of ultimate protection. The dragon of mine, who has it very rarely ever distributes it. In my time as a faram, he hasn't given this power to anyone that I'm aware of. It's so rare, I'm not even sure what all it can do. I've heard of other people in other lands having it, but again, it's very rare."

"How do I control it or use it? Is there a way to experiment with it and practice it?"

Nori shook her head. "From my understanding, the power can't be used except to save lives. I don't know how you'd practice it. You also can't use it to take away the powers of the town bully because he's annoying. It must be a threat to human life to work."

"Why is it such a rare power?"

"Could you imagine what could happen if it fell into the wrong hands and those people could use it to protect themselves from being harmed by those who were good. It would make it so no one could defeat them."

"What do you think would happen if I combined this power with a piece of flyn bark?"

"I'm not sure." Nori shrugged. "Maybe you should test it and see what happens. Then again . . ."

When Nori hesitated, Alara asked, "What is it?"

"If you do find that it's enhanced by the bark, or you figure out how to use it all the time, perhaps you shouldn't tell anyone. I think it's best if people forget about you having this power."

"Why?"

"You'd instantly become a target for anyone wanting your power."

Alara felt overwhelmed. She wasn't sure that she wanted a power that came with so much risk. She bowed her head, thinking about what this would mean. "I understand."

"This is a great power, and as with any great power, it will come with risks and opportunities. This is a burden you will have to carry alone, and as things progress, I'm sure you will understand."

Alara's head shot up, and she eyed Nori. "Do you know more than you have told me?"

Nori said nothing for a time. She eyed Alara. "I may have said too much already. Any rare power comes with risk. Now, hand me your locket or other object you want me to use to have the dragons give you back your invisibility power."

Alara handed over her locket. Nori opened it and fingered it slowly. She mumbled something, but Alara couldn't understand her.

Alara started to ask another question, but Nori put up her hand to quiet her. Then Nori opened Mirum Alara watched as Nori walked right up to five different dragons. Like when she was younger, they each stepped back when they were done.

Nori handed the locket back to Alara. "Test it just to make sure."

Sure enough, Alara went invisible. "How come you used five different dragons?"

"All of them had an invisibility power, and I wasn't sure which one had given you the power originally."

After Nori closed Mirum, Alara asked, "Do you know every power each dragon has?"

"Yes, that is part of becoming a faram. Once we were introduced and the dragons trusted me, they showed me the powers they have. This is the same way it happens with all farams. It is hard for us to pick dragons if we don't know what powers they have."

"Are there other rare powers or any that you have never seen someone receive?"

"There are, though, I'm sure, when the time is right, some of those will be displayed as well. It is possible people have them and use them, but we don't hear a lot about them. Perhaps others have them that don't know it yet. The powers never come too early—"

"Or too late." Alara smiled. "I know. They always come at the perfect time."

Acknowledgements

I am grateful for my husband, Dave, who would listen as I read him parts of the book to see if he thought it was interesting enough. When I lacked confidence, he would tell me I was good enough to do this. When the book needed improvements, he would tell me that he was sure I would get it there. He never doubted that I could make this work.

I am grateful for all my readers who gave me encouragement and feedback to make this book even better. I know a lot of them were busy, but they took time out of their schedules to read it, encourage me, and tell me how I could improve parts.

I am grateful for my editor, Christine and Scott Wilkins, who gave me valuable insight.

Last, but certainly not least, I am grateful to Heavenly Father for the times that inspiration came when it was needed most.

About the author

Kimberly lives with her husband, Dave, in Ogden, Ut. She loves to hear about the experiences people have with her books. You can email her at kasechser@gmail.com.

Follow her on

Facebook

Instagram

Youtube

Amazon

Made in United States
Troutdale, OR
07/18/2025